Readers Love ANDREW GREY

Lost and Found
"Andrew Grey knows how to tug on the heart strings and make you feel the emotions the characters are feeling."

—Sparkling Book Reviews

Second Go 'Round
"A really great, touching read from start to finish!"

—The Geekery Book Reviews

A Wild Ride
"I love a good cowboy book and throw in the fact that it's written by Andrew Grey and I'm sold."

—MM Good Book Reviews

A Daring Ride
"An emotional, engrossing and sexy ride is what's in store with this latest work from one of the best authors in the genre."

—TTC Books and More

A Courageous Ride
"Once again Andrew Grey has written a book filled with passion, romance, sex, happiness, sadness, and amazing characters you can't help but love."

—Paranormal Romance Guild

By Andrew Grey

Published by Dreamspinner Press
www.dreamspinnerpress.com

By Andrew Grey (cont'd)

Published by DREAMSPINNER PRESS
www.dreamspinnerpress.com

By ANDREW GREY (cont'd)

Published by DREAMSPINNER PRESS
www.dreamspinnerpress.com

ANDREW GREY

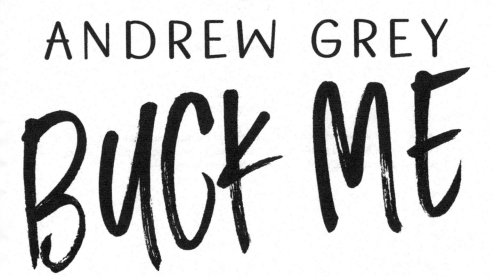

BUCK ME

DREAMSPINNER PRESS

Published by
DREAMSPINNER PRESS

8219 Woodville Hwy #1245
Woodville, FL 32362 USA
www.dreamspinnerpress.com

Buck Me
© 2023 Andrew Grey

Cover Art
© 2023 L.C. Chase
http://www.lcchase.com
Cover content is for illustrative purposes only and any person depicted on the cover is a model.

Trade Paperback ISBN: 978-1-64108-471-0
Digital ISBN: 978-1-64108-470-3
Trade Paperback published November 2023
v. 1.0

Printed in the United States of America
∞
This paper meets the requirements of
ANSI/NISO Z39.48-1992 (Permanence of Paper).

To Dominic and Lesley.
I could not have done this book without both of you.

Chapter 1

ANOTHER DAY on the ranch for Emmett Beauregard McElroy, and yeah, that was a mouthful if he ever heard one. Everyone called him Emmett or Em, thank God. When he was a baby, his mama had thought they could call him EBM or some damned thing, but his father thought it sounded like an out-of-control bowel condition and nixed it. There was precedent for using initials. His older brother, Robert Edward, had been RE, and that worked, but Emmett preferred that people use his name, especially the hands on his family ranch.

The horses, of course, didn't give a damn. Though if the horse he was working with could actually talk like Mr. Ed, he might have an easier time with the beast.

"Okay, hold still," Emmett said in as soft a voice as he could muster with Virginia. She was a champion cutting horse, the pride of the McElroy stables and the most cantankerous mare Emmett had ever met. And that was saying something. "Now just lift your foot so I can get the stone out for you."

Emmett did all the right things. He never made quick movements and never raised his voice. He was the epitome of calm as he got to the stone and pulled it out from where her hoof met the shoe. The farrier was scheduled to be out in a day or so. All he wanted to do was make her more comfortable and ensure that there wasn't any damage to the tender portion of the hoof. "There you go. That should be better." He lowered her leg and felt up it for any heat. There was none, thank God. His father would have a screaming fit if anything happened to her. "Do you want me to brush you?" He refused to show the hesitation he felt crawling under his skin.

She stomped her front hooves, and Emmett took a step back to let her get out any orneriness, then bent to get the brush from where it had fallen onto the concrete floor. A sharp pinch grabbed his ass, and he jumped about two feet straight up.

"Dammit!" He straightened fast, jumping forward as Virginia neighed, or made a sound as close to a laugh as the she-devil horse could muster. "Fine. One of the guys can brush you, ya old pain in the butt." In more ways than one.

He took her by the halter, unfastened her from the leads, and led her through the barn to her stall, then closed the damned door with more force than necessary. After putting the supplies away, he stomped out of the stable and across the yard, rubbing his right buttcheek.

"Did she bite you?" Holace asked. The bastard had the gall to actually laugh.

"Yes." Emmett turned with a hard glare.

Holace didn't even try to hide his mirth. "At least you have a matched set. Didn't Reggie get your other cheek a few days ago?"

He had, dammit. The last time he'd checked, his left buttcheek had been black and blue. Now the other was going to be the same. "Nice to know you have such a fascination with my asscheeks. Maybe you'd like to come over here and take a look?" Emmett winked, and Holace stumbled a second. His whole family and the dozen or so hands on the ranch knew he was gay. After all, there had been enough screaming, name calling, and stomping from his dad that all of central Montana knew exactly what was going on. Tears and worry from his mama, who could be just as dramatic in her own way. Needless to say, the fact that Emmett preferred bulls to heifers wasn't a secret.

"I don't want to be hearing about that gay stuff," Holace called back.

Emmett couldn't resist. "Then don't go taking an interest in my ass. I might take it as an invitation." He winked, and Holace stilled for a second before throwing his head back with a hearty laugh.

Emmett turned and walked away, but he resisted rubbing his butt again until he was out of sight. Damn, that hurt. For the past two days, he had sat to one side because of the soreness. Now that was shot to hell. But how was he going to explain to his mama that he needed to stand during dinner because a damn horse tried to bite a piece of his butt… again? He needed to get his mind on the tasks at hand, rather than worrying about stuff he couldn't change. This was his job, and like it or not, he needed to keep his nerves under control and his head in the game.

As soon as he stepped into the sprawling ranch house where he'd grown up, the scent of roasting chicken and a touch of vinegar reached his nose. He knew that meant coleslaw and probably mashed potatoes to go with the chicken. Emmett's stomach growled, and for a few seconds he forgot about his aching buttcheeks.

"That smells amazing, Martha," he said, taking off his boots before going to the large kitchen at the back of the house. Their cook and housekeeper took good care of him.

"I know it's your favorite," she said with a smile as she poured shredded cabbage into a large bowl. "I know what this family likes."

Emmett kissed her cheek and stole a taste of the salad. She scolded him, and he scooted out of the kitchen.

"Where's Mama?" Emmett asked.

"I think she's in her work room trying not to swear at her sewing machine," Martha said softly. Everyone knew his mother wouldn't say *shit* if she had a mouth full of it. Still, he smiled and thanked her before going down the hall and pausing outside the closed door. Muttering drifted through the door, and he knocked before opening it.

"What has you so riled up?" Emmett asked.

She huffed and then set aside the dress she was working on, turning with a smile. "You weren't supposed to hear that. Why do you think I had the door closed?" Her eyes were hard, even if the rest of her expression was completely composed. Giselle Eugenia Lafont McElroy had been raised as a Southern debutant, complete with cotillion lessons, afternoon tea, lessons in deportment, and even training in the arts, including painting and music. She could converse on any topic and entertain a room full of strangers as though they were old friends. She also believed that any unseemly behavior that might occur alone and behind closed doors simply didn't count—especially if it was hers. "Did you finish up with the horses? Dustin asked if you'd been in as he breezed through for lunch."

"Of course he did," Emmett said. He was surprised his father hadn't stopped in the barn to check up on him. Maybe he had and just hadn't made his presence known. His dad loved being stealthy. When Emmett was a kid, he used to think he was so clever, but every night at dinner, all the things he'd thought he'd gotten away with were discussed in front of everyone. That might have been okay if his older brother, RE, and his sister, Suzanne, had gotten the same treatment. They didn't. RE was always the golden child, the oldest and apple of his father's eye, and Suzanne, well, she was the only daughter. Emmett just seemed to exist in RE's shadow, until he was gone. And now Emmett was expected to fill his shoes. "The day he doesn't check up on me like I'm an errant teenager who doesn't know shit around here is the day he dies." It got so that Emmett could eat a full meal in five minutes and be gone from the table faster. That meant Dad had less time to enumerate his seemingly ever-growing list of faults. Emmett turned to leave his mother alone. His patience was wearing thin just talking about his father, and he didn't want to take it out on her.

"Watch your language," his mother scolded.

Emmett snickered. "I heard worse coming out of you through the door." It wasn't often that he got one up on his mama. In their family, his father, Dustin, wore the pants, but there was no doubt that his mama wore the genteel, pointed-toed shoes that could kick those pants right in the ass. "Where is Dad, anyway?"

"He was out with the men checking on the herd. He got some reports that one of the watering holes was getting a little low, so he went to check to see if some of the herd needed to be driven to lower ground." She turned back to the sewing machine. "Go and get yourself cleaned up and ready for dinner. I'm going to fight with the gather on this dress for a few more minutes." He turned. "And close the door." Apparently, the gather was going to require more words she didn't want to actually put out into the universe.

Emmett went to his room and closed the door. The one thing he had been able to convince his father to do for him had been to combine two of the smaller back bedrooms into one with its own bathroom. The work had been completed only a few months ago, and it had only happened because Suzanne would be moving out soon for her first year of medical school. RE... well, he was gone, and the loss of his older brother still hurt.

He winced as he gingerly sat on the edge of his bed, looking at the picture of himself and his brother, taken at Emmett's high school graduation. Emmett was gawky in his dark blue cap and gown, firmly in his brother's shadow. RE stood next to him, tall, broad, with bright eyes and a huge smile. The thing was that Emmett probably should have hated his perfect older brother. He'd been Dad's favorite and did no wrong, but RE had always made time for Emmett, encouraged him like his father never did, and even tried to teach him how to ride on numerous occasions. Not that it ever worked. He was nervous around horses and consequently they hated him, and he had the broken leg, two broken arms, and ending-up-on-his-ass-in-the-dirt more times than he could count to prove it. Maybe it was one of those circular logic sorts of things, his nerves making the horses hate him and then the horses making him nervous. But RE never gave up, and when he got hurt, it had been RE who took him to the hospital and sat with him while the doctor set his latest broken bone or stitched closed the cuts. It had been RE who looked out for him and stood up for him when he'd sneak off to the hayloft to read rather than shovel horse shit. It had been RE that he'd first told that he was gay, and his brother had not only hugged him and said it would be okay, but he kept his secret as far as Emmett knew— he'd said that was the sort of thing a man had to be the one to decide when he wanted folks to know. "Damn, RE, if you could see what Dad has me doing now, you'd probably crap yourself laughing." Managing the horses on the Rolling D had been RE's job. But then his brother died when a semi plowed into his truck, and now it fell to Emmett. The shock of RE's death had nearly killed his parents, and in some ways they had yet to recover. Emmett knew he was a poor substitute for his brother, but he always did his best… and had the sore ass to prove it.

He stripped out of his clothes and hit the shower, checking his backside in the mirror. Sure enough, he was indeed going to have another livid bruise. Not that it mattered, because no one was going to see his bare ass except him. Emmett washed quickly and dressed in a clean pair of jeans and a red polo shirt Suzanne had given him for Christmas last year. His mother insisted that they look nice for dinner, and not even his father dared contradict her. Jeans were only recently allowed. When he was a child, it had been dress pants and a church-worthy shirt for dinner every night. Talk about torture.

"Do you need any help?" Emmett asked Martha as he passed through the kitchen.

"No. I have everything under control. Your dad came in ten minutes ago, and he's in the living room with your mama." They always shared a glass of wine or a cocktail before dinner. It seemed out of place on the ranch, but it was one of Mama's rituals, and Dad liked to keep her happy.

"Then you're sure there isn't something I can do?" He snatched a carrot off the counter, munching on it and getting out of her way as she pulled open the oven door. Avoiding his dad was becoming his sport of choice.

"Go on in. Your dad seemed in a good mood," Martha said and shooed him out of the kitchen. Not that he wanted to piss her off. Martha took care of the entire family, but she always especially looked out for him. When he was little, she always had a cookie ready when things between him and his dad went to crap. To his father, Emmett should be a cowboy, like everyone else in the family, but Emmett had other interests—like books and even sketching and art—that his father didn't see as cowboy-like. Not that Emmett was particularly talented, but those things didn't involve horses and tying his belly in knots. The nights he ran from the table under his dad's sometimes withering criticism, she'd sneak a sandwich and a chocolate chip cookie to his room so he didn't go hungry.

"Good to know," he said softly and went into the living room, where he poured himself a glass of the wine his folks were drinking. His mother knew all about wine and made sure that there were always good bottles in the cellar. Emmett knew what he liked, though he preferred beer or a mixed drink.

"I went looking for you," his dad said as soon as Emmett set the bottle back on the tray. "But you were busy."

"Of course I was," Emmett retorted. "I'm always busy."

"Sit down," his mother said.

"I'm fine." Emmett wasn't going to explain in front of his dad that he'd gotten his ass bitten… again. Still, he turned to him. "Was everything up to your illustrious standards?" He drank half the glass of wine in a few gulps.

"Don't be a smartass," his father snapped.

"Then stop acting like I'm still a kid to be scolded." He'd managed the cutting horse portion of the family business for the five years since RE's accident, stepping into his older brother's shoes because his father expected it. Emmett had hoped to leave the ranch to make his own way in the world, become a high-powered businessman or a lawyer, or maybe an astronaut. Unlike most kids, his dreams didn't involve horses. Nonetheless, most of the time he'd even learned to manage his nerves around them.

Dad ran the entire family business but concentrated on the cattle portion. It was much larger and provided the bulk of the business income. All his life, Emmett felt as though he tried to live up to his father's expectations and fell short. With RE gone, it seemed as though he fell shorter and farther from the mark of what his dad wanted, probably because he just wasn't his brother. No matter what he did, things weren't right, even when Emmett knew he was doing exactly what his father would in the same circumstances.

The back door closed, and Suzanne called to announce that she was home. Emmett glared into his father's intense blue eyes and then turned to his mother, then back to his dad. "I don't know what time you started this morning, but you were snoring loud enough to wake the dead when I got up and started before you." He finished his wine and set the glass down before meeting Suzanne with a hug. "Hey, sissy."

She returned it. "Going a round with Dad, Em?" she whispered as she gave his backside a pat—her older-sister way of letting him know that she knew what happened. He stifled a hiss and stepped away from her.

"Here, honey, have a glass of wine," his father said, suddenly all smiles. "How was the visit?"

"Perfect. I have everything all set, classes all registered, and I found out the books I'm going to need. They're being shipped here so I can work through them in the next two weeks. The first year of med school is a killer, and I'm going to be ready." She was always top of her class in everything. Determined and driven, she and Emmett had been close growing up, but their lives seemed on different paths now. "How are the horses, Em?" Dang, she could be wicked when she wanted to be. She winked to say she was only teasing.

"Good. Virginia is as ornery as ever," he told her. "Holace is doing some amazing work with the others, and we're going to have a wonderful crop of cutting horses to sell on the open market in a few months." Each of their horses, with their bloodlines and training, sold for tens of thousands of dollars.

"I saw him working with the yearlings," his dad said. "He looked good. Maybe next week I'll come by and do an evaluation." He finished his wine and leaned back in his seat before burping softly.

"No need. They aren't ready yet. It will be a few months." Emmett might not have a rapport with the horses, but he knew well enough that none were ready. Still, his father would step in, look things over, and come to the same conclusion that he did, only with a side of grief and disruption.

"Dustin, let Emmett do his job," his mother said softly, even as his dad stared a hole in him.

Emmett returned his father's dead-reckoning stare. He used to think his father could see into his soul with that look on his weathered, suntanned face. Dustin McElroy was every inch a cowboy, pure and simple—everything Emmett knew he would never be—and sometimes the disappointment in his father's eyes was more than he could stand. "It's fine. Dad can come by any time he wants." Emmett tried to keep the hurt and frustration out of his voice.

Fortunately, Martha came in to say that dinner was ready. That ended the staring contest, but nothing was going to change between them. Maybe they were both too stubborn for their own good.

Martha had dinner on the table, and the five of them took their places. It had taken Mama a long while before she could convince Martha to eat dinner with them. "Where's Marianne?" Suzanne asked as their father started passing the food around the table.

"She's having dinner with some friends," Martha answered with a smile. Marianne was Martha's only child and the apple of her eye. She also had a tongue as sharp as a knife and said what was on her mind. There had been many times when she'd left Emmett completely gobsmacked, and his little gay cowboy heart loved her for it.

Even though Mama knew Emmett was gay—he had the tearstained handkerchief to prove it—she still held out hope that he and Marianne would get together. She pushed them on each other at every opportunity. Even if he weren't gay, Marianne was almost as much a sister to him as Suzanne was, and the idea of getting together with her felt wrong on every level.

"When does she return to school?" Emmett asked. Marianne was entering her senior year at the University of Montana.

"A couple months." Martha smiled and yet seemed like she might cry at the same time. "Just the rest of the summer, and then my baby will be completely out on her own."

Mama took Martha's hand and looked at Suzanne. "I know exactly what you mean."

"If you got your head screwed on straight, you could marry that girl, make both your mama and her mama happy, settle down, and maybe start filling this house with little McElroys to carry on the family name," his father growled, and then put his hand to his chest. He patted it gently and set down his fork. He drank some water and sat still.

"Dustin?" his mother asked.

"Just a little indigestion. Been belching all day." He performed a demonstration and picked up his fork.

Mama rolled her eyes. "Dustin, you may be doing it, but you don't need to talk about it at the table," she scolded gently and continued watching him until he began eating again.

Emmett shook his head. He had heard that little aria about him and Marianne more times than he could count, and every time he tried to argue, his mother got upset and his father got angry. It was a familiar tune, and every time he came out a loser, so he lowered his gaze and returned to his dinner, eating quickly so he could escape and just get away.

"Sorry, Em," Suzanne whispered to him and continued eating. He noticed her sympathy, but also that she didn't stand up for him either. Emmett had long ago learned that his sister loved being Daddy's little girl, and she wasn't about to do anything to jeopardize his view of her.

He shrugged. "You know, Mama, maybe it's time I do what Suzanne and Marianne did. I've been thinking of taking the college entrance tests and looking into classes, probably business. I was always good at math and things like that." After high school he had wanted to go away to college himself, but RE passed away, so he'd put that on hold to help his family. Now he really hoped he could go.

The look that passed between his parents was unmistakable. Disappointment... again. Maybe he should have those words tattooed on each of his bruised buttcheeks.

Since RE's death, he had been expected to fill his impossibly big shoes, and that meant being the heir apparent, learning the ranch, taking his brother's position, and eventually assuming control of the ranch from his father. Whether he wanted to or not was as unrelated as deep-sea fishing and the Montana Rockies. He took the last bite of his dinner and pushed back his chair. "Thank you, Martha. That was delicious as always." He gave her a smile and stood, thankful to be upright and off his aching backside. "I have some things I need to check in the stables."

His mama gave him one of her patented unhappy looks with her eyes hard and her mouth set.

"The boy has things to do." His father reached for his water with his right hand and slopped it all down his front before dropping the glass to the floor, where it shattered. He placed his hands on his chest, gasping for air as he leaned back in the chair and began to slump under the table. Suzanne jumped up and helped catch him.

"Call an ambulance, Mama," Suzanne said with authority. "Now!" she added when Giselle didn't move. Emmett pulled out his phone, made the call, and handed the phone to his mother while he helped Suzanne get his father out of the chair.

Emmett lifted his dad—he had no idea how—and carried him to the sofa, where Suzanne took over his care. He stepped back, with Mama looking fearfully at his father, who was still clutching his chest. He was as white as a sheet. Mama held the phone to her ear as she knelt next to the sofa and held his father's hand.

After the longest fifteen minutes in history, sirens sounded and drew closer, and then an ambulance pulled into the yard. "I'll go with him," Mama said.

"Okay," Suzanne agreed as the EMTs raced inside. Only then did Mama end the call and hand Emmett back his phone. "Emmett and I will follow you."

His father grabbed Emmett's hand and tugged him close, pain in the blue eyes that usually only displayed stubborn strength. "Son...." He leaned closer, his voice weak and soft, deep lines etched around his eyes and mouth.

"Yeah, Dad," Emmett said, swallowing hard. "Don't try to talk. Save your strength."

He squeezed Emmett's hand and winced. "Stay here. Someone has to look over the horses and cattle." His father let go, and Emmett backed away, a sense of renewed rejection washing over him, but he pushed it away. If his father wanted him to look after the ranch, then he would do his best to make his father proud.

Chapter 2

"YOUR FATHER actually said that?" Emmett's best friend Reid asked in total disbelief. "No damn way. Do you want me to come over there and put a little bleach in his catheter? Maybe some Bengay in his jockey shorts? You know I will. Just say the word."

Reid could always make him smile, even at a time like this. The combination of his over-the-top personality, his Easter-egg-yellow hair, and the rainbow studs in his ears declared his sexuality louder than a pink-and-lavender ten-piece band dressed as Dorothy. "It's okay. I shouldn't have expected anything different." Emmett set aside his tools and moved the horse he was working with back into the stall, avoiding hooves and teeth as much as possible.

Reid shifted his stance, right foot forward, hands on his hips. "No one should be treated like that by their father."

"He was having a heart attack and was worried about the ranch," Emmett said, but he knew he was just covering for him. His father never saw Emmett for who he was, just what he wanted or needed him to be. Emmett was stuck, and he didn't know the way out. Since RE's death, Emmett had been the person his parents relied on—and yet they only saw him as RE's replacement.

Reid huffed. "I'm not buying that, and neither should you. That man has talked you down for fricking ever. And now when he has a heart attack, it's all 'stay here and look after my ranch.' Suddenly you're the one who should look after the shit that he would never let you near when he was well. Your father guards those books and cattle records like they're made of gold, and now he expects you to pick up after him." Reid narrowed his gaze. "This coming from a man who knows you and horses don't get along, but put you in charge of them anyway." He scowled. "And don't think I haven't noticed how gingerly you're walking. If I thought you were getting a little something, I'd say good for you, but the horses bit you again, didn't they?"

There were times when having Reid as a best friend was like living with the town telephone operator, when they'd still had one. He always seemed to know everything about everyone's business. He and Emmett had been friends since the fifth grade, when this flamboyant kid walked into his class, took one look at Emmett, and decided they were going to BFFs. When kids picked on either of them, Reid shut them down with his razor-blade-sharp tongue.

"I wish the entire world would lose interest in my ass."

Reid snickered. "Honey, you must be *really* depressed, because I'd give anything to have my ass the center of attention, especially the hot, rugged, cowboy kind of attention." He fanned himself with his bedazzled cowboy hat, showing off his almost glow-in-the-dark hair. "I'd forgotten how hot some of these guys were and the way they could fill out a pair of Wranglers."

"Somehow I find that hard to believe," Emmett teased before checking out the stables. He was so used to his father deriding him for the smallest thing out of place that he instinctively checked that the stable was perfect before pulling Reid into a hug. "I missed you so damned much. I'm glad you're back from the big city, even if it is under terrible circumstances."

Reid nodded slowly against his shoulder and then pulled away. "I wonder why horses hate you like they do. Maybe it's the way you smell. I read horses use scent to warn them of danger. So I was wondering, maybe you smell like a mountain lion or something." He leaned close. "Or maybe it's rotten feed." His eyes gleamed with mischief. "I know you have this nerves thing around them, but that can't be all there is to it."

"Well, that's comforting." He rolled his eyes as he shook his head. The stuff that went through the tangle of Reid's mind was frightening. "How is your mom?" A change of subject was definitely in order, and Beth had been sick on and off for years.

"As stubborn as ever," Reid answered seriously.

"There's a lot of that going around. I'm starting to think there's something in the water around here." Or maybe it was the smell of horse and cow shit that was making everyone a little loopy.

Reid hugged him tighter. "You know my mother. She called and asked me to come back to help her decimate cancer. She never did anything by halves." He backed away and wiped his eyes. "She's going to beat cancer or die trying." He rolled his eyes, but the words were clearly straight from Beth Ziegfeld's lips. Reid's smile at his mother's humor was only on the surface. Worry filled his eyes, and Emmett pulled his friend into another hug. He had his own set of worries in the parent department, and together, they comforted one another.

"WHAT ARE you going to do?" Reid asked as they left the stables, heading for the house and the lifeblood of the entire ranch: the coffee pot.

"I don't know. Hope that Dad isn't as bad as I think and that he's going to be able to return pretty soon," Emmett answered just as his phone rang—one of his father's foremen. He paused in his steps and pulled it out. "Yeah, Glen, what's going on?"

"The feed order needs to be placed, and your dad always did it. I'm in town, and James stopped me to say that he hadn't gotten an order and needs it today if we're going to have it next week." Glen seemed a little edgy, which everyone on the Rolling D had become over the past few days. Like they were all waiting for something to happen to blow everything all to hell because Dustin McElroy wasn't there to guide the ship. The operation was sizable with thousands of head of cattle, but everything ran through his father.

"Okay," Emmett said calmly. "Do you know what we need?"

"Yeah… but your dad always did it, and…," Glen sputtered. He had been on this ranch for a decade, and Emmett knew he was smart.

"Dad can't do it, so we all have to stand in for him. You know what we need, so order it. If the feed store wants some kind of authorization, then have them call me. Until Dad gets back, you're in charge of the feed. So arrange to take delivery of it when it comes in and ensure it gets stowed in the proper place. We can talk about it face-to-face when you get back here." Emmett took a deep breath and released it slowly. There were going to be so many things like this.

"Yes, Emmett. Count on it." He hung up, and Emmett put his phone back in his pocket and turned to Reid, who rocked back and forth on his heels.

"What?" He had a tendency to do that when he was excited, and at this moment he looked like one of those old roly-poly punching bags that bounced back when you hit them.

Emmett's phone rang again, and he answered it and took care of another issue left hanging by his father's illness while they went inside and Martha greeted them with the coffee Emmett craved.

Once in the living room, Reid was too bouncy to sit. He fluttered through the comfortably furnished space. Emmett's mother had put a lot of thought into its large, masculine furniture with deep colors, which reflected his father. But it still had his mother all over it, with rich curtains and huge abstract paintings on the wall that always reminded Emmett of the land they worked every day. The paintings were so different from anything else around, and yet they fit right in.

"What am I going to do?" Emmett asked.

"Exactly what you're doing?" Reid answered, rolling his eyes as though Emmett were stupid. "Everyone on this ranch is looking to you. They ask you questions and listen to you." He threw his hands in the air. "Step into your father's shoes and take over the ranch. Someone has to run it, and your sister isn't and I don't think your mom can. You need to do it, and I've watched you step up even if you don't realize it. Get yourself up to speed on what your father was doing and what his plans were and make them happen. You're smart—you'll learn and grow into the role." He finally sat down next to him, and the energy level in the room descended by a factor of almost a hundred.

Emmett nodded. This was his chance to make a difference at the Rolling D. RE was gone, and the weight of being the heir fell to him. He hadn't thought he wanted it, but now he saw this situation as an opportunity. If he could show his father he was capable of running the entire operation, then maybe, just maybe, his father would see him as something other than as his son the disappointment. He nodded and actually smiled. Reid was right—he could do this. Heck, to a degree he already had. Finally, some of the apprehension and anxiety that always seemed present slipped away. This could be exactly what he was meant to do. He always dreamed of being a businessman, so he would see to it that the business portion of the ranch ran better than when his father did it. It sure felt right to him. Emmett sat back and finished his coffee, already planning out the evening and the next few days in his mind—with someone *else* tending the horses.

HE AND Reid were in the kitchen having a light dinner an hour later when his mother came inside, hair mussed, dark circles under her eyes, and sat blankly in her chair at the table.

"How is Dustin doing?" Reid asked as Emmett poured her a cup of coffee and set a plate of food down for her.

She ignored it and met Emmett's gaze. "The heart attack was worse than they first thought. He's going to have to have bypass surgery, and the doctors are saying that he's going to need a long recovery time. The attack damaged his heart. We're going to have to change the way we live and work." She bit her lower lip. "I don't know what we're going to do."

That was the understatement of the century. His father ran the family business with a tight fist, only letting Emmett in on parts of it. Taking on the entire ranch with all its complexity was something he'd known would eventually fall to him, but he hadn't expected it would happen so soon—he was only twenty-three. Still, it was what his family needed, and a well of excitement built in his gut as he once again reminded himself that he could do this. "I'll do all I can; you know that, Mama. Just take care of Dad and don't worry about anything here."

She smiled for the first time since his father's heart attack. "I know you will." She took a few bites of her dinner and drank some of her coffee, her movements smooth and dainty from decades of ingrained practice that made Emmett sure she didn't think about them at all. "Things are going to be different now."

"I know they will, and Dad isn't going to be able to do all the things he once did. But we have good people here, and they can learn. All they need is leadership, and that can be provided." He figured he'd spend his days with the hands and his evenings in his father's office, seeing what was what and how he was going to ensure that everything continued running the way it was supposed to. One way or another, he'd make sure that the family business continued and that everyone on the Rolling D was taken care of.

After taking a few more bites, she drank a little more coffee and excused herself. "I'm going to clean up and then go back to the hospital to be with your father. Suzanne is going to school as planned. She wanted to stay, but she needs to start medical school on time or she'll lose her spot." She left the room, and Emmett watched after her.

"I never got how your mom could put up with your dad. They seem so…," Reid said quietly. "I mean, it's pretty obvious that they love each other. But they seem like oil and water." He leaned over the table. "Your mom is so genteel and refined, and your dad is… well… anything but." Reid smirked, and Emmett half expected him to stick his tongue out. "See, I can be tactful and didn't say that your dad was a horse's ass." The lack of filter on Reid's mouth had gotten them in trouble more than once—especially that time at that bar in Missoula with the biker the size of a brick outhouse. He'd asked Reid why he'd picked such a pansy-assed hair color. Reid had batted his eyes and quipped, "And here I thought pigs were colorblind." They got out of there ahead of the guy's pounding fists, and Reid had agreed that Missoula was probably off limits for a while. They had been there to have a little fun and let their hair down away from town. They'd definitely done that.

"Tactful once in a blue moon," Emmett teased.

"So why them?" Reid asked.

"Because Dustin was stunning," Emmett's mother answered. Reid had the decency to blush and stammer an apology. Neither of them realized she had come back into the room. "He was every inch the cowboy back then, just as he is now. But when I met him, it was at a social for service members in Biloxi, where he was stationed." Some of the lines around her lips and eyes faded as her features relaxed. "I remember seeing him across the room, and he came over and asked me to dance. I agreed, and he asked me question after question… and actually listened."

"Was it love at first sight?" Reid asked.

"Heavens no. I thought he was handsome, but my parents would never have stood for me being interested in someone like him." She stood up straight, hands gently clasped in front of herself. "My parents wanted me to marry the son of a friend of theirs. He was dull as dirt, and Dustin was exciting. I snuck out to see him a few times, and we always went dancing because he said I was too pretty not to show off. After a few months, he was stationed somewhere else, and I thought that was the end. But your father wrote to me every week, faithful as anything. There was none of this email everyone uses today. He wrote old-fashioned letters, and I wrote him back. I don't even know when my feelings changed, but he returned when he got leave for three days. Your grandmother wanted him to come here, but he returned to Mississippi to see me. Then we wrote each other until he got out of the Army. By then I knew he was the one for me, though my mother and father provided a steady parade of acceptable men for me to choose from. But I knew my heart and what I wanted. When he asked me to marry him, I said yes, and my parents threatened to disown me. But I loved him and didn't think twice. We married anyway, and he brought me here to the ranch."

Reid's mouth hung open. "Did they ever forgive you?"

Giselle smiled. "It took them six years, and three grandchildren that they had never seen, before they came for a visit. My father and Dustin came to a truce of sorts." She turned to Emmett. "I know that you and your father don't see eye to eye, but he's a good man, and in his heart, he wants what's best for the ranch and for his family." She sighed and slowly moved toward the door, as graceful as a dancer. "When I see him, I'll tell him that you have things under control and that he isn't to worry." She passed behind Emmett, patting him lightly on the shoulder before leaving the room once again.

"I bet there's a lot more to that story than she told us," Reid said quietly.

Emmett nodded. "Like Grandpa threatening to run my dad off with a shotgun." He snickered. "We're from Montana. Dad probably had the bigger gun."

Martha came in to clear the table. The two of them helped her before Emmett saw Reid to his car so he could check on his mother. Then Emmett did a final walk-through of the stables before heading to his father's office.

Emmett would have thought that with the kind of discipline he required everywhere on the ranch, the office would be a model of organization. It was anything but. It took him all evening to make sense of his father's filing system, and he didn't dare move anything before he figured out what was what, in case he screwed things up. Every time the air conditioning turned on, a slight breeze fluttered the air, and he held his breath in case the papers shifted in some disastrous paper tornado. Everything was on paper or in handwritten ledgers. The computer on the desk functioned more as a paperweight than an actual piece of equipment.

"Oh God," he sighed after finally determining that one pile was paid receipts that needed to be filed somewhere in the polished wood cabinet in the corner, while others were projections, ideas, bills to be paid, and the good Lord knew what else.

This was a damned disaster, but one good thing was that the ledgers seemed to be up to date. At least he hoped to hell they were, since he saw the bills received already entered but not yet paid. The ranch finances were one thing he could actually see and get his hands around. He'd always had a mind for numbers and money, but his father never let him anywhere near the records. Now he had to figure out how his father actually ran the cattle operation and got the herds in the locations where they belonged at the right times—and all of that seemed to be firmly lodged in his father's head. Emmett had never had any luck figuring out his father, and now he had one hell of a puzzle to unravel. But for the first time in five years, RE's shadow, the one that hung over him constantly, seemed to recede. With his father out of action, maybe this was his chance to step out of it completely.

HE JUMPED when his phone rang. Emmett's neck and back ached from where he'd fallen asleep over his father's desk. He straightened up and pulled the paperclip off his cheek, hoping he wouldn't have an impression of the thing on his skin all day. "Yeah," he mumbled, peeling his sandy eyes open.

"Where are you?"

"I'm in the office, Mama. Did something happen? Is Dad worse?" He got to his feet, pulling the door open. "I was working to try to figure out where things were." He shuffled to the kitchen, where, bless Martha's heart, she already had coffee on. Martha clicked her tongue at him but said nothing as he poured a mug.

"Your father is sleeping. They brought in a bed so I could stay with him. He had a good night, it seems."

Emmett sighed. "That's good. Are you coming home today? Do you need me to bring anything up to the hospital?"

"No. We're fine, and I have everything we need. They're telling me that your father will probably sleep much of the day, but plan to come up tomorrow. He's worried about the ranch and asks about it whenever he wakes up."

Emmett had stopped up to see his father a couple days ago, but he'd been asleep, and Emmett had just sat with him and let him rest.

"I'll hold down the fort here," Emmett told her. "The horses are fine, and the guys have a good handle on the cattle." He sipped from his mug.

"Good. I'll let your father know." She sounded exhausted, her accent coming forward more prominently.

"Then I'll talk to you later," Emmett told her just before the connection dropped. He set the phone on the counter, drank some more of his coffee, and then went up to his room to change clothes and get ready for the day.

"OKAY, VIRGINIA. Keep those teeth of yours to yourself," Emmett said softly later that afternoon. He had her in the crossties and drew them a little tighter than usual in order to ensure her teeth didn't get anywhere near his backside. He checked her new shoes and liked that the hoof looked good.

"Emmett?" an unfamiliar voice said from behind him. "I was told I'd find you out here."

Emmett finished with her hoof and released it, stepping away and out of kicking distance before looking up into a pair of eyes he hadn't seen in a number of years.

"Nate." Emmett smiled at the sight of his brother's best friend. Part of him wanted to hug Nathaniel Zachary, but he didn't have a right to do that. They were friends, nothing more, so a handshake sufficed. Warmth flooded through him at the first touch and continued building as he stood in front of his first crush. He hoped to hell that he didn't blush like a teenager as he stared into the large, deep blue eyes that had starred in more late-night fantasies than he ever wanted to admit. He swallowed, looking Nate over. There were lines around his eyes now, and the straight, tall stance that supported the swagger Emmett remembered was more stooped than Emmett recalled. "It's been…."

"Since Dad's funeral," Nate said, and Emmett nodded slowly. He remembered going with his mom.

"You left town after that," Emmett said, wondering why Nate was here and at the same time glad he was. It had been too long. Seeing Nate again was like getting a part of RE back. The two had been close for so many years, and Nate had seemed like a part of their family while Emmett was growing up.

"Yeah. I joined the rodeo circuit to try to make some money and save the ranch for Mom." From the way his eyes darkened, that hadn't been successful. "We had to sell it a while ago, and I was looking for a job."

Emmett nodded. "I see. Dad's currently in the hospital, but I'll go up tomorrow, and if he's awake, I'll ask him about a job for you."

Nate tilted his head slightly to the side. "That's why I'm here. I talked to your mom a few hours ago, and she offered me one. I take it she didn't tell you. They offered me the job as ranch foreman and asked me to oversee all operations while your father is recuperating. Giselle said that even once Dustin recovered, they would need one, because she intended to make sure he cut way back on his workload. Until then, I'm to report to her."

"I see." Emmett forced a smile he hoped looked genuine as that glimmer of sun he'd felt earlier darkened, the shadow he'd spent his entire life in falling right back into place. "That's good, then." There was no way in hell he was going to show an ounce of how butt-hurt he was. He'd always thought his mother, at least, was in his corner, but it seemed that neither of his parents had any faith in him.

"Thought I'd stop by to see you. If it's okay, I'll bring my things by in the morning and get started."

Emmett nodded but didn't really hear much of what Nate said next. Just when Emmett thought he might be able to carve a place for himself, his parents brought in Nate to upset everything.

Chapter 3

SOMETIMES LIFE was more turbulent than a bronco, but both seemed to dump you on your butt in the dirt at the end, and you ended up racing for safety, brushing away the sand. Nathaniel's life had certainly had all the spins of a rodeo champion bucking horse. The bed of the pickup held three battered suitcases—one pink, because it was what he could find at the secondhand store. The rest was in boxes, aside from his saddles and gear, not that he was going to need it. Nate's rodeo days were behind him—hell, the life he'd known before his father passed away was gone as well. His life rested in a tiny apartment, the bed of a pickup, and the view of the road ahead, which finally held a glimmer of hope. It seems that life had more ups and downs than a rent boy on a pogo stick.

Nate turned into the ranch driveway, parked next to the other vehicles, and got out. At a little after six in the morning, the place was already buzzing, which was exactly what Nate had expected. The Rolling D had always been well run, and it was good to see that some things didn't change. Standing in the middle of the yard, he could almost see RE hurrying over to tell him that he was ready to head into town, Emmett following behind asking to go along, looking at RE like he hung the moon and having a ball the times they agreed to take him.

"Morning. Help ya?" one of the men asked.

"Nathaniel Zachary," he said, extending his hand. The cowboy shook it. "Mrs. McElroy hired me on as—"

"Nate," Emmett called from the door to the stables. "This is Holace. He's our own version of the horse whisperer. Holace, this is Nate, our new foreman." Nate couldn't miss the flatness in Emmett's voice. "My parents hired him, so pass the word that this evening, everyone is to come to the house so they can meet the new foreman. Make sure everyone knows."

"Sure, Emmett," Holace said with tension and suspicion before turning and going back inside the stable.

"Come on. My father has been acting as foreman of the cattle operation, but I can show you around." Emmett peered in the back of the truck, grinning as Nate pulled out the old pink suitcase. "Something I need to know?" The slight quirk to his mouth lasted just a fraction of a second.

"I needed another one, and it was what they had. Figured I might need extra clothes for working," Nate growled, keeping his expression serious. He took the suitcase and put it in the cab of the truck before slamming the door. Then he followed Emmett inside.

Damn, the boy he knew had become one hell of a man. Oh, Nate had seen Emmett a few times over the years, but not enough to get a good look at him. Emmett was compact, not bulky, but there was muscle there, and he filled out his jeans perfectly. Nate remembered how when he and RE were growing up, the two of them had been inseparable, even when RE's little brother tagged along. At first, the kid had been a nuisance, but then Emmett turned seventeen and grew into himself—and oh God, did he ever. There were nights when Nate found himself staring at his bedroom ceiling trying not to think about his friend's younger brother. Emmett was way off limits, but his teenage mind had a will of its own sometimes. RE was Nate's best friend, and Nate thought of him as a brother from another mother, but Emmett…. All of a sudden Nate was having thoughts about him—ones that he knew would have his best friend kicking his ass into next week.

"Sorry," Nate said when he realized Emmett had been saying something.

"I was asking if you'd need a place to stay on the ranch. I assumed you would, but then you didn't have much stuff." He pulled open the door and led Nate down to a very familiar room. "This is—"

"I know what it is," Nate said softly as he pushed open the door to the room RE had used growing up. Nate half expected the walls to still be covered with RE's awards and the shelf over the window threatening to fall down under the weight of his trophies. But all that was gone, and the room was just a room now, with a bed, a dresser, and a huge closet. More space than he needed. Still, if these walls could talk, the things they'd say… even today. Nate had had more sleepovers in this room than he could remember. He and RE would stay up half the night whispering so they didn't wake up the rest of the house. It didn't matter that the two of them would have to be up for chores, and more than once Dustin had found either Nate or RE leaning on a broom, sound asleep. As they got older, Nate and RE figured some things out. Like the fact that RE was interested in Molly Hansen and Nate was more interested in her brother, Claude. They shared each other's secrets and dreams. The one thing that Nate never told RE about was his budding interest in Emmett that bloomed into full fruition when Emmett turned seventeen, but had probably been there for longer. That was one secret that he always kept to himself.

"At least it doesn't look the same," Emmett said after clearing his throat. "Mom redecorated it about a year after RE's accident. She couldn't stand to see all his things any longer."

Nate could understand that. "I have a place of my own between here and town. But maybe you can show me around and tell me what's changed."

"Not very much," Emmett said with a smile. "In case you haven't figured it out, my father likes things done the same way they have been. He doesn't change anything unless it's the size of the herd, which is bigger now than when we were kids. It took five years and RE threatening to go buy his own for him to allow ATVs on the property. He felt we should wrangle the cattle on horseback... preferably the horses we raised and trained on our own."

"I see." Nate turned away from Emmett's incredible blue eyes and wavy hair that almost reached his collar, indented where his hat pressed the hair down. Emmett licked his lips, and Nate wondered what they would taste like. Before he realized what he was doing, he even started to lean closer. There was something that drew him like the unchangeable force of gravity. But Nate pushed the idea away and straightened before Emmett could notice. He was here to work, and God knows he didn't need to complicate things. This job was his chance, a gift from the gods after injuring his back one too many times after being thrown in the rodeo ring, and he wasn't going to mess it up over some old crush that seemed to have bubbled up once again. After all, going back out on the circuit wasn't an option and ranching was the only other thing he knew, but people didn't want to hire someone whose back could leave him flat on it for a week or more. The McElroys were good people and willing to give him a chance. He had to make this job work.

Emmett turned to leave the room. Nate watched him out of the corner of his eye and didn't move until Emmett was out of sight. Then he left the once-familiar room with its memories, closing the door behind him.

"WHAT ARE you up to?" Nate asked as he stepped into the stables. Emmett turned, and damned if the nearest horse didn't snap her head forward. Emmett jumped out of the reach of those teeth.

"Virginia!" Emmett scolded.

"Did she try to bite you?" Nate approached her. Virginia nuzzled her head to his chest, and he carefully rubbed her nose. "What did you do to her?"

"Nothing," Emmett protested. "She's always done that. I swear she just doesn't like me."

Nate chuckled. "Either than or she thinks you're tasty." Nate could get behind that idea.

"That horse and Reggie, the black stallion over there, have this thing going. They're both fascinated with my backside." Emmett blushed big-time, and Nate couldn't help himself.

"You have butt-biting horses? That must be some sort of specialty. Maybe when it's time to take Reggie to the sales, we can add that as one of his characteristics. We could list him as having great taste in cowboy ass. That would appeal to someone." It took him a few seconds to realize what he'd just said, and then Nate wished the ground would open up and swallow him whole.

"Yeah, well...." Emmett huffed and continued down the stables, explaining about each of the horses. "Thankfully it seems that only those two have biting issues. The others tend to try to stomp my feet or just press me against stable walls. It's no big deal."

"Wait," Nate said. "If you don't get along with the horses, then why work with them?" He narrowed his gaze.

"Because this was supposed to be RE's job. He'd manage the horses, Dad would run the cattle, and when Dad thought RE was ready, he'd take over the entire operation and Dad would semi retire. That was the plan all along. RE was the heir; I was the spare. And now that RE is gone, I'm supposed to step up and fill his shoes. That's what Dad and the family expect, and nothing else will do. That's how things work at the Rolling D. Whatever Dad envisions is what has to happen, regardless of what anyone else wants or is good at. So for the past five years I've worked with the horses and kept my mouth shut when I get bit or when my feet hurt from being stepped on or my shins are black and blue from a well-placed kick." His eyes blazed, anger simmering just below the surface. "What is complaining going to do? Dad doesn't listen to anyone, and the only ideas that matter are his."

This was messed up. "Why don't you show me around the rest of the old place?" There was nothing he could do to change things until he got the lay of the land and figured out a way forward. Hell, he might not even get the chance to do anything other than make sure the operation kept moving forward. He had been brought on as foreman, but eventually Dustin was going to come back, and as the ultimate boss, he'd have the final say over how things were done.

"Holace, do you have things here?" Emmett asked.

"Sure. I'll finish feeding and watering before putting the horses out in the paddocks for the day." He got back to work, and Emmett motioned to the stable door.

"In addition to the horse operation that's centered around the yard here, we have the cattle operation, which consists of ten thousand head spread over almost thirty thousand acres of grazing land. There's a land map with boundaries in the office. We also have rights on an additional ten thousand acres of federal land that were granted almost a century ago."

"Weren't they in dispute?" Nate asked. He seemed to remember the uproar over it when he and RE had been in high school.

"Yes. The federal government wanted to terminate them and renegotiate. Dad took them to court, and they lost. He produced the original document from the safe that granted the use of the land in perpetuity, and they folded like a house of cards. That bill is the one that Dad pays with glee each and every year, registered and certified." It was great to see Emmett smile. Nate got the feeling that it didn't happen very often. "We've been building the herd gradually over the last decade, and the plan is to get to thirty-five thousand head."

"A sizable operation," Nate observed.

"Yeah. We have a number of hands on the ranch, and I'll see that you're introduced to all of them." He now seemed tense once more. "Our main water source is the Black Creek, which flows from the mountains over there and meets Rock Creek on the property. Those two bodies of water are enough to support all our needs."

"Are there limits on what you can take?" Water use rights were almost as valuable as the land out here.

"No. That's another stipulation in the original deed and in the agreement the government wanted to change. We take no more than we need and have a number of catch basins on the property so that when it does rain, we're capturing it." He led Nate behind the house. "The rise over there wasn't useful for anything, so RE convinced Dad to put it to use. Now those solar panels generate most of our electricity in the summer. Not so much in the winter, but it works out that we pay very little for power."

The operation seemed impressive, and Emmett's knowledge of it seemed thorough. While Nate was grateful for the job and probably would have taken a position here as one of the hands, he didn't understand why Dustin and Giselle hadn't made Emmett foreman and let him take over the operation. No wonder Emmett seemed like he wanted to spit nails at any second. Nate couldn't blame him.

Emmett's phone rang, and he answered it. "I'm on my way." He shoved the phone into his pocket. "There's something I need to see in the stable." He turned and strode back the way they had come. Nate followed out of curiosity.

Holace stood outside one of the stalls, pacing nervously, foot tapping. "What is it?" Nate asked, his instinct for leadership taking over.

"We seem to have an unexpected development." He motioned into the stall.

Emmett peered inside and his eyes widened. Then he turned back, muttering under his breath. "Holy shit." Nate peered in to where a mare stood with a newborn foal nursing, just as beautiful as anything. "How the hell did that happen?"

"You didn't know she was pregnant?" Nate asked.

"She wasn't bred. Matilda here was too old for breeding, so we were putting her out to pasture. And not only did she sow her wild oats, but the old girl kept the results of her wandering eye a complete secret," Holace said, watching the mare and foal.

"Dad is going to have a fit," Emmett said.

"Why?" Nate asked, turning toward him.

"Because of this. How did she get pregnant, and why didn't we know?" He swallowed hard. "There will be a lecture about leaving paddock gates open, or the one about the birds and the bees, just to make sure I know how things like this happen. I don't remember her getting loose, and she was always in her paddock. The stallions are tightly controlled, as you can guess. Don't want them wasting their love juice."

Nate had to try to lighten the mood. "Maybe this is the second immaculate conception in history? We can tell your father it's an unexpected miracle. A DNA test will show us who the father is, and from there, we can register the little guy." He was gorgeous, with beautiful conformation. Deep chestnut in color, with a white star-shaped pattern on his forehead.

Emmett sighed. "Doesn't matter. Something still went wrong." He shrugged as though he were resigned to his fate. "He is pretty."

Nate took out his phone and snapped a picture.

"Make sure the dam has plenty of hay and oats. She's going to need her strength. Do you have a quieter place we can put them?" Nate asked.

"We'll move both of them to the birthing area in a few days. It's away from the other horses, and it will be quieter for them. If we'd have known, we'd moved her before the birth." Emmett reached out to pet the mother, but she moved away, closer to Nate. Damn, this horse thing with Emmett was real, and it sucked.

"What do you want to name him?" Holace asked.

"Lucky Bastard?" Nate teased.

"Big Surprise?" Holace offered.

Emmett turned to both of them like they were crazy, his eyes dark. Nate had seen that look when they were kids. It showed up whenever Emmett thought he was going to be in trouble.

"How about Bun in the Oven?"

"Unexpected Miracle," Nate offered more seriously when the jokes didn't seem to find their audience. "It's a good name and what he is. Horses have minds of their own. They're smart, and they never cease to amaze me. This little guy should be accepted for the gift he is, and that's it. Besides, your father isn't going to see him for weeks. Just relax. It's good news."

Emmett sighed. "You don't know my father." He turned and strode out of the stable, leaving Nate wondering just what the hell was really going on. For years he'd thought his own family was dysfunctional as hell and had felt at home with RE's family. Now it seemed that below the surface, there was just as much tension as there had been with his own father, but at least alcohol, psychotropic medications, and painkillers weren't involved. Maybe it was all cowboy fathers, because the guys he'd ridden rodeo with all had issues with their own dads.

"I practically grew up here, remember?" Nate told him.

Emmett stopped in the doorway. "You and RE had no clue. Neither of you got to know the Dustin McElroy that I have to deal with every goddamned day. Whatever RE did was perfect. He was the golden boy. So he got the encouragement, and I got whatever was left over." He stomped back. "My gramps used to say, 'Remember, we could all be plumbers. Hot on the left, cold on the right, and shit runs downhill.' And with my father, straight to me." Emmett's entire body stiffened, and he seemed about ready to explode. Fires burned with long-simmering hurt behind his eyes, and damned if the anger in his stance and the steel in Emmett's backbone weren't stunningly attractive. Nate wanted to do something to try to make things right. But what the hell could he do about it?

Emmett left the stable without another word, and Nate couldn't tear his gaze away from him, especially when Emmett rubbed his left asscheek. Nate had to wonder which horse got him this time.

"YOU'RE COMING into town with me and that's all there is to it," a man with the brightest yellow hair Nate had ever seen was telling Emmett. With his hands on his hips and blazing eyes, it was almost funny. Nate hadn't seen a guy so obviously out and proud since he'd crossed paths with some of the guys from the Rainbow Rodeo a few years back. "You've been cooped up here for days, your dad is improving, and you deserve a few hours away."

One thing Nate had to give the guy—he certainly didn't back down, even when Emmett flashed a scowl dark enough to create a rumble of thunder.

"Come on, what are you going to do here—work with Virginia so she can take another butt nibble?"

Nate strode over because he wasn't going to skulk around listening to others' conversations. The guy with the yellow hair's mouth hung open. "And who are you?"

"This is Nate. You remember him. He was RE's best friend. He was there when you and I were freshmen," Emmett explained.

"And this is the guy your mom and dad brought in as foreman?" He turned back to Emmett and nudged him in the side. "Lucky," he whispered before schooling his expression to a wicked grin. "Maybe you can help with something. The horses on this here Rolling D seem to have taken a shine to Emmett's backside. Maybe you can help explain why. See, I think it's because of how he smells." Reid pushed Emmett over to him. "What do you think? Predator? Or maybe hints of something rotten?" Reid pressed again until Emmett nearly fell against Nate.

"Hey!" Emmett growled. "Be nice."

"I am," Reid countered. "So, what do you think? Does Emmett here have a scent that makes you want to take a bite of his butt?"

Jesus, that man was wicked. Nate said nothing, but inhaled anyway. His senses flooded with sweetness, hay, and the underlying scent of musk and earthiness that sent his head reeling for a split second. He was about to answer that yes, he'd take a lick or a nibble of that ass any day of the week, but he managed to remain silent. His gaze met Emmett's, and they locked for a brief second. Nate swallowed hard, tension rising skyward by the second, and sweat broke out under his shirt.

Emmett backed away and smoothed out his shirt. Nate followed the flow of those hands as they brushed at that lean body.

Reid's eyes flew back and forth like he was watching a tennis match. Then he cleared his throat, breaking the spell. "I need to go check on Mom, but I'll be here at seven to pick you up. We'll go into town and raise a little hell. Scare a few of the shit-kicking straight people." He turned and half pranced to his yellow car, then pulled out without waiting for Emmett's answer.

"In case you don't remember, that was Reid Ziegfeld." Emmett shook his head slowly. "And I guess we're going out tonight." He didn't sound particularly excited. "There are things in the office that I should review and make sure are up to date. But if I don't go, Reid will park himself in the office, his elbows on the desk, and make huge puppy-dog eyes at me until I give in. So I guess it's easier to simply do what he wants." Emmett rolled his eyes. "Sorry. Where are my manners? Would you like to go? We'll get something to eat and can drink a ridiculous amount of beer. Come to think of it, maybe that's the best idea I've heard in a while."

Nate almost said no, but maybe it would be good to try to work things out with Emmett if they were going to work together. "Then maybe I should go just to keep the two of you out of trouble." He smiled at Emmett and might have seen the ghost of one in return. More than once, he and RE had followed Emmett and his friends just to make sure they stayed safe and didn't get themselves into hot water. In a way, this was like old times—except back then, Nate's attention wasn't so firmly on Emmett. And fucking hell, he missed RE like a limb. It had been five years, and even before that, he'd known loss, but nothing like losing someone who was such a part of him.

"Fine. I need to check on things and clean up if I'm going to go out." Emmett squiggled his nose. "And I'd say that you need to do the same. You're a little ripe." He headed for the house, and Nate wondered what the hell he had just gotten himself into. Lord knows going out with those two was going to be interesting.

Nate got in his truck and headed home to shower and change. When he returned, Emmett was on the phone talking to his mom, so Nate stayed out of the room until he hung up. "You okay?" Nate asked when he saw Emmett. "Is it your dad?"

"Oh, he's fine. Mom is just tired and worried, and she wanted to talk." He flopped in the chair. He checked the time on his phone as the bright yellow Mini pulled into the yard. Emmett snorted.

"What is that thing? I noticed it before, but I guess I didn't really pay attention."

"Reid's rental car. I swear he picked the most outrageous car in the entire state." He left the house, and Nate followed. There was no way all three of them were going to fit into that thing, so he offered to take his own truck. Reid rode with Emmett with Nate following behind as they headed for town and Hill's Tavern.

Hill's had been around forever. It was where Nate took his first legal drink of beer and where he and RE had played pool and hung out every Saturday night when he was in town. The place looked exactly as it always had—wooden chairs and scarred tables, the bar worn, gouged with decades of drinks, boots, and hands.

"Let the fun begin," Reid said as soon as they stepped inside.

"What the hell are you expecting? The Ramrod or whatever club you go to in San Francisco? Remember, we're in Montana." Emmett guided them to one of the empty tables. Nate once again wondered what the hell he had gotten himself into and how he was going to keep these two from getting into trouble.

"I know, I know. But can I at least look?" Reid pouted perfectly.

Emmett shook his head. "Don't touch, and for God's sake, don't be obvious." Nate figured that was damned near impossible. Reid had on enough guyliner to keep Elizabeth Arden in business for a year.

"Stay here. I'll get us some beers," Nate offered, and he went to the bar, where the same guy who had checked his ID growing up and passed his first beer over the bar pulled the three he ordered. It was amazing how some things never changed… and yet his life had been on a roller coaster for years before the death of his mentally ill and self-medicating father. He pushed away those thoughts as he returned to the table and passed out the beers. Emmett downed his in two gulps and immediately headed to the bar for more.

"Is someone drowning his sorrows?" Nate asked as his gaze refused to leave Emmett's retreating form.

"Of course he is. Emmett was determined to take over the ranch and run it for his father. But then they hired you, and now he's pissed as hell at them… at you… probably the entire world. His folks have never understood or cared what Emmett wanted." Reid sipped his beer. "This isn't about you, though. It's really between him and his parents. You just got thrown into the emotional manure pile."

"And he's determined to get himself completely shitfaced," Nate observed as Emmett downed a whiskey, then chased it with another beer. At this rate, they were going to have to pour him into the truck for the trip home. "Was this such a good idea?"

Reid shrugged. "Maybe not." He lifted his beer and paused before it reached his lips.

"What the fuck do we have here?" a deep voice sneered.

Nate turned and groaned. He should have known. Clinton Masters, the asshole of the county. He and RE were huge rodeo rivals all through high school and into college until RE quit to work the ranch. "If it isn't the Mouth of Montana. I heard you left and joined the fairies." The idiot thought he was clever, but no one got away with talking that way to Reid.

"Yeah. Now I spit rainbows and poop glitter. You, on the other hand, are still as vacant and brain-dead as you always were. Neanderthal man?" Reid actually seemed to ponder Clinton, and Nate turned away to keep from laughing. Clinton always was a jerk. "What I want to know is if a horse kicked you in the head one too many times. No one can be born that stupid."

Nate tensed, ready for a fight. But Clinton simply turned toward the bar. "There's McElroy Junior, or is it Number Two?" he said loudly enough for Emmett to hear him.

"Go back to your own table," Nate growled. "Before you get more trouble than you bargained for. I kicked your ass years ago, and you know I'll do it again." Nate wasn't taking any of this guy's crap. "Go on."

"Yeah, scoot your cowboy butt right on back to your little seat." Reid waved Clinton off. "Maybe I'll rub against you and turn you gay. Too much fairy dust will do that." Nate actually bit his lower lip as Clinton pondered the notion and backed away. He always was a bully.

"Later, little McElroy." Clinton glared as Emmett rejoined them, then finally went back to his own table.

"God, I hate that guy," Emmett growled as he sat and finished off yet another beer.

"We should order something to eat." Nate grabbed a menu, flagged down a server, and placed an order for the table.

"Can I get another beer and a whiskey?" Emmett added to their order. "Thanks, Missy." His eyes were already getting glassy, and Nate had a strong notion that Emmett was not going to be a happy camper in the morning.

"Come on, let's dance," Reid said, pulling Emmett to his feet. "And leave that behind. Nate will watch it for you." And just like that, Reid got Emmett out on the floor to do the two-step. Every eye in the room was on them, but for a very different reason than the way Nate watched. He wished he had the guts to cut in. Hell, he wished a hell of a lot of things.

He should be used to disappointment by now.

From the side of the dance floor, Clinton made a beeline toward Emmett and Reid, face red, looking like he was either going to explode and get ready to shoot someone. "Shit," Nate breathed and started over himself.

"No wonder you never amounted to anything, Number Two," Clinton sneered, parting the dancers, glaring at Emmett as he poked his chest. "You were always good for nothing, and from what I hear, you never amounted to anything. No one in your family did."

Emmett and Reid had stopped, with Reid looking a little scared and Emmett about two seconds from his head exploding. "Just shut up, dumbass." It seemed Reid was out of sparkly repartee at the moment.

But Emmett surprised him. He stepped forward and jabbed Clinton in the chest. "You piece of shit. You could never beat RE at anything. He wiped the arena floor with you every time. Always said you were a sad excuse for a rodeo cowboy."

Damn, the alcohol must have hit Emmett all at once. Nate hurried forward to get him out of there.

"You want to step out of your big brother's shadow? Show everyone what you're made of?" Clinton puffed.

"Any McElroy can beat the hell out of a piece of shit like you." Emmett got right up in Clinton's face. Nate tried to grab Emmett around the waist to pull him back in case they came to blows, but Emmett squirmed away.

"Fine, then. Broncs at the county rodeo next month in front of everyone. You gotta stay the full eight seconds, which is something I'd like to see." He laughed.

Emmett took a swing at Clinton, missed by a mile, and would have fallen to the floor if Nate hadn't caught him.

"Look at you. I can't wait for the entire county to see you fall flat on your ass." He was already crowing as Emmett groaned. Nate led him back to the table.

"What the hell did he just do?" Reid asked as Nate got Emmett seated. "He can't ride a bronc—he'll break his neck." Reid glared at Nate as though Emmett shooting his mouth off was his fault.

Emmett's eyes widened as though he had just realized what he'd done, and then he passed out on the table.

Chapter 4

MAYBE HE was dead. Yeah, that would actually be good. Emmett moved his head without opening his eyes, and his stomach threatened to rebel. He felt worse, so he had to be alive. At least part of him.

Emmett opened his mouth and didn't want to close it again. He held his tongue out away from his lips. It tasted like something had crawled in there and died, probably from the fumes. He smacked his lips and groaned at the awfulness. He didn't even try to swallow—his mouth and throat were so dry he knew it would hurt like hell. Emmett cracked his eyes open and wondered where he was. The room was strange, as was the huge crack in the ceiling. Hell, maybe he was in some sort of torture chamber and the ceiling was going to fall down and crush him. Was that a thing? Wait, he needed to think. Where was he? What had happened and why the hell did his back ache like he'd been sleeping on a pile of rocks?

"Do you remember anything from last night?" Someone thrust a mug in his direction, and Emmett sat up and took it. He sipped slowly as hot, strong coffee slid down his throat.

"No...." Emmett groaned as his brain tried to grow past his skull. He took another sip. "I take it I had too much to drink."

He got a chuckle for an answer. "You passed 'too much to drink' a full two beers before I could get you out of the bar." The voice rang with anger and impatience. "Do you remember anything at all from the bar?"

"I remember dreaming." Emmett drank a little more coffee and set the mug aside with a groan. Each movement made him regret waking up alive. He raised his gaze to where Nate stood in a pair of boxers and an old T-shirt. Damn, the man had great legs. And holy hell, the way he filled out that shirt was something the gods would be jealous of.

Okay, so maybe this wasn't the time for that, but he was hungover—really hungover—not dead, and Nate was... as he had imagined.

"Think," Nate prompted.

Emmett held his head as it throbbed like hell. "I remember this dream, and you were there, and so was that asshole Clinton. God, I hate that guy, and now he's invading...." Emmett gasped. "That wasn't a dream."

"No, it wasn't," Nate said flatly.

"Did he and I argue? Oh God, we did." He held his head as snippets of last night started returning: Clinton being a dick and him opening his mouth and accepting a challenge of some sort.... The playback went in and out, but Emmett groaned. "That was real?" He groaned long and loudly enough that he made his own head ache as he remembered accepting a challenge to ride broncs. "What the holy hell was I thinking?" What the hell was he going to do now? There was no way he could do this. Suddenly he thought he might be sick, and then the images of last night clarified, and he felt worse and just knew he didn't have that luxury. This was worse than anything he could possibly throw up.

Nate left the room, and Emmett was so engrossed in recollections of his own stupidity that he didn't even lift his gaze to watch Nate's backside as he strode down the hall. "The drinking was doing the thinking, and you went along for the ride," Nate commented when he returned with a glass of water and a couple of pills. "Take these and drink all the water. It will help."

Emmett complied before picking up the mug of coffee once again. "What the hell am I going to do? And what the fuck was I thinking? I can't ride a bronc. I can barely get on the back of one of the lesson horses." He had given up trying to ride the damned beasts years ago. Emmett's hand shook, and he felt like he was going to be sick. All that damned alcohol and it stayed down, but the idea that he'd shot off his mouth and agreed to enter the county fair in the bronco-busting competition sent him hurrying down the hall to find the bathroom. Thankfully he made it in time.

"Are you all right?" Nate asked outside the door.

After a minute, the convulsions ceased. "I'm okay. Just puking up my shoes." And God knows what else. He flushed and cradled the cool porcelain for comfort. Something had to make him feel better after this little revelation. And dammit, there was no fucking way on God's green earth that he was ever going to be able to take this back. His head still pounded, and Nate's knock on the door only made his heart hurt worse.

Nate came in and chuckled before handing him another set of pills and some water. "Let's try this again, shall we?" He seemed amused.

"Asshole," Emmett swore and took the pills and water. "You're not supposed to delight in other people's misery." He downed both the tablets and water, grateful for something to rid his mouth of the sour taste.

"Why not?" Nate asked, helping him up. "I was the one who brought you back here and actually carried you in last night. You passed out in my truck, and I undressed you and put you to sleep on my sofa. At least you weren't sick last night."

Emmett let Nate help him back to the sofa. He sat down and for the first time realized he was in nothing but his underwear. Great, just what he needed, for Nate to see him practically naked, looking like shit after puking his guts out. He sat still and waited for the pills to kick in. "Thanks," he told Nate. After all, the guy had looked out for him and gotten him home.

"Your friend Reid got himself home." Nate left the room, and Emmett leaned forward, holding his head once again, trying to get his mind to work. "And damn, when you've had a few drinks, you talk like nobody's business and you don't back down, that's for sure. You're usually so quiet and reserved." Nate returned to the room and set his clothes on the end of the sofa. "Drink some more of the coffee, it will help. And let the pills and water do their job. The hangover should start to dissipate in a few hours."

"If I'm lucky maybe I'll be dead by then. That should get me out of the crap my mouth got me into." Emmett drank some more of the coffee and then slowly got to his feet, managing to step into his jeans without falling down. This whole situation was ridiculous. He'd been upset that his family—his own damned mother, for God's sake—had brought in Nate to manage the ranch while his father was laid up. His parents didn't think he was capable of doing the job, and what did he do? Go out, get drunk, shoot his mouth off, and prove them right.

"I'm heading to the ranch in five minutes. I'll give you a ride out there." Why did Nate have to be so nice? It would be easy to hate the guy if he'd been a real jerk, and hating him was what Emmett needed to do. Nate had taken away his chance to show his parents that he was up to the job of managing the McElroy operation. He could finally show them that he wasn't a complete screwup, and they took that away from him.

Emmett pulled on his shirt and socks, then managed to get his boots on without making his head explode. The pills must have been starting to work, because he didn't feel as awful by the time he got in the truck. The sun shone right in his eyes, sending a jolt through his head, so he closed his eyes, sat back, and did his best not to think about the mess he'd made of things. Just thinking about it made his stomach lurch and his head ache all over again. Once he could think straight, he'd figure out a plan so he didn't embarrass the whole family at the fair. But for now, he needed to shower—because he stank—sober up, and get himself to work. Maybe an idea would come to him and he could see a way out of this mess.

Yeah, right. He was never that lucky.

EMMETT'S HEAD still ached, but at least his mouth tasted better after he gave his teeth a good brushing, and he no longer smelled like a distillery after his shower. He changed into clean clothes and called his mother, but he got her voicemail. Reception in the hospital was usually awful, so he left a message asking how his father was and hung up.

"Do you want something to eat?" Martha asked as he entered the kitchen. Emmett's stomach rebelled at the thought of food, and he shook his head. "Then how about this?" She pressed a glass into his hand.

"What is it?" Emmett asked as he looked it over.

"Surefire hangover remedy. Drink it down in one go and don't stop." She narrowed her gaze, and Emmett didn't have the fortitude to refuse. He did as she said, drinking the whole thing, and danged if he didn't feel better... for two seconds, until the heat in the stuff took over and he bent over, gasping for breath and desperate to put out the fire in his mouth. Sure*fire* remedy was for damned sure, with plenty of emphasis on the *fire*.

"Are you trying to kill me?" Emmett asked between gulps as he downed two glasses of water in rapid succession.

"No."

"But damn, you nearly burned my mouth off." He handed her the glass back, and she grinned.

"Maybe. But your hangover is gone." With that little pronouncement, she left the kitchen, and Emmett grabbed his hat and left for the horse barn, his head much clearer.

The main door was already open, but he didn't hear voices as he went inside. Emmett checked the mangers, pleased to find them full and the barn inhabitants munching away. He turned and then thought better of it when Virginia stuck her head out of the stall and neighed as though she were laughing at him. "I'm onto you. No more biting, you old nag. Dad may love you, but I'll sell your raggedy ass if you go trying that again." He whipped around. "You too, Reggie. So help me, there's an auction in a few months. I'll stick both your horsey asses on the block and get some horses without teeth." He was so tired of getting bitten, stepped on, or kicked by these damned hayburners.

"Heard about last night," Holace teased as he strode in the barn and right up to Virginia. He patted her neck and stroked her nose as though the old bat were a kiddie trail horse. "What were you thinking? There's no way you can keep your skinny butt on a bronc for eight seconds." He snickered, and Emmett scowled at him. "Sorry," Holace added. Often the hands thought of him as one of them... at least to a certain extent. He had never been set up by his father to be respected or as someone in authority.

Emmett strode nearer. "What have I told you about making cracks about my butt? Maybe you have this fascination because of latent tendencies? Are you trying to send me a message?"

Holace stepped back, sputtering and shaking his head, waving his hands. "I like the ladies, thank you very much."

"And my ass, apparently," he said flatly, trying to send a message to Holace. It got him off his game and it was the only way he could get the big cowboy to shut up. Emmett turned away, careful of the two biters, and checked the rest of the barn. "Have all the horses been exercised today?" It was time to get down to business, and with his father gone, maybe he could have a chance to show what he could do. The hands all appreciated action.

"Not yet. I have some training sessions this afternoon." Holace fed each of the horses a carrot as he moved down the aisle through the barn. "All teasing aside, how are you going to stay on the back of a bronco?" Emmett had known Holace since he and RE were boys, and he got more latitude than the other men. "You sure shot your mouth off last night, and Clinton is spreading it all through town that you're going to ride a bronc and that it will be his chance to prove that he's better than any McElroy." There was no humor in Holace's eyes when he faced Emmett. "He's building this up like the entire ranch's honor is at stake over this."

"Shit," Emmett swore. "He was going after RE, and I couldn't let him do that." He had also been drunk and smarting from the kick in the pants his parents had given him. He'd had something to prove, but all that was going to happen was he was going to make a fool of himself and the ranch itself.

"Can you call this thing off?" Holace asked. "Figure out a way to get out of it. Move to Saskatchewan, or ask some girl to marry you and move to Florida with her." He was serious, and Emmett glared hard.

"Fuck off, Holace. I know I'm the last person on fucking earth to try to sit on a wild damned horse. But I am not going to run away from a stupid bet. I am a McElroy, and damn it all, I'll figure out a way to make the eight seconds if I have to superglue my butt to the saddle." He turned and stormed out of the barn, knocking into Nate as he went. God, the guy was a bundle of muscle. Nate held him to stop Emmett from falling, and he gave in to the closeness just long enough to get a good musky whiff of him. His head swam for a second just from the headiness, and then he pulled away and glared to cover up the attraction. "Are you going to give me more grief?" he challenged, and Nate took a step back. "Good." Emmett stormed off to the equipment shed, jumped on a four-wheeler, and took off, only pausing when his phone vibrated in his pocket.

He recognized the number. "Hey, Mama," he answered, doing his best to keep his voice sounding normal.

"Son," his father said, sounding hoarse and weak. "How is everything there? Is Nate getting settled in? How are the horses? Hayley should be getting ready to foal soon, and I got the breeding schedule all set up in my ledger. You just got to follow it."

"Pop, I know the breeding schedule. I put it together, and we already talked about it." He sighed, wondering why his dad was worried about it. "How are you feeling?"

"Tired, but I'm fine." He breathed hard and sounded awful. "I made some changes to the schedule. I thought it over, and I think we need to do some things different. I updated the schedule a few days ago. Look in my ledger book."

Emmett should have known—he spent weeks researching each horse and their characteristics before putting together that schedule. He consulted with all the men and got their opinions. Then he worked like hell to put together something his father could be proud of and even reviewed it with him in detail before getting his blessing. He should have known that the old man would just pay him lip service and then do whatever the hell he wanted. Emmett had never done anything right in his father's eyes, so why should things suddenly be different?

But Emmett knew he was more than what his father saw, and he had a plan. If his father was going to be gone for a while, then he was going to run the ranch as well as, if not better than, his father. The phone shuffled.

"Emmett?" his mother said. "Your father is asleep. Just do whatever he wants. The doctor says he's going to be okay, but he can't have any stress or shocks right now. Dustin is completely worn out, and even when he can come home, he's going to need plenty of rest and quiet." Even she sounded tired. "I know you'll do all you can to help." She paused and spoke to someone in the room. "I have to go. We'll talk to you later." She ended the call, and Emmett jammed the phone back in his pocket and took off once more.

After an hour and feeling much calmer, he returned to find all hell breaking loose in the yard and Nate in the middle of it, looking every bit like sex on a stick. For a second Emmett forgot everything else.

"You get out there and round up those head before they get very far. Holace, get the supplies in the back of the truck to repair that fence and get them to the break. We'll drive the cattle back through the hole and then close it. Emmett, where have you been? We need that four-wheeler." He jumped on almost before Emmett could get off, and then they were gone, leaving him behind once again like he didn't fucking exist.

An engine grew louder, and Nate flew back into the yard. "What the hell happened? Get on." He pulled to a stop. Emmett paused as his gaze caught Nate's, and damn, Emmett wondered if the banked heat that flashed in them was for him or a result of the situation. Nate always had that ability to make him wonder just what was going on behind those eyes—if what he saw was real, could possibly be real, or if it was just his imagination. Emmett climbed on behind Nate, wrapping his arms around his waist, hands sliding along his hard, flat stomach. He inhaled and his head swam for a split second, and then they took off with Emmett just able to grab on to his hat.

"THIS WAS intentionally cut," Emmett told Nate as soon as he was able to examine the fencing.

"Dammit," Nate hissed and pulled out his phone. "Sheriff Bridger, Nate Zachary. I'm the temporary foreman at the McElroy place, and someone purposely cut some fence. No… we got it under control. Could you stop by the house? If we're out here handling fence…. Yeah, I'd appreciate it." He hung up.

"What was that for?" Emmett asked.

"Someone cut this fence. Why? They knew the cattle would find it and we'd have to bring them in. I just want him to check on the place in case this is a diversion." The men were already driving the loose cattle back through the opening.

"We got 'em," Holace called as a couple dozen head filed back into the pasture.

"Are the others checking for strays?"

Holace nodded. "They didn't go far because they found some really good grass." The last of the loose head passed through, and the guys unloaded the fence material. "We got this," Holace told them.

Nate motioned to Emmett, and he jumped on the ATV with him, and they took off back toward the house. Once again, Emmett sat right close to Nate, his hips pressed to Nate's backside. For a few seconds, old fantasies rose up from long forgotten places in his brain. He held on and leaned slightly against him as they sailed over the flat green land.

"Not much of a diversion," Emmett said, holding tighter as the ATV bumped a little. Not that he needed to, but what the hell. This was probably as close as he was ever going to get to Nate, and he might as well take advantage of it. Emmett knew he needed to get his head out of the clouds as far as Nate was concerned, but old fantasies died hard, especially when he was right there, pressing back against him.

"We were lucky. It could have been hundreds of head and taken us days to round them all up. That would have spread us thin." He took off at full speed, pointing ahead with Emmett holding on tighter. "Grass fire. Want to bet it was set on purpose? The wind is blowing it toward the horse pastures and barns." He sped up until they were moving as fast as the machine would go. Emmett hung on for dear life and jumped off as soon as Nate slowed. Together they hooked up hoses to the water spigots before dragging the hose and wetting the grass in front of the fire. The call went up, and others joined in just in time for Emmett to get his feet tangled in one of the hoses. He stepped, the hose didn't move, and down he went in ash, grass, and mud. "Damn it."

Emmett groaned as wet sank into his clothes. He opened his eyes to Nate standing next to him with a slightly puzzled expression. He didn't say a word but offered a hand to tug him back up. Emmett picked up the hose because he needed something to cover his embarrassment—and the way warmth rushed into his cheeks from the heat in Nate's eyes. That heat always seemed just below the surface whenever Nate looked at him. It was both exciting and unnerving, and yet Emmett couldn't turn away. For a few seconds, Emmett thought that heat might have grown as he watched.

"There aren't horses around. You don't need to be jumpy," one of the men said, and the others laughed. Nate turned away at the same time Emmett did.

Emmett turned the hose toward the last of the flames and set his jaw, growing more embarrassed and angry by the second, mostly at himself for being so damned clumsy.

"You want us to get the mud off?" Holace asked with a grin that Emmett wanted to punch off his face. Instead, he kept his attention on the task at hand. Going off into a temper tantrum wouldn't help anyone.

"Just get the hell to work and get this fire out before I turn the hose on all of you," Nate bellowed. "Less talk, and pay more attention to where the flames are trying to jump." He pointed and got the men to douse the last of the fire. Emmett wet down the burned areas, grateful to Nate for the interference.

"Wet it all down so nothing starts up again, and then get the water off and the hoses rolled up and at the ready. If we have ourselves a firebug, I want to be ready in case they strike again." Nate was sure on top of things. He hurried away as the sheriff arrived. They followed the burn back to the point of origin.

With a scowl, Emmett handed his hose to one of the laughers, meeting their gazes hard and not backing down until they broke eye contact and started looking embarrassed. He was tired of that behavior, and he was going to put an end to it. He should have done it long ago. There were times when he missed RE so much. It didn't matter if Emmett tripped or if the damned horses didn't like him. RE didn't seem to care and made things better. If Emmett fell, RE was there to pick him up, no matter what. Filling his shoes was a nearly impossible task, but somehow he was going to at least fill part of them and stay on that bronc at the fair next month for eight damn seconds.

"It's right here. Things are dry, but not as dry as they'll get." The sheriff leaned down, sniffing. "I don't know. It could have been anything. I don't smell gasoline, but that doesn't mean it wasn't used. Could have been a coincidence, but I doubt it. Someone is pissed at you all for some reason." He straightened up, the leather of his belt creaking a little as he moved.

"We'll keep an eye out," Nate said.

The sheriff wandered through the area but didn't seem to find anything else. "I'll write up a report, and you call if anything else happens. I don't suppose you kept anything from the fence break?" He shook his head. "The area would be pretty well trampled by the cattle, I suppose."

"Unfortunately, yes. We had to get the cattle back."

"I'm not faulting you all. There's no way of knowing. Just if anything else happens, call so we can get out here faster to check out the scene." Emmett couldn't help wondering if he thought all this was a waste of his precious sheriff donut-eating time. The guy looked like he ate enough of them, and Lord knows the election was a popularity contest and Sheriff Holter was always popular. If rumor was correct, he took his popularity from both sides of the coin.

"We will, and thanks for coming out. I appreciate it." Nate flashed a smile and then shook the sheriff's hand. They all trudged back to the cars, and Nate stood, watching as the sheriff pulled away. "Slow, lazy ass," he muttered under his breath.

"From the way you talked to him on the phone, I thought you guys might be friends or something," Emmett commented before striding back to the barn. His shirt and jeans stuck to his skin, and he squished a little when he walked. The heat would take care of all that soon enough, and he still had things to do, and first on the list was to get his butt on a bronc. If he was going to have any sort of chance against Clinton, he needed to figure out how to ride a damn bronc.

"Holace," Emmett bellowed. "Get Ringo in the chute!" He pretended not to notice how the men all stopped, gaping at him, not moving. "Do it or I'll fire your ass." He continued inside, not stopping to see if his order was carried out. In the tack room, he put on RE's old chaps and stalked out to the bucking ring.

Holace had Ringo in the chute like Emmett had asked, and all the men gathered around the ring. Horses might not fucking like him, but Emmett didn't care. He intended to show the men just what he could do. Emmett was RE's brother, and hell, he wasn't going to let him down. No way. With his father gone, it was up to him to run the ranch, and they were going to take him seriously.

One of the men manned the door of the gate while Holace kept the horse steady as Emmett climbed into the chute and got on the horse. He could almost hear RE's voice. *Steady—breathe and keep calm. Let your mind tap into the horse and figure out what he's going to do. Keep yourself free and easy, ready to go with what the horse does rather than fight it.*

"Are you sure you want to do this?" Holace asked.

"Yes." Emmett could feel the horse under him huffing and ready to go. He nodded, and the chute opened. Ringo shot out of the chute and into the air. It felt like the damned horse was flying, and Emmett right along with him. No wonder RE had loved this so damned much—the feeling like he could do anything at all. It was amazing, the power, the adrenaline, the feeling of floating on air—

Followed by the *thud* of hitting the ground and not being able to fucking breathe. He tried to pull air into his lungs and failed. God, what a letdown. Okay, so maybe that part wasn't so fucking great.

"Get that horse under control!" Nate bellowed at the top of his lungs while one of the other men helped Emmett to his feet and over to the fence. He held himself upright, not willing to show weakness as Holace and the guys got Ringo out of the arena. "What the hell were you doing?" Nate asked, his face inches from Emmett's. "You could have been killed or worse. You were damned lucky you landed the way you did. You could have broken your neck." His eyes were wide.

"But I did it. I rode that fucker. You saw it—everyone saw it. I actually rode him." He was finally able to pull in air. "I'm a cowboy just like the rest of them, and I can do this shit too."

Nate pulled back a little. "Was this some macho piece of shit thing? Get on the back of the craziest horse in the county because you got something to prove? Well, all you did was get yourself thrown and ended up in the dirt."

"But I rode him," Emmett said.

"No. You sat on the back of the horse. Clark opened the gate, the horse took one jump, and you went soaring in the other direction. The entire time you thought you rode the horse, you were in the air and on your way to the ground." He shook his head.

"I didn't…?"

"No. You didn't make eight seconds. You might have made one, and you could have gotten yourself killed in the process." Nate turned toward the other men. "Get Ringo back in his stall and give him some extra oats. He deserves it for not killing Emmett." He strode away.

Emmett picked up his hat from where it rested on the ground outside the fence and smacked it against his leg. Maybe he was a damned fool—hell, the family fool. He had proof now. Maybe it was for the best that his mother brought in Nate. There was no way he could run the ranch. He wasn't cowboy enough.

He wasn't good at a fucking thing.

Chapter 5

AFTER HIS spectacularly dismal performance the day before, Emmett had made himself scarce. When Nate asked about him, Martha said that he was in the office working on the books and that he didn't want to be disturbed. She'd seemed none too happy about it as she carried a pretty much untouched tray back to the kitchen.

"Are you serious about keeping this bet with Clinton and trying to ride one of those damned horses in the county rodeo?" Nate asked Emmett the following day as Emmett was on his way to the barn.

Emmett paused his stomping steps. Everything about the man said to stay away, from the way he stood to the glare of fire in his eyes. "Don't you have something better to do other than give me shit?" At least there was a hint of amusement in those huge, sad eyes.

"Jesus, knock the chip off your shoulder. Shit happens to all of us, and there's no need to act like an ass about it." Nate crossed his arms and puffed his chest out a little. "I was asking for a reason, and if you'd stop with the out-of-control teenager attitude...."

Emmett put his hands up. "Fine. What is it you want, oh great and powerful ranch foreman?"

Nate rolled his eyes. "From snottiness right into sarcasm in less than two seconds flat. That has to be some sort of skill. You know, if you bottled that shit, you could sell it to... exactly no one. So knock it off." God, sometimes Emmett acted just like the little pain in the ass he always was when they were kids.

Emmett sighed. "Okay, what do you want?"

"First thing, have you called your mama today?" Nate asked.

Emmett flipped him the finger. "Just because you were RE's best friend doesn't mean you get to play the big brother. Those days are over." God, Emmett was almost cute when he got all huffy. "And yes, I talked to her. Dad is doing better, and they're hopeful he'll be strong enough to come home in a few days. Mama isn't happy about that and is trying to convince the doctor to keep him a few extra days because

she knows as soon as the old coot comes home, he'll try to go to work."
The glare he fixed at Nate would freeze a tsunami in seconds. "Is that
all you needed?"

Nate growled under his breath. "No. If you remember, I asked you
about the bronc riding. Are you really intent on doing this? No matter
what Clinton Masters says or thinks, no one is going to look down on
you if you don't do this. You were drunk, and half the town was there and
saw it. They also saw the county asshole baiting you."

Emmett squared his shoulders. "And your point is?"

"Just answer the question. Is your mind made up to do this?"
Nate asked, keeping his words measured before he had to do what
he and RE used to do when they were kids and Emmett got to be a
real pain in the ass. After all, he was still big enough to give Emmett
a noogie.

"I'm not going to back down." In that moment, Nate saw that
Emmett's pride wasn't going to allow it no matter what happened. And
Nate had to admit to himself that the utter determination in Emmett's
blue eyes was sexy.

He sighed. "Then fine. Tonight at five, come to the old storage
shed. RE and I used to practice out there years ago, and I'll do what I can
to help you." Someone had to help the guy. Otherwise he was going to
end up breaking his neck.

Holace called for Emmett, and he nodded before striding off
toward the barn. Nate watched after him, enjoying the tight, slightly
bouncy rear view, wondering how one cowboy could be such a pain in
the ass.

NATE SPENT part of the afternoon getting things set up for Emmett's
lesson. He wasn't sure if he was going to show up, but Nate had said he'd
be here, and he kept his word.

"What's all this?" Emmett pushed open the door that the wind had
blown closed just a few seconds before.

"You said that you were determined to ride a bronc in the rodeo.
You know that people don't just hop on a horse and ride the wildness
out of it. Riding a bronc takes skill, finesse, training, and practice." Nate
gripped the rope string near his head. "This is where you start."

"An old barrel horse?" Emmett stepped forward. "We used to play on this when we were kids." He stroked the blanket Nate had strapped over the old oil drum. "I used to man the ropes and try to knock you or RE off." He smiled, and it went almost to his eyes. "I could never get either of you to fall off. But there was that time I got one of the hands to hide in here, and he worked the ropes. You sailed into the padding like you had wings. That was so funny."

"You used to ride too, remember?" Nate asked. He could almost see the younger Emmett, so determined, with such energy, and yet he could never stay on for more than a few seconds. Of course he and RE did their best to make sure Emmett got thrown off. "So hop on and let's see if the years have been good to you." He held the ropes, and Emmett climbed on. "Okay, remember, one hand on the rope and use the other for balance. Don't let it touch the animal. When the bucking starts, it's almost second nature to try to hold on with both hands, but that isn't allowed. Use it like this." Nate demonstrated for him, raising his arm over his head. "Use your legs to grip the horse." He positioned Emmett's hand. "Okay." He started pulling the ropes, and the barrel bounced a little. "Move your hips, arm, and the rest of your body. Most of all, don't try to fight the horse. You will lose no matter what. The horse has more power than you. So muscling isn't going to work."

Nate pulled the ropes harder, adding more bounce and movement before switching to another rope to add additional direction. He pulled harder, Emmett's legs already beginning to slide around. He continued the movement, and Emmett slid off onto the padding, ending up in a heap.

"Well, that sucked," Emmett griped as he got up.

"So? Get back on," Nate told a skeptical Emmett. "That's what you do if you want to go anywhere." He waited until Emmett was on once again. "Now use your legs. You have them, and they're strong. So grip with them. Gravity gets wonky on the back of a bronc, so use your legs to anchor yourself, because once they come up, you're toast."

"Right. Like I can actually do this. Horses hate me. Even the ones that love children and stand still for hours with them will lean over and try to bite me." Emmett climbed back on the barrel. "At least this thing isn't going to leave my ass black and blue, I suppose."

"Probably not. But I'm not promising about the rest of you. Now concentrate and use your legs. Yeah, like that. You aren't going to hurt the horse by gripping him. This isn't a damned trail ride. This is a horse that wants you off his back as fast as possible, and he doesn't care how he does it or if he stomps your face into the ground when he's done." Nate began rocking the barrel. "See, just sway with the movement. Get a feel for what the horse is going to do." He began pulling harder. "Yeah. That's it. Now hold on." Nate began pulling hard, and Emmett held on a second or two before going flying again. "That was longer."

"This was a bad idea, and it's going to be a disaster."

Nate pulled him to his feet. "Get back on and try again."

"What good will it do? I'm going to make a fool out of myself no matter what." Still, Emmett climbed back on.

"Remember, all you have to do is stay on for eight seconds. It doesn't have to be pretty, and you don't need to get the most points. All you need to do is stay on until the buzzer goes off. Then you can tell the asshole of the county where he can stick his piece-of-shit attitude." Nate wanted that for Emmett, and he knew he could do it. While nothing was guaranteed, especially in rodeo, Nate was sure anything was possible. Their families never got along, and Clinton always seemed to hate harder than anyone else. It probably didn't help that RE had always beaten Clinton at everything.

"Yes. Just eight seconds."

Nate smacked Emmett on the shoulder. "And stop trying to count the time in your head. It doesn't work. You put all your concentration into the ride and let the timekeeper do its work. You'll hear the buzzer." He stepped back and pulled hard on the ropes. Emmett fell right off, and Nate snickered. "You gotta be ready."

"Did anyone ever tell you that you missed your damned calling? You should be teaching elementary school… to delinquent children… armed with knives." He climbed back on and glared at Nate, but this time he was ready and went with Nate for a few seconds before ending up on his face.

"You need to concentrate. Remember, no two broncs are alike."

"I know some of them are as mean as hell. And then there are the ones that are worse," Emmett grumped as he grabbed his hat and climbed back on.

Nate had to give him credit for not giving up. Nate must have dumped Emmett on his cute, tight ass two dozen times before they called it quits. "You've had enough for tonight," Nate said, giving Emmett a hand up. His legs seemed a little wobbly. "It's time to get something to eat. We've been at this for hours." Once he got Emmett up, he nearly fell again, and Nate caught him as he pitched forward.

Emmett's huge eyes met his, and that familiar heat that Nate experienced whenever he was close to Emmett flared to life, fast and hot. He knew he needed to stay away. Emmett was RE's little brother, and he didn't need Nate perving on him. Just because Emmett was gay didn't mean he was fair game.

Still, damn, the man was warm and smelled cowboy sexy as all hell. He was also one heck of a compact package, and Nate had spent more than a few nights wondering what he had under those tight jeans and work shirt would feel like. He'd gotten an impression having Emmett behind him on the ATV, pressed right up to him.

"Nate? Emmett?" Jeremy, one of the hands, asked from outside. "What are you two doing out here?"

"We'll be right there. Just checking out the building for soundness," Emmett called out, then straightened up and backed away. "Don't tell anyone what we're doing. If I can stay on the bronc, then great, but if I don't…. It would be humiliating to prepare for weeks and still suck. Besides, if I tell them, then Mama and Dad will get wind and Mama will have a fit of epic proportions."

Nate scowled. "Are you serious?" he hissed.

"Come on, Nate. I appreciate you helping me, I just don't want a neon sign. 'Hey, Emmett is trying to ride again, let's go watch.'" He had that teasing tone just right, and Nate couldn't really blame him. The men seemed to love watching Emmett fall on his ass. Maybe if they helped him instead of using him for entertainment the guy might have some confidence.

"Fine. We'll keep it on the down-low," Nate agreed. "And I'll get some supplies, because this place is fucking filthy and could use some work anyway. That can be our cover." He pulled the door closed and waited for Emmett to step outside. Then he shut and latched it.

"Thanks, Nate. How about we go find out what Martha has for dinner? And I need to call Mama."

"And I'd like to talk to your father. I've got some ideas I'd like to run past him if he's up to it." Nate strode across the yard, taking in everything. "Jeremy, are the herds all bedded down? Fences checked?"

"Yes," Jeremy called back as he got in his truck. "I'm headed to town, but I got my phone."

Nate waved as Jeremy pulled out.

"Holace, what's all this?" Nate asked about the horse trailer parked near the main barn.

"Got two mares going to the stud tomorrow. Per Mr. Dustin's plans," he answered.

Emmett growled and then sighed.

"What?" Nate asked.

"Nothing. Just do what Daddy wants," Emmett snapped loudly enough for everyone to hear before veering off toward the house. Nate let him go.

"Emmett and Mr. Dustin made the breeding plan, and just before he went into the hospital, Mr. Dustin threw it out and came up with his own." Holace shook his head. "Mr. Dustin always made those decisions, and we'll do what he wants—they're his horses. But what we all developed with Emmett was better." He started back toward the barn.

"Holace? How often does shit like that happen?" Nate asked. He got a shrug in return before Holace disappeared into the barn. Nate continued to the house, where he found Emmett talking to his mother on the phone.

"A few more days? ... I see. ... Okay. They're planning to release him on Monday if everything checks out? Okay. ... Suzanne is coming too? Great...." He might have said the words, but he sounded about as enthusiastic as he would be about having a horse step on his foot. "Is there anything you want us to do for him here?" He listened for a while, and then it seemed his father came on the line. Emmett tensed immediately and spoke to him for a few minutes before handing Nate the phone.

"Dustin."

"Everything up to snuff?" Dustin asked right away.

"Yes. We're fine. The herds are okay and where they should be." Nate was about to ask his questions, but Dustin cut him off.

"Excellent. Just hold things together until I can get back into the saddle. Giselle and I appreciate you coming on board to look after things. We really do." He seemed to lose some of his energy, and Nate got the idea that he wasn't interested in anything he or anyone else had to say. *Just hold things together.*

Giselle came back on the line and said that Dustin needed to rest. "Thank you for everything, dear. You're a good friend to all of us, and we really appreciate it. I need to see to it that he gets his dinner." She ended the call, and Nate shook his head and put the old cordless phone on its cradle. Talking to Dustin and Giselle was a little like getting whiplash *before* they ran over you with a car.

"Mr. Emmett always has that look after he speaks to them," Martha said just as he turned around.

"I see." Nate had always thought that RE had the best family. The thing was that maybe RE had… back then. The Dustin and Giselle he remembered from his time with RE were indulgent and encouraging. They had lavished attention on RE and were gracious. Now they seemed so different, closed off to everyone except each other. It was a shame, but Nate supposed that losing RE had affected them. That tragedy had had an effect on everyone, but Nate thought that it might have affected Emmett the most.

"Are you staying for dinner?" Martha interrupted his thoughts. "I made plenty. Sometimes around here I never know how many people there are going to be."

He nodded. "Thank you, Martha. That would be great. Emmett and I have some records that we need to go over afterward. I always loved your cooking."

"Go on with you," she chided, but she still smiled. "Your sweet-talking ways aren't going to get you anywhere." Martha returned to the kitchen, and Nate went in search of Emmett, figuring he was in his father's office.

"Why should I even bother?" Emmett asked as soon as Nate pushed at the partially closed door. "I spent weeks working on that breeding schedule and he fucking agreed to it, and then this…." He wadded up papers and chucked them into the barrel-shaped trash can. "Next time I'll save myself the grief and let him do it all."

Nate came forward and stood behind Emmett. "You know that's why your father is in the hospital. He's been doing it all for years and it's too much. Dustin is a great man, and he knows this business better than just about anyone. How else could he have made this place a success when a lot of others have been struggling for years?"

Emmett turned to him, expression as dark as hurricane clouds. "My father is a hemorrhoid on the ass of life."

Nate snickered. "Is that the best you can do?" Nate teased, though he thought it was pretty good. "I mean, really."

Emmett crossed his arms over his chest. "Then by all means, throw some shade my father's way," he countered. "The reading room is open."

Nate threw his head back. "Have you been watching RuPaul late at night after your parents have gone to bed? I'd think that was the time for porn." He leaned close. "Do you have a thing for drag queens?" He grinned, and Emmett stilled, tense.

"How do you know about all this? It seems to me that someone else has been spending time with the drag queens." Emmett glared back. "Any heels in your closet?"

Nate snorted. "The only heels I have are on my cowboy boots." The mirth in Emmett's eyes was enticing, and Nate licked his lips before he could give it a second thought. Damn, for years he had wondered how Emmett's full lips would taste, and they were right there. All he had to do was take what he wanted. Emmett even leaned forward a little. Their eyes were locked, and Emmett, damn, he smelled good. Nate's heart pounded and his pulse raced. The room grew warm, and Nate held stock-still. Emmett didn't draw back or move an inch, as if he too were caught in the spell that neither of them could pull away from. And there it was, Emmett's tongue sliding over his bottom lip, making a quick appearance. Then it was gone, but that was one hell of a tell, and Nate leaned even closer, hoping Emmett wanted this as badly as he did.

"Guys, dinner is almost ready," Martha called, and Emmett straightened up. Nate did the same as Martha appeared in the doorway. "Get washed up. You two can finish up in here once you've had something to eat." She turned and left, and Nate followed right behind, inhaling deeply.

God, Emmett had him on edge. Nate had been strong for a long time, but being around Emmett seemed to be wearing him down. Emmett was his best friend RE's brother. Heck, with all the time he'd spent here with RE, Emmett had been like *his* younger brother, so acting on this attraction was wrong. But damn, it was getting harder to control himself the more time he spent with Emmett. Nate needed to back off. They worked together, and that had to be it. The fact that Emmett pushed all his buttons was immaterial. Nate and Emmett would work together until Dustin was back on his feet and healthy, and then Nate would move on and all this would be behind him.

With that resolved, Nate went to the bathroom, washed up quickly, and joined the others at the huge table just off the kitchen. "Hi, Marianne," Nate said when he saw Martha's daughter. He hugged her and stepped back. "Where have you been?"

"Out trying to get a job for after graduation," she answered. "I have a line on a few of them, but no luck so far." She seemed happy as he pulled out a chair. Emmett stalked into the room and sat down across from Marianne. Nate sat at the end of the table, with Martha next to her daughter. "Mama wants me to stay in the area, but there isn't much here."

Martha passed the dishes around the table.

"The pork chops look amazing," Nate commented as he took two and a huge helping of potatoes. "Thank you." Salad and vegetables followed around the table.

"What sort of work are you interested in?" Emmett asked. "You're studying business?"

"And Ag," Marianne said. "It's the kind of business we have around here. I've been thinking of leaving, but Mama would have a fit." She winked, and Nate knew she was probably pulling her mother's chain. "I've got a few feelers out, and we'll have to see if anything comes of them. I still have one year in school, so I'm not desperate… yet." She smiled, and Nate noticed how Emmett returned it and then lowered his gaze to eat.

"Is Giselle still trying to fix you and Emmett up?" Nate asked.

Emmett nearly did a spit take, and Marianne laughed. Martha groaned and pointedly looked anywhere but at Emmett or her daughter.

"Yes. But eeww," Marianne said. "That would be like dating my brother… my *gay* brother." She shivered, and Martha rolled her eyes.

"Miss Giselle is still hopeful," Martha said.

"Delusional is more like it," Emmett muttered, and Martha smacked his hand. "Come on. Really? Mama has her own ideas, and they aren't rooted in reality sometimes. But arguing with her does no good. She just digs in her heels further." Emmett shook his head while Martha rolled her eyes again. It seemed everyone understood the lay of the land except Emmett's mother.

"When Emmett brings home the man of his dreams, she'll get the message," Marianne said, and Emmett blushed deeply.

"Marianne," Martha scolded. "There are times when I wish you wouldn't say the first thing that comes into your head." She returned to her dinner.

"We all have issues with our family. I rode rodeo for years to try to pay off my father's gambling debts. That was a huge waste of time and effort, and all that I ended up with was being unable to ride any longer, the ranch gone, and my mother so deep in her grief at losing her home and husband that she needs around-the-clock care." Nate hadn't meant to say so much. It had just come out.

"Yeah, well…," Emmett said softly.

"I guess you're right. But I draw the line at dating Emmett to make his mother happy," Marianne insisted.

"Like I want to date my little sister," Emmett agreed. "There are limits."

"So what are we going to say when she starts pushing us together like she always does?" Marianne asked. "You know that she'll start as soon as she gets home."

Emmett snorted. "I'll just tell her that you and I talked, and we've discovered that we both share a grandpa fetish and that we're madly in love… with the sheriff." They held each other's gazes for about two seconds, then burst into laughter.

"You're both very mean," Martha said before grinning.

Nate smiled, loving the mirth in Emmett's eyes. It had been a while since he'd seen a real smile from Emmett. Yeah, Nate had his family issues, but they were largely behind him. His mother was well taken care of, and he visited her when he could. There was nothing he could do about his father, and the past was just that. Emmett, on the other hand, was still dealing with his parents, and they clearly didn't think too much of their second son, which was a shame. Emmett had his problems—everyone did—but he was determined, and he didn't give up. There was something very attractive about that kind of courage.

"You know, you're right. We are being mean," Emmett agreed, and Martha nodded. "But are we lying? I mean, the sheriff does have a certain appeal in that uniform of his." He leaned over the table to Marianne. "There's also that tool belt," Emmett growled.

"He does have a nice butt in those pants. He must work out." Marianne appeared to think a few seconds. "And he has a steady job with a pension." She put her hands together as though the thought was perfection. Martha patted her arm, and Marianne rolled her eyes.

"Don't be ridiculous," Martha scolded with a touch of rebuke.

"Then stop Giselle from pushing us together. It isn't going to happen. I'll pick the man I want to marry myself. Giselle's taste is most definitely not mine."

"And what exactly is your taste in men, little lady?" Nate quizzed, and Emmett scowled at him.

"Let's just say that I tend to go for men who are a little larger, taller, and have intense brown eyes. I also like a man who can ride." All three of them about choked at the same time, and Marianne howled with laughter. "I also want a man who isn't gay."

"That's plenty of that talk," Martha scolded. "Everyone eat your dinner, and there is to be no more sex talk, especially from you. Do you want me to have a heart attack?" She met each of their gazes with a hard look that would brook no argument.

"Come on, Mom. There is so much subtext in this house you need a primer to decipher it. But without Dustin and Giselle, we can at least talk about it. I mean, Emmett is gay, but Giselle refuses to accept what that means, so she pushes me at Emmett, but she never says anything. She just seats me next to him at every meal. Dustin, meanwhile, at every meal, talks about the ranch, asks what everyone thinks, and then ignores them until they're done so he can make a pronouncement on whatever he's already decided." Nate's eyebrows shot to his hairline, and Emmett almost choked on his water. He began to cough, and Nate patted his back.

"Marianne!" Martha snapped.

"Do I lie?" she pressed. "Come on, Mom. They live in their own world, and as long as things are exactly the way they want them, they're happy."

"Marianne," Emmett said quietly, "you are right, but this is still their house and their land. So they don't have to listen to anyone. We always have a choice, and that's to leave and do something else." He sighed and returned to his dinner. "I used to dream about running away to the rodeo like RE and Nate did. But then he came home, and there's the little fact that I'd end up cleaning the stalls and trying to keep my backside away from the damned horses and their teeth."

"What did you want to do?" Nate asked, deciding this conversation had probably gone on longer than it should. "I mean, when you were kid, what did you want to do when you grew up?"

Emmett turned to him, those eyes filled with hurt. "I wanted to do whatever you and RE were doing. You rode horses, so I tried riding. Even the pony didn't like me. Then you and RE started rodeo, and I wanted to try that. You know how well that worked out. The one thing I was good at was the cattle. Those I understand. They want to be part of the herd. They're prey animals, and I understand how that feels. But RE was supposed to manage the horses, and Dad managed the cattle, so...." He shrugged yet didn't turn away, and it seemed Emmett was speaking just to him. "This is my home, but there hasn't been much for me here. There never was. I mean, RE was perfect. He could do anything, and my father adored him. RE was the perfect son for my rancher father and former debutante mother. He knew what to say at every occasion, and the horses followed him around like he had apples in his pockets. How can I live up to that?"

"You don't have to live up to anything," Nate told him gently. "RE was who he was. He was your brother, but he was far from perfect."

"And the notion that your brother and father always got along isn't right either," Martha said with a half smile. "Those two used to argue all the time, about you sometimes, but also about the ranch. RE wanted to modernize, and your father resisted change of any kind. They used to go round and round about it all the time. So take RE down from that pedestal and give yourself some credit and be yourself."

"They did?" Emmett asked. "I don't remember any of that."

"Because your father and brother didn't fight. They argued, but when they came out of the office, everything was okay. They respected each other." Martha got up and began clearing away the dishes. "I understand your father will be home on Monday."

Emmett nodded. "That's what Mama told me. I'd suggest having everything cleaned and ready in their room for Sunday in case they release him early." He took care of his own plate and cleared Nate's and Marianne's as well. "Thank you for a wonderful dinner." Emmett lightly kissed Martha's cheek before retreating to the office.

Marianne leaned over the table, her hand resting on her hips expectantly.

"What?" Nate asked.

"I was about to ask you the same thing. What the heck are you waiting for?" she asked as though he were completely stupid. "That man just looked at you as though the sun rises and sets on your butt, and you seemed completely oblivious." She shook her head. "Sometimes men are so stupid."

"Excuse me?" He straightened up.

"Come on. I've sat here for one meal with the two of you and all you did was eye-fuck each other through the entire meal."

"Marianne, language!" Martha called from the other room.

"Knock off the bat hearing, Mom. If you don't like what's said, then don't listen," she snapped back, looking toward the kitchen. "Geez, I'm trying to help." She turned her attention back to him. "And it's true. Every time you looked at each other, my ovaries shriveled up a little because it's true, all the good men are either married or gay. Thank goodness I go back to school in a few months—not that the pickings are all that much better there. A quarter of the guys are looking for a little woman to bring home to Mom, another quarter are looking for someone to just bring home. A good portion are there to party, and whatever brains they had got washed away in the booze or went up in a puff of smoke. That leaves maybe a quarter of the male student population. And most of the ones worth having are already taken or have set themselves up in a nice garden apartment, perfectly decorated, with hot and cold running guys who listen to Madonna, Bette, Lady Gaga, or Barbra and only have eyes for each other."

Nate couldn't compete with that, and he left the table, heading for the office.

Chapter 6

EMMETT PORED over the ranch records as the door opened behind him. "There were things you wanted to review. But if now isn't a good time...," Nate said.

Emmett wasn't sure he wanted to do this now, but Nate was here already. Ranches were great places to be alone or commune with nature... until you really wanted to, and then there seemed to be a ton of people around all the damned time.

"It's fine." He rolled the chair back. "Dad did a good job of keeping the records, and everything is in order."

"But...?" Nate said.

"Well, I got the bank statements, and I've been reconciling them with the records—and there's extra money all over the place. I mean, it's like Dad hid money in every single account. The house account has thousands extra, the main ranch account almost a hundred grand, and the cutting horse accounts almost as much." He turned to Nate. "It doesn't make any sense, unless Dad just let the accounts grow and grow over years without ever bothering to actually balance them." Emmett sighed. "I always thought Dad was really on top of the business end of things."

Nate pulled over the other chair and sat down. "I don't know what to tell you."

A sharp crack had Emmett freezing momentarily, and then Nate was up and out of the chair. "What the hell was that?"

Emmett grabbed his arm. "It was a gunshot." He had no intention of letting Nate go anywhere if someone was shooting outside. A second shot followed, and Emmett pulled open the gun case and handed a rifle to Nate, keeping another for himself.

"I need to get out there." Nate pulled open the door.

"Emmett," Martha asked as she met them at the door.

"Call the sheriff and get him out here now," Nate ordered. "Stay in the house and away from the windows in case there are more shots." He was already on his way to the back door, and Emmett followed behind. He wasn't letting Nate go this alone.

"Did you hear that?" Jeremy asked. He was dressed in just a pair of jeans, hurrying across the yard toward them. "I didn't see anyone."

"Get the rest of the men and turn on every light we have." Nate was already flipping switches near the back door, and floodlights illuminated the yard.

"On it." Jeremy hurried over to the barn, and lights flashed on all around the structure.

"The horses," Emmett said and took off after him. The damned things might hate him, but he wasn't going to let anyone shoot the hayburners. Once inside, he took a head count and relaxed when none of them seemed hurt.

"Emmett," Nate called from outside, and he came to the barn door as Nate pointed across the yard to his truck. The back and front windows had spiderwebbed, and radiator fluid dripped from the front onto the ground.

"My truck," Emmett said softly. He'd bought it just three years ago, and it had been truly his—not one of the ranch vehicles, but something he had saved for and paid for with his own money. It was something that was his, not the ranch's and not his parents'. It represented a sense of freedom, and he had picked it out. "Why?"

Flashing lights signaled the approach of the sheriff, and Emmett let Nate greet him. Not that he could look the man in the eye after the crack he'd made to Marianne earlier. "How many shots did you hear?" Sheriff Bridger asked as he strode over.

"I heard two, but we were inside the house," Emmett answered.

"I think I might have heard three," Jeremy said, and Holace nodded his agreement. "But I'm not sure." Emmett stayed where he was while the sheriff looked over the mess that was his truck.

"Everyone stay back. It looks like one shot went through the windows and one into the front of the truck." He continued walking slowly around. "There's definitely a third shot, right into the engine block." He pointed to the hole in the hood of the truck. "I'll get some guys out here to gather what we can from the scene."

"Come on inside," Nate said gently, tugging Emmett toward the house. "There's nothing you can do out here."

Emmett was stunned, and Nate guided him into the house and to the table, where Martha immediately tried to feed him. It didn't matter that they'd had dinner less than an hour ago—if you needed comfort, Martha fed you. "I'm going to go out and check with the sheriff, but I'll be back soon." Nate patted his shoulder and then left the house.

What the hell was happening around here? His truck, the fence, someone setting fires. It didn't make sense. What could someone want or expect to gain from any of this? His family wasn't going to be run off their land no matter what. Somehow Emmett thought this was personal, not so much against the ranch, but aimed at him. The truck had definitely been very personal and meant to send a message of some sort, but Emmett was damned if he knew what that message was.

The sheriff and Nate came in the back door, then took off their boots and sat at the table. "Emmett, who have you pissed off?" the sheriff asked.

"Me? No one other than Clinton, and he's an ass to everyone." Besides, why would Clinton bother with this? It was likely he'd get what he wanted when Emmett flew through the air and landed on his face in the rodeo arena.

"Emmett... someone specifically went after your truck. The other ranch vehicles were right there, and none of them were touched. Instead, they put three shots through yours."

Emmett snorted. "And I'm supposed to have the answers why?" He turned to the sheriff, deputies, Nate, and surrounding cowboys all staring at him. "Well, you can forget that. I don't know why someone would want to kill my truck. You know, maybe the entire universe is out to get me." He threw his hands in the air. "I give up. Maybe I should just crawl into a cave somewhere and live the rest of my life as a hermit." Fuck it all. This pity party he had going on needed to stop. If he wanted others to treat him with respect, then he needed to start by respecting himself.

A few of the cowboys snickered. "With your luck, there'd be a skunk in the cave." A chuckle went through the assemblage, and Emmett rounded on Aaron, the offender.

"No, I think that's your own scent you're smelling," he snapped back. "And I definitely wouldn't want to share a cave with you."

Aaron stepped back and partially hid behind Holace. At least the kid had some brains.

"As for you, Sheriff, I don't know why anyone would want to shoot my truck. I haven't been in town in a while. With Dad in the hospital,

I've been staying here to help make sure everything is taken care of." He pondered who he could have pissed off as he looked out the window toward his truck. Damn, someone hated him.

"What about Foster?" Holace spoke up. "Remember him? Your dad fired him—caught the kid stealing and threatened to call the sheriff. The way he looked at your dad, I thought he was going to kill him on the spot, and he's the type to try to get his own back, even if he was in the wrong."

"Would that be Foster Hadden?" Sheriff Bridger asked.

"He left town," Aaron said much more softly than before. "I thought he said he was going to stay with a sister before he left."

"If he did, he's back," Holace supplied, and Emmett was about as thrilled as the last time he had dental work. "I saw him at the diner just the other day. He looked like hell. I asked what was new, and he said he'd just gotten back and was looking for a place to stay."

Emmett sighed. "Great, just great." Could his life fall apart any more?

"I'll stop by and have a little confab with Mr. Hadden just as soon as I finish up here. You all go on about your work, unless you have something helpful to add. We'll finish up with the truck and see if we can get any information from the bullets used." He seemed to know what he was doing. "Young man, you be careful. I'm going to make sure cars patrol this area over the next few days. You all keep him safe. If someone is after young Emmett here, then he's going to need protection."

Holace took a step forward. "We may pick on him a little, but we all know how to look out for our own. And Emmett is one of our own."

"That's good, but for God's sake, don't go shooting anyone." He actually smiled. "The paperwork for that kind of crap is murder." He grinned at his own joke, but Emmett wasn't feeling humorous at the moment. Still, the play on words was kind of funny.

The others trickled in, and soon enough the table was full of cowboys, talking quietly and eating. Men who worked hard the way they all did worked up huge appetites. Emmett wasn't up to talking, so after half a sandwich, he went to the office and closed the door. He sat in his father's chair, wondering how he could ever have thought about filling his shoes. And yet he knew that was what he truly wanted. He was smart, and he could see the big picture when others didn't. But Emmett wasn't his father, and he was never going to be. Maybe he was a fool to think he could run the ranch in his absence, but he sure as hell intended to try, if for no other reason than to show his father that he could. The men looked up to his father and did what he wanted in an instant, snapping to when he gave instructions. They would never do that for him. Emmett knew they saw him as…. God, did he dare think it? As a cowboy clown. And maybe he was the clown in this western ranch circus—the one everyone laughed at, but never thought about whenever anything serious needed to be done.

He felt rather than heard the door open and then close, and then Nate's hands rested on his shoulders. "The sheriff said he was done and was taking things back to the office. He asked that we leave the truck where it is for a day or so in case they need to look at it again. He did say to call the insurance company to get things started and that he would make sure we had a copy of the report for them."

Emmett nodded, but he didn't really care at this point. It was just a truck, after all. Once the insurance company got done, he'd go out and get a new one. "Thanks for taking care of that." He expected Nate to leave, but he sat down in the other chair.

"Are you going to hide all evening?"

Emmett slowly swiveled the chair to face him. "I think I earned that right after someone decided to put my truck out of its misery. What the hell did I do to piss someone off enough that they decide to attack me like that? I mean, it's just a truck, and I can get another one. But why is someone doing this?"

"You know," Nate said softly, "this may have nothing to do with you at all. You and your dad both have dark gray trucks. The cut fence, the fire, the truck—it could all relate to your father. It could have been your father that they were after. So maybe we need to think about who could be after him. I brought that up to the sheriff, and he said he was going to look into it. But it isn't like he's going to question your dad in the hospital after he's had a heart attack."

Emmett lifted his gaze. "I hadn't thought of that." At least it was an explanation that meant he didn't have a target on his back. He hadn't been thinking of anything other than his own misery the past few hours, and that needed to stop now.

"Things are rarely as bad as they seem," Nate told him as he leaned closer.

Emmett snorted. "Let me guess, your superhero name is Platitude Man."

"Maybe. But at least you smiled." Nate grinned, and Emmett rolled his eyes, turning back to his father's books. But he didn't see the neat rows of numbers or balances. They just swam on the page as Emmett thought and then snorted.

"What's that for?" Nate asked, catching Emmett's gaze. "What? You look like the Joker or something."

"Imagine whoever they are coming after my father. Dustin McElroy. That has to take the cake in the book of stupid criminal tricks. As it is, no matter what, my father will hunt them down. And when he finds them, they'll either get the hell out of Dodge or Dad will shoot them and bury the body under a carcass the next time one of the head has to be put down. No one will ever find a thing." Emmett smiled broader and then laughed outright. "My father has run off more idiots than you can imagine over the years. The list would probably take up a good share of the Montana census."

Nate scratched his head. "Your father can be a force of nature."

"Hell, he's the one who taught tornadoes how to spin faster, for Christ's sake. Even after having a heart attack, my father would still take this guy out and have a good time doing it." Emmett couldn't image anyone willing to take on his father. When his dad caught Foster stealing, he threatened to beat the shit out of him, scaring the guy enough that Emmett thought he was going to wet himself. He believed in the old cowboy ways of justice, and that meant if he caught you pulling shit on his land, prepare to be shot first. No questions—just the burial to follow.

"Yeah. That's true. But if what's happening is because of something your father did, then we're going to have one hell of a time getting to the bottom of it. You've been here for years. Is there anyone that you could think of that would do something like this?" Nate asked. "You worked with some of the men your father fired."

"And they were lazy asses. Dad didn't fire someone for one mistake. He believes in working with people. But if you stole from him or just didn't care, then you got let go." Emmett tried to think of someone who was unbalanced enough to actually attack the ranch. He shook his head. "It's possible that some long-simmering grievance has bubbled up. It's common knowledge in town that Daddy is in the hospital, so maybe someone had figured that with him gone, the Rolling D is vulnerable."

Nate shrugged. "I don't think we're going to get to the bottom of this one tonight." He yawned. "There were things you wanted to go over earlier."

"I can't do it tonight. My mind just isn't on all that right now." He was worn out, and maybe it was time for him to head to bed. Hopefully tomorrow would be better.

"How long has it been since you've been off this ranch?" Nate asked, his gaze intense and yet warm. Emmett shrugged, and Nate's eyes widened. "Let me guess. You haven't left since that night you got drunk, have you?"

"Yes, I have. I…." He tried to think of an example and snapped his lips closed. "I don't need to go anywhere."

"You sure as hell do. Call your friend Reid, or I'll call him. We'll go into town and get us a beer or something. I won't let you drink too much, but you need to get out of this house and off this ranch, if only for a few hours."

"Are you serious?" Emmett asked. "What about the fact that someone just shot up my truck?" There was no way in hell he was going anywhere.

"Yeah, about that. You know that this town is full of folks who talk. So maybe we need to find out who's doing the talking? I'm thinking that there's too much we don't know and somehow we need to find out, and the one place to do that is in town."

His slight smile had Emmett's reluctance dropping away. This was such a bad idea. The last time, he'd shot his mouth off. Plus, every time he closed his eyes, he was seeing Nate—at night, in his daydreams—and he didn't need more temptation. The man was sex on a stick and very much off limits.

"Call your friend Reid if you want and ask him to meet us at Hill's Tavern. We can have a drink, you can get over whatever reluctance you seem to have built up about going into town, and maybe your friend will pull you out of your shell a little. It could be good for you." Nate crossed his arms over his chest, glaring at him, just daring him to offer an argument.

"Fine. Though I think this is rather stupid."

"So is you going to bed at nine o'clock like an old man. And don't argue with me. I know that's what you were thinking."

Dammit. Emmett thought about arguing, but he couldn't come up with anything that didn't sound lame even to him. Instead, he snatched up his phone and dialed Reid, who answered on the first ring. Emmett explained Nate's idea.

"Oh, thank God," Reid said dramatically. "I have been climbing the walls here. I love my mother, but I am so bored, I'm starting to wish she had simply drowned me at birth to put me out of my misery." Reid was in classic flutter tonight. "I'll make sure she's settled in and then I can meet you there in half an hour." He hung up, and Emmett snickered.

"What?"

"You asked for it. He's excited." Emmett leaned forward, Reid already having lightened his mood. When he inhaled, he got a good whiff of Nate, and in an instant, Reid wasn't the only one whose heart was going a mile a minute.

"Good," Nate said, and Emmett snorted. "What?"

"Let's just say that when Reid gets excited, he gets gay-cited. He's likely to show up in a rainbow suit with fairy wings and a wand shooting glitter all over everyone." Maybe that was what Emmett needed—a real glitter bomb kind of night.

Nate shrugged. "Get your hat and boots on, because we're going out."

"I have boots on," Emmett said.

Nate lowered his gaze. "Okay, let me be clear. Put on boots that aren't scuffed all to hell, and let's go have a little fun. And don't worry, Cinderella, I'll have you home before you turn into a pumpkin."

REID MET them outside the tavern, and just as Emmett had predicted, he was over the top. Bright red boots and a pink shirt topped the otherwise black ensemble. At least there were no fairy wings.

"Come on, I'm thirsty," Reid said as he grabbed Emmett's arm. "Besides, I'm horny as hell, and maybe there will be a hot cowboy I can cut from the herd and take home for a ride."

Behind them, Nate choked.

"God, I missed you," Emmett said as they went inside. The tavern was busy as hell, with country music from the digital jukebox on full power. The energy in the room seemed electric and only grew more excited when people saw the three of them enter. A few guys turned to where the short-tempered asshole Clinton sat with a few of his box-of-rocks friends, Brad Connors and Weston Marcourt. Emmett swore if the three of them put their brains together, they'd have enough for one mind, and it would be filled with resentment and old grudges. "Maybe we should go somewhere else," Emmett offered. There was no sense begging for trouble.

"Ignore the Twinkle Triplets over there. Though I do think that Brad is kind of hot... in a vapid and vacant sort of way." Reid snickered, and Nate directed them to the only empty table in the place. Fortunately it was on the other side of the room from the brain void.

"Is that the kind of thing you like?" Nate asked Reid.

"I've been here taking care of my mother for weeks now. The ups and downs of chemotherapy and radiation are worse than any roller coaster, and I think it's getting to me. To top that off, there are hot cowboys everywhere, all with muscles from working hard, tight jeans, and great big Do Not Touch signs. It's fucking depressing." He heaved a dramatic sigh. "So yeah, I think I'm getting desperate enough that if he was actually interested...." Reid shook himself. "God, I need to go back to San Francisco where I can find gay men by the bunch. I think this drought is starting to affect my glittery fabulousness." He groaned and then straightened up, squared his shoulders, and stood as tall as possible.

"Where are you going?" Half the cowboys in the place gawked at Reid like he was some exotic species of bird that they needed to get their guns to shoot, then take home to stuff and place on their mantel.

"To the bar. Being a wallflower isn't going to get me a cowboy to ride into the sunset." Reid leaned close, speaking softly. "Unlike you, I don't have a big hunk of cowboy eye candy looking at me as though I were an all-you-can-eat buffet." He swished away on his own personal pink, glittery cloud as Emmett watched, his mouth hanging open. Sometimes Reid was totally crazy, and this had to be one of those times.

Emmett shifted his gaze and didn't see any of that "buffet" gazing that Reid described, no matter how much he might wish that Nate thought of him that way.

"Can I bring y'all something?"

Emmett lifted his gaze. "Hey, Sally Beth. What are you doing working here?" He hadn't seen her in quite a while. "Last I heard, you had moved to Cheyenne."

She rolled her eyes. "My soon-to-be ex-husband, Brad"—she glared at one of the three rocket scientists in the corner—"got a job there, which he managed to lose after three months, along with what he had left of his brains. The idiot didn't even have the good sense to stay there. He followed us back. Our son and I are living with my parents." She sounded beaten down.

"What sort of work were you looking for?" Emmett asked as Nate cleared his throat.

She snorted. "Around here? You have to be kidding me. Everything is so gender roled. I grew up on my grandpa's ranch. I've done it all, but all I could get was this job."

Nate nodded and caught Emmett's gaze, the two of them thinking the same thing. "When Mr. McElroy gets home next week, come on out to the ranch. We always need hands experienced with cattle and horses."

"And the fact that I have these?" She pushed up her ample bosom.

Emmett snorted. "As long as you don't intend to take them out and flash me with them. As a gay man, you may scar me for life. But seriously, if you can do the work...."

"We'll talk to Dustin," Nate interjected.

Sally Beth looked so relieved. "Thank God. Living with my mother is stomping my last nerve. Now what can I bring you?"

"Just a couple of beers and whatever the dancing queen over there is having," Nate answered, their heads all turning to where Reid had pulled Kevin McClusky out onto the dance floor.

"Does your friend know that Kevin is having it on with him?" Sally Beth asked.

Emmett nodded. "I bet Kevin doesn't know that back in San Francisco, Reid teaches martial arts at one of the top dojos in the city. If he tries anything, Reid will down him in two seconds, and Kevin can give up any hope of ever having children."

Sally Beth whistled. "I'd pay money to see that, the big redneck." She tapped the table. "I'll get your beers, and thank you. I could use a real chance at a life." She hurried away, and Nate leaned over the table.

"What are you thinking?" Nate asked.

"That Holace could use some help? I remember that Sally Beth has a sweet touch with horses."

Nate nodded his agreement, and once their drinks came, they clinked glasses. Now Emmett just needed to convince his conservative father that a woman on the ranch wasn't going to set every man off into a fit of runaway hormones.

"Her grandfather trained amazing horses, and from what I heard, he taught Sally Beth everything he knew." They paused their conversation once she returned. "Come to the ranch on Tuesday and we'll see if we can make this happen."

"I need a place for me and my son. Brad keeps watching me to make sure I don't do something wrong so he can try to swoop in." She bit her lower lip before setting down the beer mugs.

"You asshole." Reid's voice cut through the crowd, which grew quiet as everyone took in the floor show. It seemed Kevin had tired of playing whatever game he had in mind and had Reid in an arm hold. Emmett felt Nate tense, but he just sipped his beer. Emmett had seen shit like this before.

"Did you really think I was interested in a butt-waver like you?" At least the insult was original. Emmett had to give Kevin points for that.

Reid tensed and then relaxed, his arm flying back, catching Kevin in the solar plexus. He let Reid go, and in an instant, Reid whirled around and caught Kevin in the groin. He doubled over.

Emmett was about to grin at Sally Beth, but Reid wasn't done. He pushed Kevin forward, and he ended up on the floor. "Now who's a butt-waver?" He smacked Kevin hard on the ass, the clap ringing through the bar. "Oh, and douchebag, you definitely need to do a lot more squats if you want your ass to be up to gay-man standards." Reid strutted back to the table, all eyes on him.

"That was one hell of a display, but did it get you anywhere?" Nate asked as Reid lifted his beer and drank half of it.

"Of course it did. The rednecks are now going to be scared shitless of me, and anyone that's interested is going to make their desires known, because a guy who can kick ass and take names is hot." He didn't even look around. "Now that everyone has pretty much returned to normal, there are three or four guys in the room who keep looking over."

"You see any?" Nate asked. "Because I got two, and I never would have picked Beau Sumner for walking on the dark side."

"I got one, but I think he's just curious," Emmett said, since the guy had turned away and didn't look back. A gay man would do his best to sneak another look.

"Is Beau the cowboy in the brown hat, blue shirt, with jet-black hair just peeking out from under the hat and the perfectly trimmed mustache?" When Nate nodded, Reid grinned. "Good. Because me likey some of that. Especially the full lips, and that man has come-fuck-me eyes if I've ever seen them." Reid finished his beer and levered himself up from the table. "Time to separate a little walking cowboy sex from the rest of the herd." He winked. "Don't wait up," he sang as he headed off.

"Good God," Nate chuckled.

"Exactly. Montana may be Big Sky country, but with Reid in town, the sky is dim by comparison. He rivals the sun for attention, and he usually gets it. Reid has always had this way about him." Part of Emmett was jealous. He was one of those people who rarely got noticed... or more accurately, he seemed to have so many bright, attention-getting people in his life that people didn't notice him by comparison. Reid, RE, his father... all of them had garnered attention wherever they went. If Emmett got attention, it definitely wasn't the good kind.

"Can I get you refills?" Sally Beth asked.

"Sure, but that's all, because I have to drive home," Nate told her. "Say, I want to ask you. We had a little trouble at the ranch earlier this evening. Is there any talk about it?"

She shrugged and then shook her head. "Not that I've heard. But I'll keep my ear out if that helps."

"Good, and let us know which quarter it seems to be coming from."

Sally Beth nodded. "I gotcha." She left, and Emmett swayed a little in his chair as the music changed.

"You know, one of these days, after Reid's mother is feeling better, I want to visit him in San Francisco. There are a number of clubs there, and I'd love to go just so I could go dancing." He looked out over the floor. "I know that gay marriage is legal and all that, but I'd like it even more if people weren't such dicks." He'd really like to be able to just dance.

"It takes time for people to catch up and figure things out," Nate said as Sally Beth placed their beers on the table. Nate handed her some cash, and Emmett did the same, making sure she got a good tip. "Thanks. We'll finish these and free up the table."

"I'll see you Tuesday." She hurried away happier, and Emmett drank his beer, still watching the dance floor.

"This is nice. I haven't been out with someone just to have a beer in a long time. Well, at least not without someone getting drunk and…." He sighed, and Emmett turned just as Clinton decided to pay them a visit. Emmett could have gone all night without having to talk to him.

"You going to be ready for next month?" He seemed tickled. "It's going to be wonderful putting you McElroys in your place. Your entire family has lorded it over everyone for too long, and now you're going to fall flat on your face."

"Yeah, he'll be there. And you better be there. We all know the kind of stock you come from. When the going gets tough, you Masters shit yourselves and run the other way," Nate chimed in. "Now go back to your friends and leave us alone. You issued your stupid challenge, and Emmett has agreed to ride."

"Do I need to call the police?" Sally Beth asked from behind Clinton. "You can spend the night in jail with some very interesting company, or you can pay up and go home." Dang, she was something else. "The owner is tired of you causing trouble in here."

"This is a public place—"

"No, it's not. This is a private establishment, and we can refuse service to any asshole we like." She spoke loudly enough that the entire bar could hear, and a chuckle went through the crowd, which left Clinton's cheeks beet red. "And you better tip your server, or next time, if there is one, you'll be wearing your beer instead of drinking it." She pointed, and he slunk back to his table, threw down some bills, and then left the bar, his two friends following. "God, I hate that man."

"Which one?" Emmett asked.

Sally Beth grinned. "Brad wouldn't have been a bad husband if it weren't for his friends. But as it is, he's useless, and my son deserves better."

Emmett finished his beer and stood. "We'll see you Tuesday." He waited for Nate, and they left the tavern and climbed into the truck. "You okay to drive?"

"Yeah. I left half of the second one." He pulled out of the parking lot and drove out to the ranch. Emmett watched out the side window as the cab filled with Nate's scent. He kept glancing over, taking in the way Nate's thighs stretched the denim. He found his mind wandering the way it usually did when his thoughts turned to Nate. This dancing around each other was driving him crazy. As soon as they pulled into the ranch, he'd make some sort of move and see what happened. Reid had told him, in his own colorful way, that he thought Nate was interested, and if he was right, then maybe it was up to Emmett to make the first move. Maybe Nate would push him away, or maybe Nate would pull him closer, deepen the kiss and—

The tone of the tires changed as Nate slowed and pulled into the ranch drive. He rolled the truck into his parking space next to what was left of Emmett's truck.

Emmett did his best not to look at it. He didn't open his door and turned to Nate. He licked his lips and leaned closer to him, the seat creaking softly under him. Nate's gaze wandered for a second and then locked on Emmett's. The temperature in the cab skyrocketed, and Emmett's heart beat faster as excitement coursed through him. "Nate… I…." Maybe it was time for him to put his cards on the table and tell Nate how he felt—and what he had dreamed of for so damn long. Emmett leaned over the gap between them, his lips parting—

A knock on the window startled him enough he jumped and hit his head on the ceiling. Holace grinned through the window, and Nate opened the door. Emmett did the same.

"What's up?" Emmett asked, hoping Holace hadn't seen their almost kiss.

"Come on. You gotta see." Holace hurried off around the side of the main barn to the weaning shed where Unexpected Miracle and his mother were. Holace turned on one light that illuminated part of their yard. "I was about to bring them inside."

"Is something wrong?" Emmett asked looking over the fence, trying to see the problem.

"Look at the colt," Holace said. "The little guy is absolutely perfect. Look at his conformation already."

"He is a pretty thing."

Holace cleared his throat. "I'm going to recommend to your father that we get him tested to find out who the sire is. We need to prove it, because this little guy is going to be an amazing horse—I can feel it. Whatever accident resulted in his birth is likely to be more of a miracle than any of us thought."

Emmett patted Holace on the shoulder. "Thanks. At least Dad isn't going to completely blow a gasket." And at least something was going right. "I'll see you in the morning."

Holace went to turn out the lights, and Emmett followed Nate back to his truck.

"Night, Emmett." He smiled and got inside. Emmett sighed as he left, wondering how quickly his luck could change.

Chapter 7

"YOU HAVE to pay attention to your balance and move with the horse instead of against it," Nate said as Emmett fell off the practice bronc yet again. The longest he had made was about five seconds. Most of the time, after a couple decent bucks, Emmett was down on the padding. "Use your hand, lean into the movement. Don't try to counter it, because you can't."

"I'm trying," Emmett gritted and got up from the floor. He slapped his jeans and then climbed on once more. Emmett got into position, and Nate grabbed the ropes and waited for Emmett to nod. Then he yanked with everything he had, trying to give Emmett as authentic an experience as he could. Emmett rocked his hips and survived the first roll as Nate pulled against the flow, sending the barrel horse bucking. Emmett managed to keep his feet down and remained seated, but the next jump did him in, and he went flying off in Nate's direction, hitting him and sending them both down to the mats.

Nate ended up on the bottom with Emmett on top. Instantly, Emmett's heat went through Nate's clothes, his eyes gazing into Nate's. Nate held his breath for a moment as they widened in surprise. He wondered what Emmett was going to do. He hoped he might take it further, but was that a good idea?

Then Emmett slowly drew closer, watching Nate like a hawk. He met Emmett, who kissed him hard, stealing Nate's breath away. Nate went with it, winding his fingers through Emmett's soft hair, energy coursing between them. Within seconds Nate was lost in Emmett's slightly sweet lips, his hips bucking slightly, pants way too fucking tight, cock desperate for release. He felt like a teenager again. Emmett shimmied on top of him, their hips gliding together. Nate wound his other arm around Emmett, holding him tightly as he returned his kiss with the passion that bubbled up from his soul.

"It's about fucking time."

They stopped instantly, and Nate glared at Marianne, who stood in the doorway.

"Mom sent me to find you to say that dinner will be an hour." She didn't turn away, and Nate sighed.

"If you're so happy about it, then you wanna leave?" he growled, but Marianne looked over at the practice horse.

"So this is where you've been hiding." Since apparently she wasn't going to leave, Emmett lifted himself off, and Nate got to his feet and helped Emmett up. "Teaching Emmett how to ride so he can beat Masters?"

"That's how things started," Nate said, wiping his mouth. "Do you want to let us get back to it?"

"What, the training or the kissing?" She snickered.

"Girl...," Emmett growled.

"Well, at least this will ensure that Giselle's matchmaking days are over. How long ago did you two finally figure things out?" She looked at each of them and then shook her head. "God, was that your first kiss?" She fanned herself and shook her head. "Damn... that was definitely a scorcher." She walked around to the other side of the horse. "What are you waiting for, more kissing? Emmett, get back on. Nate and I will man the ropes, and for God's sake, stay on this time. Oh, and don't let that kiss scramble your brains. A bronc will do that fast enough."

Nate wondered again if this was a good idea. The thought of Emmett getting hurt dissipated the heat from the kiss like the sun burning off the morning fog.

Emmett climbed back on the training horse and got into position. When he was ready, he nodded, and this time he lasted maybe four seconds before tumbling off. "I'm never going to get this thing."

"Everyone gets bucked," Marianne said. "Including world champions. All you need to do is last the eight somehow."

"With the way I'm going, my only chance is to superglue my ass to the saddle."

"Hah," Marianne said. "You'll still get bucked, and all you'll end up doing is mooning the entire crowd while the seat of your jeans is still in the saddle." She grinned.

"Use your hips and adjust your balance. This is all about balance. And the thing is, we can't simulate the horse twisting here. Only the bucking and jumping. But keep your head and your balance and you'll be okay." Nate smiled. He understood how frustrating this was. "Now try it again." The truth was, he hated seeing Emmett fail, but it was the only way to learn, and if Emmett was determined to ride, Nate had to make sure he was as ready as possible. Nate blinked and reminded himself he needed to keep his mind on his task rather than on that kiss.

Emmett climbed back on, and they started bucking when he nodded. Marianne held her own on her end, and Nate did his best. This time Emmett held on for longer before finally ending up on the floor. "That was close to the eight," Marianne pronounced.

"Yeah. And you used your hands and hips much better. It's coming along." Nate grinned widely. "And I think we're going to end this on a high note for tonight." He gathered things up and followed the others outside, gathering up some trash and carrying it outside as a cover, then closing up the shed just as Emmett asked Marianne to keep this quiet.

"Really?" Marianne asked. "This is the coolest thing you've ever done."

"See?" Emmett retorted. "That's just it. I just want this over with and as few people to see me get humiliated as possible. So just keep it to yourself, okay?"

"If that's what you want." She checked the time on her phone. "We'd better get in for dinner or Mom is going to have a fit."

Nate hurried because he didn't want to get Martha upset, or she'd serve him peanut butter and jelly for days. He shuddered at the thought.

"THANKS FOR a great dinner," Nate told Martha, wondering what he was going to do with Emmett. The kiss earlier had been boot-meltingly hot, and he wanted to do it again. But then, he kept going back to the fact that Emmett was RE's younger brother. He sighed. Both he and Emmett were no longer kids, and Emmett wasn't *his* younger brother, even though they had grown up together. Kissing him had been great and not at all weird, as he'd feared it would be. He stood and left the table, not sure what to do.

"You and I have to go through things in the office," Emmett said and got up from his place. Nate followed, entering the office, and Emmett closed the door. "What's gotten into you? If you aren't interested in me, then I can take that. But I keep getting these on-and-off signals, and I don't know what they mean."

"You're RE's little brother. The guy who used to follow us around all the time. What are your parents and friends going to think? I'm older than you, and…." He rubbed the back of his neck. They weren't kids any longer, and four years probably wasn't as big a deal now as it had once been, but still….

"Yeah, you were RE's friend and mine. But I grew up—so did you. Big deal. I think I first noticed you when I turned sixteen, but you and RE were always off doing your own thing, and, well…." Emmett shrugged.

"Damn," Nate groaned. "That was about the time I noticed you…." His cheeks heated. "Well, you were RE's little brother, so I felt like such a perv watching you. It was just easier to stay away. Then you got older and hotter and…." He was so danged nervous.

"So you liked me?" Emmett asked in apparent disbelief. He chuckled, and before Nate could step back, Emmett had his arms around him, pulling Nate to him. "I can't tell you how many nights I lay in bed, thinking about you."

Nate swallowed. "So this isn't pervy to you?"

Emmett closed the distance between them, his breath ghosting over Nate's lips. "Does it feel pervy to you? I'm an adult, and so are you. I can make my own decisions, and the whole possibly pervy situation was over long ago." Emmett sighed. "Look, RE is gone, but I like to think that he would be happy that the two of us are friends."

Nate cocked his eyebrows. "Is that what we are?"

Emmett shimmied his hips, and Nate whimpered. "I don't know what we are. I mean, we've kissed, and I want to do it again." He took Nate's lips with power, tugging on his lower lip before pressing him back against the door. The panels dug slightly into his back, but Nate didn't care. All that mattered was the heat radiating off Emmett's body and the way Emmett quivered in his arms. He seemed to know what he wanted and took it. That was hot as all hell, and Nate hugged Emmett to him, kissing him right back.

"Yeah…," Nate said as Emmett pulled back, and Nate took the opportunity to catch his stolen breath. "We can…." He slid his hand down Emmett's back and cupped his butt. Emmett groaned and pressed nearer, his hips gliding along Nate's. "Is this really what you want?"

"Dammit, yes. I've dreamed of this since I was sixteen. After you left, I was so angry with you, and then you came back and took the job I thought I wanted."

"So is this like hate sex?" Nate asked, smirking.

"Fuck no. If I wanted hate sex, I'd seduce Clinton. I've had feelings for you since I was sixteen, and they were anything but hate." Emmett tugged at the hem of his shirt. Nate lifted his arms, and Emmett drew the shirt over his head before dropping it on the floor without dimming the interest in his gaze. "Are you interested in taking things further?"

Nate couldn't find his voice, so he nodded. This had been a long time coming, and for years he'd never thought it possible. He swallowed hard. "I want this." He was about to ask if Emmett did, but then Emmett tugged off his own shirt and tossed it aside, and damn, Emmett was smokin'. He wasn't bulky, but sleek and lean, with long muscles that rippled under his hands. "Damn, I *really* want this."

A knock had them both jumping away from the door. Emmett fell onto his father's sofa, while Nate only managed to stay upright because he caught himself with the desk. "Yes?" Emmett said as Nate put his hand over his mouth.

"I'm going to my room for the evening. Do you need anything?" Martha asked.

"We're good, thank you," Emmett said. Nate hoped she didn't try to come in, and they stayed quiet until her steps faded. Then Emmett grinned before burying his face in the pillows.

"What?" Nate asked.

Emmett lifted his face, tears running down his cheeks. For a second Nate worried that Emmett was hurt or really upset. He hadn't seen Emmett cry since they were ten and he fell down a ravine and scraped up just about everything. "I feel like we're sneaking around behind my parents' back." He wiped his eyes from laughter, a wicked smile forming on his lips. "So I guess what I need to know is how naughty do you want to be?" He got up from the couch and stalked closer. "My room is just down the hall. My mom and dad are gone, and we have the whole house to ourselves." He batted his eyes and looked every bit the naughty teenager.

"You little shit," Nate teased. "Are we going to stay in here all night? Because that sofa isn't near big enough for what I have in mind. Either that or I could just go home and see you in the morning." He sure as hell hoped Emmett didn't choose that option. He reached for the doorknob, and Emmett took his hand and led Nate through the living room toward the bedrooms.

"Boys," Martha said from behind them just as they left the living room.

Heat blossomed on Nate's cheeks remembering that they were half undressed. There was no doubt where they were headed or what they had planned for the evening. But Emmett just turned toward her. "Please don't be making noise all night long. Some of us need our beauty sleep." She grinned knowingly.

"We won't, Martha, and for the record, you don't need any beauty sleep because you're gorgeous. Always have been." Nate grinned, and Emmett tugged him down the hall.

"What's that supposed to mean?" Martha called from the doorway to her and Marianne's area of the house. "I still need to rest."

Emmett paused outside his door. "That I'm not making any damned promises. If you got earplugs, I suggest you use them." He pushed Nate into the room and kicked the door closed, cutting off whatever else Martha might have said. Emmett immediately pressed Nate to the door, his kisses deep and desperate. He had so much energy that it seemed to come out in almost frantic movements, as though he had to do everything all at once before he lost his chance.

Nate cupped Emmett's cheeks in his palms. "You and I have all night, and I have no intention of letting you go to sleep, so relax just a little." Emmett was a live wire, and Nate wanted to calm him down before his head exploded or something. "I'm not going anywhere, so you have nothing to worry about." He pressed Emmett back toward the bed and down until he sat. Then he kissed Emmett hard until he collapsed onto the mattress. "How long has it been?" Nate asked. He needed to know what kind of experience Emmett had.

Nate had been with guys before, but they'd been rodeo hookups—a few guys on a semiregular basis, like fuck buddies, but nothing serious. On the road, serious relationships were damned rare. There was too much to pull people apart, but Nate hadn't exactly gone without. Emmett had always been here on the ranch, and the opportunities for guy-on-guy fun weren't exactly around every corner.

"It's been a year or so."

"Reid?" Nate asked with a spike of jealousy.

Emmett narrowed his gaze. "Jealous? And no. Reid and I are friends, always have been. Two gay boys taking on the world. Well, Reid took on the world and still does. He's my best friend and has been since before he left for the West Coast. But we never did anything like that. It wouldn't feel right. Besides, Reid isn't my type."

"Oh." Nate climbed on the bed and ran his hand up Emmett's belly and chest, his fingers tweaking a pert nipple. "And what is your type?"

Emmett hissed and then had the audacity to act like he was thinking. "Well, there has always been this certain guy. But he was off limits because he and my brother were such good friends...." He closed the distance between them and wound his arms around Nate's neck, drawing him downward. The kiss cut off further questioning. Emmett loosened his hold and slid his hand down Nate's back, sending a shiver through him. God, Emmett knew how to touch him as he skipped his hands along Nate's sides before deftly popping open the button of his jeans.

The pressure around his hips eased as Emmett slipped the fabric open and then tried to push the jeans away. It seemed they didn't want to go. Nate tried kicking the things off, but they remained stubborn. With a growl, he climbed back to his feet and shucked the damned things before taking aim at Emmett's.

"What the hell is it today?" he growled as he yanked off Emmett's stubborn pants and tossed them aside.

"Hell if I know. Maybe it's all the stress."

Nate didn't want to talk about that. Everything from shot-up trucks to his failures in life could be dealt with later. Right now, he wanted one thing: Emmett naked in this damned bed. He pulled away the last bit of fabric, taking in the work-hardened sexiness that lay in front of him. Emmett was lean yet strong. Muscles long and sleek, a stomach carved from years of hard ranch work. There was no fat on this sexy man, and Nate watched him squirm a little while he stripped away the last of his own clothes, standing still as Emmett's gaze raked over him.

"Holy fuck," Emmett whispered. "You're like a statute in one of Mom's books." Emmett slid closer. Nate was about to lean over to kiss him when his entire thought process fried itself in a flurry of sensation as Emmett slid his lips down his cock, taking him in in one slow movement. Emmett hummed softly around him, and Nate could only stand still, his right leg shaking with nearly overwhelming excitement. Emmett was less tentative than Nate had thought he'd be. Not that he was complaining for a second.

Emmett slowly pulled back and then lay on his side, motioning to Nate with a single finger. Nate didn't have to be invited twice and joined

Emmett on the bed, immediately surrounded by Emmett's embrace. Emmett pressed him back on the mattress, gazing down at him. "I think I like being the one in charge," Emmett told him.

"Okay." Nate smiled. He didn't mind when someone else took the lead in bed, and if that was what Emmett wanted, then he wasn't going to—"Oh God." Emmett found that spot at the side of his neck, licking right there. Nate groaned and stretched to give Emmett better access. "Emmett."

The guy was a surprising live wire and exuded energy and excitement. Maybe that came from frustration. Speaking of which, Emmett slid his cock against his, adding to the urgency of the moment. Nate hugged Emmett close, trying to slow him down a little and drawing him up into a kiss. Nate loved kissing, and doing it with Emmett was a joy. He had long wondered what his full lips tasted like, and now he knew: a hint of spice and sweetness combined with heat and passion. Emmett straddled him, returning the kiss while Nate slid his hands down Emmett's back, cupping his hard, firm butt. "I want you, Nate. Is that all right?" Emmett asked.

It took Nate a second, given his clouded mind, to realize what Emmett was asking.

"Yes," Nate whispered, and Emmett fumbled for the bedside table while Nate kissed all the skin in reach, lightly tongue-tickling Emmett as well until he dropped some slick and a handful of foil packets on the bed. Nate glanced at the small pile and then back at Emmett. "Hopeful, aren't you?"

"What? I have more in case we need them," Emmett retorted.

Nate chuckled. "You're a real Boy Scout." He wondered just what Emmett was thinking.

Emmett shook his head. "Better. I was in 4-H, where we learned all about the birds and bees from the rabbits and horses. I've been saving up for a long time."

"I'll say. You know we don't have to use all of these," Nate said. He was getting a little nervous about exactly what Emmett was expecting.

"We don't. But how about we can't stop until we do?" Emmett asked, and Nate held him tighter.

"I like that idea." He kissed him and drew Emmett down, stroking his back and buttcheeks. Damn, the man was stunning to the eyes, the hands, the tastebuds, and even the ears. The happy sounds he made were a delight, and Nate loved pulling them out of him.

How long they kissed and explored, Nate had no idea. Time seemed irrelevant. He and Emmett settled into an easier rhythm, probably since Emmett realized Nate was going to take his time. They tasted and stroked, learning each other.

Nate handed Emmett a condom. The rip followed by the snick of lube, slick fingers teasing and giving Nate a glimpse of things to come... damn, Emmett learned fast, and Nate's mind clouded with anticipatory passion that nearly drove him insane. How Emmett learned to play his body like this Nate had no idea, but by the time Emmett pressed into him, Nate was more than ready.

"Take it slow," Nate whispered to Emmett, who paused before breaching him.

"Nate," Emmett breathed. "You mean you...? Have you...?"

Nate nodded. It had been a while, but he didn't want to have that conversation now. He relaxed, and Emmett pressed forward, Nate's body opening, taking Emmett inside. It had been a long time—years, in fact— since he had taken the bottom role during sex, but Emmett seemed to need to be in control for a while. And damn, the burn built and then subsided, leaving Emmett filling him and gazing into his eyes with an almost otherworldly sense of excitement.

Emmett leaned forward, his thick cock buried inside him. "I won't hurt you."

Nate guided him close enough for their lips to almost touch. "I know. You never have. I've watched you for a long time, and this seems so important for reasons I can't put into words." It was like this was happening, and yet he couldn't believe it. It had to be a dream.

"You don't need to," Emmett told him and slowly withdrew before sliding deep once again, his hips gliding, the movement smooth and oh so enticing. Nate moved right along with him, desperate for more. Emmett ran his hands down Nate's thighs, and he pulled his legs upward as Emmett lowered himself, instantly sending lightning shooting through him.

"Jesus!" Nate cried, and Emmett repeated his motion, the pleasure like ripples in a pond, building on each other until Nate could hardly think. His entire body vibrated with it. He drew Emmett into a kiss that only added to the heat that seared between them. "Oh God," Nate found himself chanting, and he couldn't stop it. This was too much to keep inside. "Yeah. More."

Emmett added more energy, and Nate soared, gripping the bedding to try to keep himself grounded. He needed to keep from flying apart.

"Emmett… I…." Nate gasped, unable to from words, but it seemed he didn't need any. Emmett stroked him in time to their movements, and Nate realized that his own pleasure was out of his hands. Emmett was totally in control, with all his energy going in every direction, and there was something wild and amazing about that.

"Just go with it," Emmett gasped, sweat shining in the light coming in through the windows. He looked like a sleek, glistening god over him, and Nate seared that image into his mind. This was Emmett, and for tonight at least, he was his.

Nate's control became more and more brittle with Emmett at the helm. He tried to stop the building pressure, to prolong the passion between them, but that control was Emmett's, and as soon as Nate gave up the last of his hold, his release washed over him, sending him flying to the heights of the atmosphere, floating with Emmett joining him just moments later.

NATE LOST track of the number of times he and Emmett fell asleep only to wake and start all over again. Sometime during the night, they fell into a deep sleep, and the next thing Nate knew, light shone brightly through the window, the sun beaming right into his eyes. He rolled over, moaning softly to turn out that damned light as he tried to go back to sleep. It didn't work.

Emmett's arm lay cross his side, and he mumbled something about it being Sunday and to let him sleep. Then he rolled over, his naked back and rear end a sight to behold. Nate wished he could stay where he was, but nature called, so he carefully got out of bed and found some of his clothes on the floor. He pulled them on and left the room to use the toilet before heading down to the office to get the rest of their clothes. Nate tried to be as quiet as possible and managed to make it to the office door before he encountered a glaring Martha, arms crossed over her chest. Dammit.

"I did warn the two of you yahoos to keep down the noise. But did you?" Her lips formed a straight line, and Nate swore this had to be what hell looked like. "Every time I settled down to sleep, you and Mr. Oh Jesus in there would start up again! What the hell, boys? And let me tell you, the both of you need to be aware that you're loud. For God's sake, there are people in this house who need to sleep and who haven't had a husband or anyone to warm their bed in a long time." Now a twinkle shone in her eyes. "Do you have any idea what it's like to hear that—"

"Oh God," Nate groaned.

"Exactly, *that*… over and over. And that boy needs to get a new damned bed, because it squeaks. It was bad enough when he was a teenager, but it's worse with the two of you." Now Nate wanted to die, and he bet if and when Emmett got this little talking-to, he'd wish the earth would open up and swallow him whole. "Now get dressed and go back in there to wake up Mr. Right There and tell him that breakfast and a good case of embarrassment and humiliation will be waiting for him in the kitchen. Especially when Marianne gets up."

Oh God, he didn't want to hear her sharp-tongued assessment. Martha's was bad enough, thank you very much. She turned on her heels and walked back toward the kitchen. Nate went into the office, got their shirts, and slunk back into the bedroom, where Emmett was still asleep. He turned to the closed door and then to Emmett and figured what the hell—in for a penny, in for a pound. Nate stripped down, climbed into bed, gently rolled Emmett on his back, and woke him up in the best way possible.

"Oh God, Nate!" Emmett groaned. Nate paused a second to wonder what Martha was going to serve them for breakfast after this, but hell, he didn't really care—so he returned to the delicious and sexy task at hand.

WHILE EMMETT was in the bathroom, Nate borrowed one of his clean shirts. It was a little tight, but it worked. Then he went to the dining room and sat at the table, purposely not looking at Martha, who plopped a mug of coffee in front of him with a grunt before returning to the kitchen.

Marianne sat down too, and he dared a glance at her. He expected more churlishness but got two thumbs up before she fanned herself. "I told you," she half sang.

"Told him what? Are you responsible for this?" Martha snapped.

Marianne snorted. "If I am, then all I'm going to say is that it's about time. Oh, and that we all are going to need earplugs. Nice lungs, by the way." She winked at Nate and sipped her coffee, grinning behind the mug. "What I'm wondering is if the guys in the bunkhouse heard last evening's performance. I can sleep through just about anything, but that was something else."

Nate stood. "Okay, that's enough."

"Of what?" Emmett sat down, his hair still wet from the shower.

"You." Martha rounded on Emmett fast. "You seem to have developed quite a set of lungs and put them to good use all last night." She plopped plates on the table so hard that they rattled before settling into place.

"We weren't quiet," Nate told him.

Emmett sipped his coffee, completely unfazed. "And why should I be? I live here and it's my home. If I want to bring someone dreamy and hot home and have 'Oh God, You Have Got to Be Kidding' sex with him, then I should be able to. After all, I work hard, and I have the right to play hard. Oh, and Marianne, if you have a nice man you want to bring home, go right ahead." He was clearly enjoying this, while Martha looked like she was ready to blow her top. "Relax, Martha, I'm kidding." He turned to Marianne. "Clearly if you want to have great, eye-rolling, 'Oh My Freaking God' sex, just go to his place. It will be safer." He dodged Martha's swipe from his teasing.

Nate chuckled to himself watching Emmett tease them. It was amazing to see him start to act a little more like he had years ago. Nate had worried it might be impossible for Emmett to ever play and laugh again.

Martha pointedly glared at all of them. "Clearly it's a 'Have Fun with Martha' morning. But I will warn you two, your mother and father—"

"Why do you think we had to get it out of our systems? Mama and Dad come home tomorrow, and this house will instantly turn into Repression City. We breed horses and cattle for a living, but we wouldn't talk about that sort of thing among humans if our lives depended on it."

"So we'll go to my place," Nate offered. He was delighted and surprised at Emmett's attitude. He had expected embarrassment but got feisty instead. Maybe Emmett was beginning to come out of his shell. Either that or the shy, beaten-down Emmett truly was a product of his father, and with him gone, a happier, more confident Emmett was making an appearance.

"Oh, thank God. Any more nights like that and I swear I'll be a zombie," Martha commented as she sat down, yawning into her own coffee.

Emmett caught his gaze. "But they don't come home until tomorrow." Dang, he was wicked. "Now what's for breakfast?" He rubbed his hands together.

"It's Sunday, and I'm taking the day off. You can make your own breakfast." Martha got up and headed back toward her room.

"Great," Emmett said as he got up. "How many pans does it take to make bacon? Three or four?" He headed for the kitchen. Martha grumbled as she pushed him out of there and got busy making breakfast.

Nate sipped his coffee as he checked his phone for messages. "Look at this." He passed over the phone so Emmett could see the message from Sally Beth.

"That's odd. If you'd have asked me, I'd have expected Clinton and his friends."

Nate took back the phone. It seemed that talk about a truck being shot up at the ranch had started from one of the hands out at Siras Milford's place, which was outside Clinton's circle of influence as far as he knew. "I thought he and your father were friends."

"They are… or were. Though it doesn't necessarily mean that Siras is behind it. Dad could have fired someone and Siras could have hired them." Emmett bit his lower lip before taking another sip of his coffee. "I think my father has some explaining to do on this one, because this is sounding more and more like they were after him rather than me."

"FOR PETE'S sake," Marianne groused later that afternoon, "this isn't that hard." She climbed on the training horse, and Emmett took the ropes. He and Nate pulled, and she whooped and rode the things as though it were easy. When she finally fell off, it was to grins and a bow, which Emmett scowled at.

"How do you know how to do that?" Emmett asked as she stood.

"Your brother taught me. Mama was pissed as hell about it when she found out. But RE always said I was good." She stomped over to him. "Don't be afraid of it."

"I'm not," Emmett said. "It's the damned horse and what he'll do to me. Ones I've known for years want to take a bite out of me. What will these do? Stand on their hind legs and tap-dance on my head?" He climbed on anyway.

"It's just a horse," Nate told him. "Loosen up and relax. This is supposed to be fun."

Maybe that was the problem. Emmett was taking this so seriously that he wasn't enjoying it. Guys didn't ride broncs or bulls for the money or the fame—they rode because they loved it. "It isn't a job or a chore. When I was on the circuit, there was nothing I wanted more than to ride. There were times when I was bruised from head to toe and I rode. I had a broken arm, so I taped it and still rode, then let them set it once the event was over. That's the kind of thing these guys do, and it's because there is nothing more exciting than sitting on the back of one of these animals and challenging it. The whole thing is primal—it gets your heart racing, and if you succeed, then you've done something most men could never, ever do. That's the whole purpose. So forget about Clinton and everything else you've attached to this whole thing and just try to enjoy it. If you do that, then the rest will come." Nate checked how Emmett was sitting and the way he was holding on. "Are you ready?"

Emmett nodded, and Nate started pulling. Marianne yelled encouragement as Emmett stayed on, his hips rolling and arm waving.

"That's it," Nate called just as Emmett fell off and onto the mats. "Closer," Nate said, pulling him up.

"Yeah. But not good enough."

"He's too quiet," Marianne said. "Emmett, yell, whoop, say something. Let out what you're feeling. Don't hold it inside. We all heard you the other night, so I know you can do it."

"What does yelling have to do with it?"

Marianne shook her head, but Nate patted his shoulder. "It helps center you. Don't ask me how, but yelling and whooping helps, it really does. Your nerves are getting the better of you, so just let it all out." He paused. "Okay. Do you remember that time when we were teenagers and we went to Chicago on vacation with your parents, and they let us take the car so we could go to Six Flags Great America for the day? We went on all those coasters, and you got scared until RE said we were going to have a screaming contest on the Batman coaster. After that we couldn't get you off them. This is the same thing." He wasn't sure what else to tell Emmett. The fact that he couldn't stay on baffled him. There was no reason for it, and yet he might have made eight seconds once in all the time they'd been practicing.

"Okay. Let's try one more time and that'll be it," Emmett said. This time he whooped and yelled at the top of his lungs until he ended up on the mat three seconds later.

"Let's call it a day," Nate said, hefting Emmett to his feet. "Are you hurting?"

"Nothing but my pride," Emmett grumbled, brushing off his clothes. Marianne grabbed a box of trash that they'd put together at the beginning of the session for cover, and Nate took one as well. They carried them out while Emmett secured the door closed. After dumping the trash, they headed inside.

"Suzanne," Emmett said, meeting his sister at the door. Nate remembered her as a gawky teenager, but she was nothing like that now. "I thought you were coming back tomorrow."

"My schedule changed at the last minute, so I came today and have to go back tomorrow night." She hugged Emmett hard. "I only have a day, and I wanted to see Dad and check up on you before classes actually started."

Nate caught Emmett's slight wince even if Suzanne didn't.

Suzanne released him. "I saw your truck, or what's left of it. What the hell happened around here?" She glared at Emmett as though his truck being shot up were somehow his fault.

"I know you're worried, but back off, Suzanne," Nate told her and got shock in response. "We're looking into some incidents around the ranch, and so is the sheriff."

"But he must have done something to piss someone off," she countered.

"Or he happens to have the same color truck as your father," Nate pressed, and her expression turned to confusion. "Yeah, you know your father. Who is more likely to piss people off?" He cocked his eyebrow, and Suzanne's expression softened and she nodded. Then and only then did Nate greet her. "Are you settling in there?" Nate asked and gave her a hug as well, but it felt forced. "It's good to have you back." He stepped away, and Suzanne's attention shifted back to Emmett.

"I understand Mom hasn't left the hospital," Suzanne said. It seemed Nate had shut down the previous subject well enough.

Emmett nodded. "Dad is coming home tomorrow, but Mom has been sleeping there with him."

"I'm going up in a few minutes, and I'll get her to come home if for no other reason than to make sure everything is ready for him here." She turned and went inside, and Emmett stomped off toward the barn. Nate followed him, stopping at the door as Emmett muttered and tossed hay bales around.

"You'd think I didn't do a damned thing around here," he cursed as he broke open a bale and fed each of the horses. "Maybe I should leave and find something else to do. There has to be somewhere I can make a living that doesn't come with getting bit on the ass by horses."

"Emmett," Nate said gently.

"What is it with my entire damned family? I work like hell, and yet they seem to think that I'm a complete screwup. Mom has been with Dad, Suzanne settling in at school, and I've been here with you, holding the ranch together while people are cutting fences, setting fires, and shooting up my truck."

"Which we need to talk to your father about," Nate reminded him. In some ways, things had changed for him and Emmett, and yet at times, especially when Suzanne had rounded on Emmett, Nate felt himself stepping into RE's role as big brother, and that was strange for him. He didn't want to think of Emmett as a little brother. After last night, they were on the road to becoming something very different, and yet those feelings were still there and made him uncomfortable.

"Yeah, but Suzanne...." He seemed so down.

"Is your older sister, and she can be a pain in the ass, just like when we were kids." He stopped Emmett as he stomped over to grab another bale. "The horses are fine. They have plenty of hay and water and will be good for the night."

A throat clearing had both of them look toward the door. "The pain in the ass is right here." Fire burned in Suzanne's eyes.

Nate didn't back down. "You heard that? Good. Now maybe you'll do something about it. You know how your parents treat Emmett. I've seen it, and so have you, I'm sure."

"Nate, it's okay," Emmett said from next to him. "If anyone is going to fight with my sister, it's going to be me." He stepped forward. "And Nate is right—you are being a pain in the ass. You weren't the one who was snubbed and told to stay home and watch the ranch after Dad had his heart attack."

"They trust you to look after it," Suzanne said.

"Right. They trust me so much that Mom hired Nate. She calls me once a day, tells me how Dad is, and then he comes on the line to make sure I'm being a good little boy and doing exactly what he wants." Damn, he'd built up a full head of steam. "I developed a breeding plan, went over it with the old bastard, got his fucking blessing, and then he changed it on me behind my back. He does that all the damned time. But not to you or to RE. Both of you walk on water."

Holace walked into the barn, looked in both directions, and backstepped his way right on out again. *Smart man.* Nate wondered if he should step in, but instead he moved behind Emmett to back him up.

"I hate this," Emmett said. "Because RE wanted to work with the horses, I've had to try to fill his shoes, and these fucking beasts hate me." Virginia stuck her head out of the stall and stretched her neck to reach for him. He turned and smacked her on the nose. "Stop that, now!" he snapped. "Enough of all of it. I'm going to speak with Dad when he gets home, and we're going to have it out. I'm taking over the ranch finances, because it looks like he's made one hell of a mess of them."

"Things are tough all over right now," Suzanne said. "Dad said that the ranch was holding its own but that paying for med school was going to be tight."

"Is that what he told you? He keeps talking about expanding. Does he even realize he has huge amounts of money sitting in the various ranch accounts? He just let it grow and never reconciled the accounts. There's gobs of it, and no one knows it's there or is managing it. The books are up to date, but the processes behind them are a mess. But guess what? He won't listen to me." He stalked closer to Suzanne, who took a step back. It was about time that someone took Emmett seriously. "We could bet a hundred bucks. I'll tell him what I found, and he'll just say I should mind my own business and go work with the damned horses. Or ask me some stupid question to get me to be quiet. It's what he does." Emmett heaved for breath like he'd just run five miles. "Was there anything else you wanted to ask about?"

Suzanne's mouth moved, but nothing came out for a moment. "I got a scholarship and made a deal with the state of Montana. As long as I practice in a rural area for three years, they'll pay for half the cost, and my scholarship will cover the rest." She still seemed shell-shocked.

"That's wonderful. I'm so proud of you. I know you worked hard and long to get in, and this validates the extra work you did." Emmett smiled, and now it was Nate's turn to be shell-shocked. "Will you practice in this area, then?"

"Maybe," she answered haltingly.

"Good. Now why did you come out here?" Emmett asked.

Suzanne sighed. "It wasn't to get the full force of the anger you seem to have built up for years."

Emmett crossed his arms over his chest. "Well, that sucks for you, but at least I feel better. So why, then?"

"To find out why Martha is sound asleep on the sofa in the living room with her feet up. She never slows down during the day. Whatever the reason, I figured I'd get out so the house was quiet." She approached, and when Virginia stuck her nose out again, Suzanne patted it gingerly. Virginia nudged her chest as though looking for a treat. "Was the big man mean to you? He wouldn't be if you didn't try to bite him." She spoke softly. "Any clues about Martha?"

Nate turned to Emmett, who blushed and turned away.

"All right, boys, spill it. What did you do?" she asked pointedly. "Em?" He refused to turn around, and Nate found himself under her steely gaze. He put up his hands in surrender. "Emmett, either tell me or I'll tickle it out of you like I did when you were a kid. I made you puke once. Don't force me to do it again." Emmett turned to look at her, his face as red as Dorothy's ruby slippers. "Em?"

"Well...." He got out one word. "I can't talk about stuff like this with my sister."

"What stuff? What did you do, and what kind of mess is going to need to be cleaned up? Did you two stay out and come in drunk, singing at the top of your lungs?" She put her hands on her hips, tapping her foot. Nate knew from experience that was so not a good thing.

"We didn't get drunk, but he and I did—" Emmett began.

"Oh, to hell with it. Let's just say that in the throes of passion, your little brother is not quiet," Nate told her. "Do you want additional details, or is that enough of the scoop to satisfy the Montana busybody inside you?" Now it was his turn to scowl.

"I'm not the only one who's loud," Emmett countered. "I seem to remember a certain cowboy who made more than his share of noise." Now the two of them glared at each other.

"I see. So the two of you went to Emmett's room last night and...." She grinned. "Was that the first time?" Both of them shifted their glares in her direction. She nodded and smirked. "Well, it's about damned time."

"Why does everyone say that?" Emmett asked.

"Because we all have eyes. You used to follow him around, and you mooned over him whenever you didn't think anyone was looking. I talked to RE about it once, and he told me I was crazy. He said the two of you had just known each other a long time and that Emmett looked up to Nate. RE was a wonderful brother, but he was dense about some things, like most guys are."

"You knew even back then?" Emmett lowered his arms.

Suzanne shrugged. "You used to watch him all the time. I figured out you were gay about the time you turned fifteen or so. All the other boys were looking at the girls when they went to the county fair, but you stayed close to RE and Nate and had no use for girls. I mean, RE used to talk up my girlfriends, but you never did at all." She acted like it was no big deal, and Nate gave her credit for that. At least she supported Emmett. "Then after Nate left, you watched the other boys, and of course there was Reid. That man was a dead giveaway." She laughed. "It never mattered to me, and I always thought with the way you and Nate watched each other that given the chance you two might just work things out." She patted Nate on the shoulder.

"But what do you think RE would say?" Nate asked. He'd been wondering that a lot lately.

"I don't know, and I really don't think it matters. When I told him what I suspected, he didn't seem upset. I like to think that if the two of you are happy, then RE would be as well. He loved you both most in the world. Nate, you were his best friend, and Emmett was his little brother." She hugged Emmett and then him. "Now all you have to do is figure out how you're going to get Mother to give up on her little crusade to marry you off."

Emmett began to laugh until tears ran down his cheeks. "What's so funny?" Nate asked.

"I have the answer for that, though Dad may have another heart attack. You and I could simply have a repeat performance from last night. That would get the point across."

Suzanne's mouth hung open, and Nate snickered as he rolled his eyes. "I think the idea is to get your message across without killing our parents," Suzanne chided. "I'll help you, and I'll talk to Dad too." Nate supposed that was as much as they could expect from her. Not that he was counting much on her help. Suzanne would be leaving tomorrow, which didn't give her much time.

Chapter 8

EMMETT DIDN'T sleep well. He really should have gone to Nate's house for the night. Instead, he stayed at home and worked well into the evening to make sure everything was ready for when his parents got home.

"It was quiet last night," Martha teased as he sat at the table.

"Nate went home," he said softly, holding his head. He felt hungover even though he'd had nothing to drink.

"I know, honey. Though I won't say I missed the noise, I can say that when you meet that special person, it's hard to be apart from them, especially at the beginning." She patted his shoulder and brought him some coffee and pancakes.

"It isn't that. Well, not *all* that, anyway. My father is coming home today, and…." He sighed. "It isn't as though I want anything to happen to him, but it was nice not having him look over my shoulder all day every day." The pressure of having to do everything up to his father's standards, whether it was important or not, was something he had been grateful to be away from. Still, it was what it was, and he drank his coffee and ate breakfast, thanked Martha, and went out to check on the horses.

"Hey, Emmett," Holace called from the ring where he was working with one of the young horses. The horse looked good and was coming along well. "I checked on Unexpected Miracle, and the little guy is doing great. Both mama and colt are happy."

"That's great. How is everything else?" He leaned on the fence, watching Holace work with the yearling. His form was wonderful, and Emmett loved watching him move.

"Good. All the barn work is up to date, and I've had a number of the horses exercised. We do have a stallion coming in today to breed with a number of our mares. Normally the stallion stays put, but your father wants multiple mares bred to him, so they agreed to transport. We'll let him get settled for a few days and then he can meet the ladies."

"Sounds like you're on top of things." Emmett turned as Nate's truck pulled into the yard. He met him, and they headed out to check on the herds. Both of them wanted everything to be as perfect as possible, so they checked that all of the herds were where they were supposed to be and that they all had water and weren't in any distress.

"They look good," Nate said from the front of the ATV.

"I agree," Emmett told him. He wrapped his arms around Nate's waist and held him tightly as they rode across the largely empty land. It gave him a sense of peace that he knew wasn't going to last for very long.

"STOP FIDGETING," Suzanne said softly as the large car that his mother had hired pulled into the drive. Emmett followed Suzanne to the car as his mother and then his father got out. His dad seemed to have aged five years in the time he'd been away, but he still turned to look things over. "Nobody burned the place down," he commented before looking at Emmett's truck. "What the hell happened?"

"The sheriff is looking into it," Emmett said quietly.

His father paused, hand on the car, probably to steady himself. "What the heck, boy, you're waiting on the sheriff? Find out who did this and give them hell. That's what I'd do. You don't let someone get away with shooting up your truck."

"The insurance company is going to have it fixed, but the sheriff has asked us to leave it a little while longer," Emmett told him.

"Fucking hell, boy. You not even going to get mad?" His dad slowly walked over to him. "You need to stand up for yourself. Taking shit isn't going to get you anywhere."

"Dustin," his mother said gently, "don't excite yourself."

His father didn't look away. "To hell with that. He's just letting people get away with shit. What the hell kind of man does that?"

Emmett stepped closer. "Did it ever occur to you that we both have the same color truck and that they were trying to send you a message and not me?" He glared back into his father's almost black eyes. "We had fences cut, and look over there. Someone set fire to the field. That doesn't have anything to do with me. You want me to stand up for myself? Fine. Who did you piss off, old man, and why are they after you? How's that to start with." Emmett turned to Suzanne. "I suggest you help Dad inside and get him either in a chair or in bed."

"Em," she said.

"Now!" he snapped at her. "He needs to rest, and then we can talk later." He stepped back, and Suzanne helped their father inside.

"You didn't need to do that," his mother scolded in that way she had of making him feel like a child again. Or at least he felt like that's what she was trying to do.

"Then he doesn't need to treat me that way. I've been taking care of things here, along with Nate, since he got sick, and there is a lot he needs to answer for. He's always after us to do things right. Well, I found the things he's been hiding, or maybe things he isn't as good at and has been skating by on for a long time. I ought to be worthy of his respect. He may not love me the way he did RE, but I'm worth more than the dirt under his boots." He didn't want to insult his dad, but the man had pushed his buttons in a matter of seconds. "I'm going to let him relax and spend time with Suzanne before she has to leave, but the two of us need to sit down and talk."

His mother pursed her lips, a sure sign that her protective instincts were coming out. "You need to give your father a chance to rest. You know him. I'll be able to keep him inside for a day or two at the most, and then he's going to want to get out and back to work."

"Yes, I know. He's going to want to stick his nose into everything," Emmett told her as the breeze whipped a few of his mother's loose strands of hair. She tucked them back, but they didn't stay. "While he was gone, everything was taken care of here. Nate and I worked really well together, and the ranch is in excellent shape."

Speak of the devil, Nate rode up on a four-wheeler, pulled to a stop, and climbed off. "Giselle," he said with a smile and kissed her cheek. "It's good to have you back. We've missed you."

She turned to Emmett. "It doesn't seem that everyone feels that way."

Of course she'd take what he said in the worst way possible and then try to guilt him over it. Emmett's first reaction was to lower his eyes and turn away, but he didn't. He met her gaze and refused to look away.

"What is it, Emmett?"

"Nothing. Just that your guilting isn't going to work any longer."

She didn't even pause. "I met this very nice nurse up at the hospital. She took care of your father most days. She's divorced, no children, pretty, and she's such a hard worker." She opened her purse and handed him a slip of paper. "I told her that you'd call and maybe have dinner or something." She flashed that Mama-knows-best smile.

Emmett was about to blow his top. She had done this sort of thing with Marianne for years, and now she was trying to fix him up with strangers. It was embarrassing. He took the piece of paper, looked at the number, and then ripped it to tiny pieces and dropped them at her feet.

Nate lightly pressed a hand to his shoulder, letting Emmett know that he was there. "Emmett," he said softly.

Emmett turned, closing the distance and sliding his hand around the back of Nate's neck, tugging him into a kiss hot enough to melt steel. Damn, it was almost enough to make him forget that his mother was standing right next to him. He tugged at Nate's lower lip as he pulled away, breathing in his scent for a second.

Then he took Nate's hand. "I think Martha is going to have lunch ready. We should go on in." He led Nate toward the house, leaving his flabbergasted mother to follow.

"That wasn't nice," Suzanne said, meeting them at the door. She winked and stepped back so they could enter.

"She tried to fix me up with a pretty nurse. I'm done with her denial." He went inside. "You know, I bet in medical school they taught you that a refusal to accept reality is one of the signs of insanity. I'm gay, and I've told both Mom and Dad that a number of times. They can accept it or not, but I'm done playing their games. All the games."

"There's no need to... show that kind of behavior... in public," his mother scolded as she came inside.

"What behavior? And since when is our ranch public?" Suzanne interrupted. "Emmett is gay. He likes men, not women. He's told you, but you refuse to get it. What's more, Emmett likes Nate, and I think it's cool. They've had a thing for each other for a long time and now they're acting on it." She took her mother's hand. "It's good, Mom."

She sniffed, and Emmett hugged her. "I'm happy, and you need to stop and just accept me for who I am." He loved his mother, but both his parents seemed to be living in a world of their own creation, and it was frustrating.

"But what about grandchildren? I thought that RE would marry and have kids. But he's gone. You will never have any if you stick with this gay thing."

Emmett turned his head to heaven and shook it slowly in sheer frustration.

"Giselle," his father said, sounding tired as he took his place at the head of the table. "The boy is light in the loafers, and he always will be. Leave him alone."

"Daddy, we don't say that. Emmett is gay, and that's it. He isn't going to marry a woman. So what?" She sat down next to him.

"But he won't have children," his father said. Emmett had never had any idea how important that was to his father.

"Maybe I will someday." Emmett squeezed Nate's hand just because he needed the support. "I don't know." Suddenly they were on a discussion of how gay people could have children, with Suzanne explaining the process. His father looked like he'd much rather be anywhere else on the planet. Emmett's mother at least seemed mollified... for now.

And then they both turned to Suzanne.

"Don't either of you go there. I have to finish medical school and do a residency before I will even consider having children. I have to find a guy I'll consider living with, let alone marrying, first." She took some of Martha's amazing sliced ham and put it on their father's plate before passing it on. "What's with the push for grandchildren?"

"Your father and I aren't getting any younger, and we just want to know that things are in good hands." She wiped her eyes and turned from the table. "Sometimes I miss your brother so much, and then with almost losing your father.... I think we worry about the future."

And there it was. The truth that Emmett had always known was there. It didn't matter what he did—they were never going to see him the way they had RE. He wasn't valued or respected by his parents. They saw him as a poor fill-in for his older brother and nothing more. Hell, his father had discounted him with a single derogatory sentence. And they were always going to see him that way. Emmett was never going to be able to fill RE's shoes, and he might as well face it.

"MOTHER ASKED me where I was going," Marianne said that evening in the training shed. Emmett put on his chaps and boots before climbing on the barrel horse.

"What did you tell her?" he asked. "I swear I could take a trip around the world and all my parents would do is ask if I had fed the horses before I left. Either that or my mother would try to fix me up with a girl to take along with me." The whole thing still had him angry.

"Just give your mother a break," Nate said. "She'll come around, especially with Suzanne on your side." He smirked as he positioned himself at the ropes. "After today, I bet she'll think twice before trying to set you up again. Though if she does, another demonstration of your feelings wouldn't be amiss. Are you ready?"

"Yes." Emmett got in position and nodded. He was determined to do this and paid attention to every roll, using his legs to grip and his arm as balance. Instead of just trying to stay on, he attacked the damned thing, giving as well as he got.

"What happened to you?" Marianne asked after he fell off again.

"What? I ended up on my ass." He brushed himself off and got back on.

"Emmett," Nate said to get his attention. "You lasted at least ten seconds. That was the best ride you ever had. Now let's do it again, and then we need to teach you how to fall so you don't break your arm or your head."

Emmett got ready and then nodded and took another ride. At least something was starting to go right. But as usual, that was the harbinger of everything returning to the way it had been. One good ride, and then he couldn't stay on for crap, so eventually they closed up.

"I'm going to head on home. I need to be here early tomorrow morning. We have a lot to get done." Nate kissed him gently at the back door.

"Nate…," Emmett said as he headed off toward his truck.

"Will I see you later?" Nate asked, and Emmett nodded with a smile. Then Nate took off, and Emmett went inside, where his father sat at the table, seemingly waiting for him.

"I think we need to talk," his father said seriously.

Emmett pulled out a chair and sat down. "Yes, I think we do."

"You seem to be under the impression that this is your ranch and that you make the decisions here," he began.

"And you seem to be under the impression that you can run this place on your own. The last week in the hospital should have told you that isn't possible." He crossed his arms over his chest. "But it doesn't matter what you think, I guess. It's what I think and want that matters… to me, anyway. And I guess that I have some decisions to make about what my future is going to look like."

"What are you saying?" his father asked. "You aren't happy here? You always loved the ranch." He seemed genuinely confused.

"RE loved the ranch, Dad. He lived for it. I remember the day you put him in charge of the horses. He was thrilled and loved every minute of it. But RE's dead, and I'm not him." He leaned over the table. "The horses hate me. You get that, don't you? Every time I go within reach, Virginia tries to bite me."

"As a kid, you loved the horses. You used to ride your pony all the time." It was obvious to Emmett that his father hadn't paid attention to him at all.

"That was RE, Dad," Emmett said. And just like that, he realized that he'd been invisible to his father for years. His father had always paid attention to his brother, and he'd just assumed that Emmett was a younger version of him. It was sad, and it only reinforced the idea that he needed to make his own way.

"It was?" His father leaned to the side and pulled out his wallet. He opened it and pulled out some old pictures. "See. Here you are on your first pony."

Emmett sighed. "That's RE."

His father pulled out a picture of Suzanne in her first cowgirl outfit. It was red, and she grinned from her perch on the pony. Then he handed Emmett another photograph. Emmett shook his head. "That one is RE too." His father had carried photographs of his children in his wallet for years, and he hadn't ever realized that none of them were of his youngest son. What in the hell did that say about what his father truly felt about him? He huffed and wondered if he had a place on the ranch at all. Emmett could try to fit in all he wanted, but maybe he would always be a round peg in his parents' square hole, and there was nothing he could do about it. "I can't be RE, Dad. He's gone, and I won't be the also-ran that you try to get to fill his shoes. I'm sorry."

Emmett left the table and went down to his room. He passed Suzanne along the way, wished her a safe trip, and hugged her. Then he packed some clothes in a bag. "I'll see you in the morning," he told his father as he passed. He grabbed the keys to one of the ranch trucks and headed out of the house. He needed to get the hell out of there. He was tempted to get in a truck and just keep going.

Outside, the night air felt cooler. He climbed into the truck and drove the few miles to Nate's apartment. He knocked on the door and Nate let him inside. "What happened?" Nate asked, pulling Emmett into his embrace.

"Nothing I didn't already suspect." But he didn't want to talk about it, not with Nate right there. His emotions were too close to the surface, and if he rehashed what had taken place, he was likely to end up shouting the windows out, and Nate didn't deserve that. He had tried to be strong because he thought that was what he needed to be for his family. But it was clear that deep down, they didn't really give a damn.

"Who is this?" another guy asked from behind Nate, his tone impatient and dripping with discomfort. Emmett jumped back as the guy set a couple beers on the rustic chest coffee table in the middle of Nate's tiny living room.

"Emmett," Nate answered.

The guy, dressed in jeans and a pressed white shirt, approached, holding out his hand. "Langley Rogers. It's good to meet you." He didn't sound particularly pleased. They shook hands anyway.

"Langley and I used to room together on the circuit a few years ago," Nate explained quickly. He didn't pull on his collar like a character in bad television melodrama, but the discomfort seemed to come from both directions. Emmett found it confusing, and that was more than he could take on top of everything else.

"Is that what you're calling it?" Langley asked, sitting on the sofa, stretching out and making himself at home.

"Maybe I should just go." Emmett whirled around, heading back for the door. It seemed he had interrupted something and had completely misunderstood what the other night had meant. God, leave it to him to screw up even this. He and Nate hadn't made lifelong promises to each other. Hell, they hadn't even talked about what happened the next morning. Emmett had just assumed that since that night meant something special to him, it was the same with Nate. "You two have a fun night, and I'll just head on home."

"Wait a minute," Nate said, rounding on his friend. "You ass. Emmett doesn't know to ignore half the shit that comes out of your mouth, and if you don't behave, your mouth is going to have two split lips and your ass isn't going to be able to sit for a week after I get done kicking it." Nate was pissed. "Langley is straight. He loves women—all women. In fact, the guy is the least choosy person I have ever met when it comes to the ladies—blond, brunet, young, old, grandma, distant cousins, you name it, he's done it."

"Hey!" Langley protested.

Nate wasn't finished with him. "Abilene, remember her?" He smiled at Emmett. "He was smitten until he found out she had four kids and three grandchildren." Nate shook his head.

"You're never going to let me forget that, are you?" Langley groused, and Emmett took a seat on the sofa, with Nate settling next to him.

"Nope." Nate grabbed both beers and handed one to Emmett.

"What about me?" Langley asked.

"Go get yourself one," Nate told him with a grin. "That's what you get for teasing Emmett." Nate settled back on the sofa and put an arm around Emmett's shoulders. "What happened that has you upset? Your father? Did you talk to him?"

"Not really. We talked *at* each other, and then I realized some things and needed to get the hell out of there." He shrugged and drank some of the beer. It was cold and bit a little going down, which was good. He thought about asking for some whiskey, but getting drunk wouldn't help.

"What do you do, Emmett?" Langley asked.

"I work with my family at the Rolling D Ranch," Emmett answered. "What about you?"

Langley hesitated, and Emmett could almost see the calculation behind his eyes. "I'm looking for work right now. I heard Nate was working as a foreman at a big spread, and I was hoping he might have some work for me." He drank some and set down the bottle. "Life has been hard since the rodeo. The best places all have their hands and they hold on to them, and the other places... aren't where I want to work." He finished the beer and sat back. "But I suspect that there aren't any openings here."

Nate shook his head. "I don't think so. Not right now. We have someone coming in tomorrow about helping with the horse training. But she has very special experience, and we don't even know if we can convince Dustin to take her on. For a regular cow puncher... there aren't any openings." He set his bottle on the table. "I could have told you that over the phone if you'd called."

Emmett got the idea that there was something else going on. It wasn't his place to ask, but he was curious.

"I needed to get away," Langley added.

"From what... or who? Is there a jealous husband who's looking for you?" Nate asked, and Langley didn't answer. "Shit, man, did you get some girl pregnant and now you're trying to hide out?"

"No. Well, yes, but it isn't what you think. I found out a couple months ago that I have a son. His mother is down in Cheyenne, and she's having a hard time. I've been sending her money, but I don't think it's enough, and then I lost my job."

"You have a son?" Nate asked. "Why don't you move there and be part of his life?" Emmett had been wondering the same thing.

All the bravado and humor drained from Langley's expression. "I was, and I tried to get work. But I had no luck around there. So I moved farther afield. I need something so I can send Jenny the money she deserves so she can raise little Kenan. I was hoping you might have something here, or know someone who was hiring." He shrugged. "If not, then I'll move on and see what I can get."

"I don't know," Emmett told Langley. "I need to speak with my father about staffing, but he just got out of the hospital, and on top of that, the two of us aren't on the best speaking terms right now. You know families. I suspect that will change once one of us swallows our pride a little. And since my father has never done that a single day in his life, it will have to be me." Maybe he could get through the next few days with his father resting, but he was going to have to talk to him about Sally Beth.

"I'd appreciate anything you can do. I've been around cattle and horses most of my life." Langley seemed to relax a little. "I was hoping I could crash here for a day or so."

"The sofa is open if you want it," Nate said and then smirked. Emmett knew what was next and preemptively smacked his shoulder. "But you're gonna need earplugs."

"Nate," Emmett warned.

Langley rolled his eyes. "Good God. Are you two at the screamer stage? I should have known by the way you can't seem to stop touching one another. Maybe I should just go sleep in my truck."

"Or Nate could learn to be quieter." Emmett flashed him a warning look.

"Okay. I get the picture," Langley said.

Nate finished his beer and set the empty can aside. "I take it things haven't been going your way in the love department?"

Langley shook his head. "Are you kidding? Ever since I found out that I have a kid—and he looks just like me, handsome as anything...."

Well, things aren't as freewheeling and easygoing. I can barely help take care of him, let alone chance the possibility of another one."

"Have you thought about a relationship with the mother?" Emmett asked.

Langley nodded. "Jenny and I talked about it and agreed that would be piling one mistake on top of another. Kenan is something else, but we aren't in love with each other, so getting married was only going to make both of us miserable." He pulled out his phone and brought up a picture so they could look at him. "But I have to help. He's my son, and I don't want to be one of those dads who turns his back on his kid. I won't." The vehemence in Langley's voice made Emmett jump a little. "I've already been there. I won't have him go through that."

"Okay." Emmett leaned forward. "You need the job so you can help take care of your son."

"It's complicated. Jenny has issues of her own, and she's doing the best she can. I'm not in any position to look after Kenan, but if I could, then yeah, I'd like to have a relationship with him." He nervously scratched the back of his neck. "I don't know, and I don't have any real answers. Right now Kenan is doing well with his mother, and I promised that I would help support her and the baby." The conversation had gotten awfully heavy really fast. "Anyway, that's why I'm here. I need to try to find some work."

"We'll do what we can to help." Emmett wasn't making any promises, but he would do what he could for Nate's friend. As things stood at the moment, he wasn't sure what kind of help he could be.

"If there's no work, then…." Langley seemed resigned, and Emmett couldn't blame him. They got calls at the ranch all the time from people wanting employment. His father usually took care of them, which was probably good, because Emmett would want to try to help each person if he could.

"Let's talk about something happier. Emmett here is learning to ride broncs," Nate said.

Emmett shook his head. "I thought you wanted to talk about something happier. I have one real gift in life: the absolute hatred and scorn of horses. The damned things try to bite me at every opportunity. My friend Reid thinks it's the way I smell. Personally, I think it's how I taste, and the damned beasts can't get enough."

"Then why broncs?" Langley asked, leaning a little closer out of curiosity.

"I let my pride get the better of me. The town asshole was saying bad things about my brother. I was drunk and let my mouth run away with me. Now I'm supposed to prove my manhood and defend the family honor by riding a bronc in the local rodeo." He rolled his eyes. "I know it sounds stupid, but I really want to beat Clinton Masters. He's the biggest jerk in town, and taking him down a peg or two would be amazing." Just thinking about him got Emmett's insides to boiling.

"So this guy got on you about your brother," Langley said. "Big deal. Let your brother deal with him."

"RE is dead, and Clinton could never hold a candle to him." Emmett had thought quite a bit about why Clinton had gotten to him, and Emmett knew it was because of his brother. "He was the only person who really saw me for the person I was. My parents don't. RE worked with the horses, and after he died, that became my job."

"Shit. And they don't like you? That must be hell."

"You could say that." Emmett shrugged. "What about your family?"

"Mine are better left to themselves. Hell, I think it would be best if my family were staked out in the woods to let the wolves feed on them." Langley grinned. "Though the wolves would probably get indigestion and die of food poisoning."

"Jesus, what is it with cowboys? Do we all have toxic families that don't have a clue? I know that Nate's here isn't at all the best. Mine seem to think I'm just a replacement for my brother, and yours would fail at being carrion." Emmett stood and looked at Nate. "I promise here and now that if I ever get the chance to be a parent, that I will do a better job than mine." He then sat down and finished his beer.

Nate chuckled. "You know, you had me right up until the burp. Then you turned into my father."

Emmett sat in shock until Nate reached over to tickle him, and Emmett skittered away.

"Nate...." He moved to protect his vulnerable spots, laughing.

"Anyone for another beer?" Langley asked.

"Sure," Nate said. "And there's a frozen pizza in the freezer. Go ahead and put it in the oven if you want."

"Ewww, frozen pizza," Emmett teased.

"Not all of us have Martha, and besides, these aren't bad. I get them at the small grocery chain store in town. It's actually a little spicy." Nate left to check on stuff in the kitchen, and he and Langley returned with more beers. It seemed like Langley drank two to every one that Emmett did. When the pizza was done, Nate brought it in. Nate was right—the pepperoni was spicy. Emmett ate a couple slices and chased them with beer to cool his mouth.

"I got a question," Langley asked, his words slurring slightly. "Did either of you ever think about being with a woman?"

Emmett shook his head. "Did you ever think about being with a man?" he shot back. Since coming out, he had been asked many versions of that question, and he didn't care for any of them.

Langley shrugged, and Emmett turned to Nate. Maybe his friend wasn't as straight as Nate thought he was. Reid told him that sometimes guys would sleep with any woman who came along just to prove that they didn't have an interest in other guys. Like a lot of what Reid said, he'd thought it was a little out there, but maybe Reid had been right after all. It could also just be the fact that Langley had had too many beers and he was just reacting. "There was this one guy on the circuit. He was as pretty as any girl. Remember him? Jason… or something?"

Nate nodded but seemed speechless. "Did you and Jason ever…?" He left the sentence unfinished.

"No way. I had too many girls interested in all this." He waved his hand in front of him. "He was pretty, though." Langley burped and sat back, the alcohol working its depressive magic.

Emmett had had enough and began clearing away the empties as well as the trash from the pizza. When he returned, Nate had gotten some blankets and a pillow for the sofa. Langley took off his boots and lay down, pulling up the blankets. He would likely be asleep in a matter of minutes. Nate turned out the lights and took Emmett's hand, led him to the other room, and closed the door.

Nate's lips tasted of spice, hops, and under it all, the musky flavor of Nate that drove Emmett crazy. He pressed Nate back toward the bed, working at the buttons of his shirt as they kissed. Emmett got the shirt open, his hands exploring the planes of the man underneath, the soft coating of hair on his pecs a delight under his skin. Nate was amazing to look at, touch, and taste. Emmett was determined to make the most of all his senses.

"I'm starting to think you always have this much energy," Nate whispered. "Not that it's a bad thing."

"I'm glad." He cut off more of Nate's conversation by putting their lips to better use. He worked off Nate's belt and then his jeans and pushed them down. Nate stepped out of them, and Emmett rubbed him, pressing him to the bed.

"What is this?" Nate asked as he sat on the side of the mattress. "It's like you want everything all at once."

"I do," Emmett whispered. "It's been a couple of days, and do you have any idea how hard, pun intended, it was to watch you riding out on that horse in the morning?"

"You've seen me ride before," Nate said.

Emmett guided his gaze upward. "Yes. I've seen you at the rodeo and on horseback. But all those times, you were RE's best friend. Now things are different. You're more than that, so you look different." He pulled off his shirt and shucked his jeans. "When you're on a horse now, I see the cowboy, the hard-riding, hardworking, hard-playing cowboy. And it's sexy." Nate was different now. He was more than he had been before. It was hard to explain, but Nate had changed, or at least the way Emmett saw him had changed.

"Okay. I think I can understand that. Maybe someday I'll see you on horseback," Nate offered, and Emmett shook his head.

"Other than the bronc I tried to ride before you said you'd help me, I haven't been on the back of a horse in years. Not since I was a kid, actually." He smoothed his hand down Nate's cheek. "That was when I figured out that being on even the gentlest pony was dangerous for me."

Nate wrapped his arms around Emmett's waist and rested his head on his belly. Emmett wound his fingers through Nate's hair and stayed still. This was one of those intimate moments when words and actions weren't necessary. Just standing together, quiet, vulnerable, and content was enough for the moment. "It's something I've learned to live with for the most part."

"What did your parents think?" Nate asked.

"Just like now, they barely noticed. RE was always the star, and since he was a great rider, they watched him, and I went and did something else. He rode, I read. He did rodeo, I studied in school and then took a few online business classes after I graduated. RE was the star of the family, Suzanne was the brain among brains, and I was largely an afterthought." It was true and had come into stark relief today when his father didn't know enough about him to even realize that he didn't have a picture of his youngest son in his wallet. Hell, he'd just assumed Emmett was a carbon copy of his older brother and could just step into his shoes. "It seems the only one who ever saw me for me was RE." This was not what he wanted to be talking about right now.

"Come on." Nate let go and slid back on the bed. He pulled down the covers, and Emmett slipped off the last of his clothes and climbed into bed.

"But…."

Nate soothed him down onto the bedding. "Not every time has to be like a wild stampede. Sometimes it's good to just let things happen." He stroked Emmett's belly. "Go ahead and close your eyes. Just go with it." Nate gently rolled him over, his hands gliding up and down his back. Emmett stretched out, sliding his arms under the pillow. He sighed and closed his eyes, trying to let go of the disappointments of the day. It sucked that he'd had to face just how unimportant he was to his father. "Do your best to relax. You're wound so tight you're going to snap at any moment."

"I'm trying," Emmett whispered.

"Okay," Nate agreed and added more pressure, digging his hands into the muscles of Emmett's shoulders, working them deeply. He finally felt them relax and his mind settled on nothing, the wheels slowing and finally disappearing altogether. "That's it." Nate continued stroking. "What is this?" he questioned as his hands slid along Emmett's side.

"I have a skin condition. It dries out a lot and gets rough." He tried not to think about it. "This time of year it isn't so bad because of the humidity, but in the winter when it's dry, it gets worse." He hadn't really wanted Nate to see that. "I have it on the backs of my knees too."

"I see that." Nate paused, and Emmett listened as the drawer slid open. "I'm getting some oil." He popped it open and spread some on his hands. "There's no scent."

"Thank goodness." He didn't need to go into the litany of skin irritants he had to stay away from. Emmett didn't like to talk about them; it made him sound like a child.

Nate's caresses returned, this time lubricated by the oil, which soothed the rough patches and made Emmett feel better. There were times when his skin felt as brittle as dried bark, but this really helped.

"How long have you had this?" Nate asked.

"Since I was a kid." He closed his eyes once more and just relaxed into the touch, not really interested in talking. Especially not about his eczema. "God, that's good." He loved the touch. Nate straddled his legs, hands sliding lower until they kneaded his butt, then slid back upward. Nate was teasing, and Emmett loved it, letting his mind float on the sensation.

Nate paused, and his weight disappeared. With just gentle touches, he rolled Emmett onto his back. Keeping his eyes closed, he opened himself to Nate, letting him have dominion over his body and the pleasure he engendered. It was difficult for him to just let go, but he did, and Nate was so gentle yet enticing, pulling him out of himself.

"Nate," Emmett whispered, relaxed and excited at the same time. He didn't want things to change, but the relaxation part of the massage gave over to excitement as the parts of Emmett's body that came under Nate's attention shifted. "Are you trying to kill me?" He wanted to stay relaxed, but Nate definitely had other ideas.

"No. I'm trying to get you excited… and it's working." The stroking became more intense, and Emmett groaned. He didn't want things to be over too soon, but Nate was just too damned good.

"Yeah…." Emmett groaned, and Nate chuckled, his hands slipping away. Part of him wondered what the hell happened, and the rest breathed deeply as Nate climbed into bed next to him and pulled Emmett close.

"We have all night," Nate whispered.

"But what about Langley?" Emmett asked.

Nate simply tightened his hug. "He had enough to drink that he'll sleep through the night and isn't going to hear a thing. If he does, he was warned." Nate sucked lightly on his ear, and Emmett groaned. He could really get used to this all-night stuff.

"MORNING," EMMETT said as he and Nate went into the kitchen. They were already dressed.

On the couch, Langley pulled the covers over his face. "Don't be so damned cheerful."

Nate hurried over and smacked him. "Come on. Is this because of what you drank? You're turning into a lightweight."

Langley groaned, and Emmett figured the beer was part of the problem.

"We have to get to work, and you need to get your butt out of bed. Remember, ranch work starts early."

"I know." Langley pushed back the covers and got up. "Let me get myself presentable and I'll get out of here and go into town to see if I have any luck."

"Try the diner. There are a lot of people there in the mornings. Chat up the servers, but don't make a pass. They know everything in town and can point you in the right direction," Nate told him.

Langley hurried away, and Emmett poured coffee. He needed coffee. He and Nate hadn't gotten that much sleep, and honestly he wasn't looking forward to the conversations he needed to have with his father later today.

"You about ready?" Nate asked.

"As I'll ever be." He set down his mug. "Ever since I was a kid, talking to my father has always seemed like this ominous thing. I think yesterday was the first time that I really gave it back to him, and I have no idea how he's going to take it or what the fallout is going to be." Whatever it was, he'd deal with it.

Langley returned from the bathroom, and Nate handed him a travel mug as they all headed out. Emmett wondered why it felt a little like he was going out into battle. But his worries were unfounded—when they arrived, his father was still in bed and his mother had decided to sleep in as well. Not that Emmett could blame either one of them.

"I'll give them something to eat when they get up," Martha said in a half whisper.

At least they were resting. "Did Suzanne leave on time?" Emmett took a bite of pancakes and wished he had taken more time to say goodbye, but he'd been too angry when he left and had needed to get away.

"Yes. She left a few minutes after you did and messaged that she arrived back to school just after eleven." She set juice on the table, glaring at him. "You need...," she began and then stopped. "Sorry. It's none of my business." She returned to the kitchen, and for the first time in his life, Emmett didn't take the bait. He wasn't going to press Martha for what she thought. He needed to figure things out for himself and deal with his parents in his own way.

Chapter 9

"SALLY BETH!" Nate called as she got out of her truck.

"You said to come." She seemed nervous.

"Yes. Glad you did," he told her and motioned her over. "Holace?" he called into the barn and received a grunt in response. It seemed quite a few people were in a foul mood. Holace came out, wiping his hands, his sour expression changing on a dime.

"What are you here for?" Nate hadn't seen Holace smile like that before. "Nate?"

"Sally Beth has been working at Hill's Tavern in town. Emmett and I thought her talents were wasted there and that she might be able to help out up here. What do you think?"

Holace extended his hand to Sally Beth. "I say hell yes. Sally Beth here is the best horsewoman I've ever seen. Second-best horseman too, for that matter." After himself, of course. "We'd be lucky to have her."

"She has a son, and I was thinking she could move into the foreman's residence. It's not being used, and I don't need it. The place will need to be cleaned out a bit. It's been kept up, but there's lots of dust and stuff. That will give her and her son a place to live."

"Sounds like a good idea. You want me to give her a tour of the place?" He seemed more than eager. Nate nodded, and Holace took Sally Beth into the barn while he went inside the house, where he stepped into a silent battle.

Dustin sat at one end of the table with Emmett at the other, just finishing his breakfast. Both stared at each other but didn't say a word. Emmett finished eating and folded his arms over his chest.

"Sally Beth is here," Nate told Emmett.

"What for?" Dustin demanded.

Emmett stood up and leaned partially over the table. "Because she's a damn good horseperson and I'm not. In fact, I suck at it. I thought she and Holace could work together to further build our cutting horse operation. I have plans to grow it, and we're going to need some additional manpower to make that happen. Nate and I worked out that she could use the foreman's residence."

Damn, this was like two old soldiers staring at each other across the battlefield. "You thought this out, didn't you, boy?" Dustin snarled.

Nate was just about to add his opinion when Emmett touched his arm and shook his head once, never breaking his father's stare. "Yes, I have. I'm shit with horses, as I've told you. She isn't, as you know, and we could use another trainer if we want to continue to grow."

"You have plans?" he asked, and Emmett nodded. "Well, I'll be damned." He said it as though that were a surprise. It occurred to Nate that what Emmett had said the night before was true. Dustin didn't know his son at all. "Okay. We'll give her a go. But if there's any monkey business with the men...."

Emmett smiled and rolled his eyes. "What do you think is going to happen? Everyone on the damned ranch will suddenly stop working and stand in the barn door with their tongues out, ogling her all day like sex vampires after their next estrogen fix?" That had to be one of the weirdest allusions Nate had ever heard. "Sally Beth can do the job, and she'll shut down any unwanted attention from anybody."

Martha set a plate in front of Dustin, and he slowly began to eat. "Is there anything else?"

"Actually, there's a lot of things I want to go over with you. But waiting a few days isn't going to hurt." Emmett probably figured he should quit while he was ahead.

"Fine. I'll be out to look things over once I'm done eating."

Giselle glided into the room and stopped behind Dustin, settling her hands on his shoulders. "You most certainly will not. Nate is doing a fine job of overseeing the ranch, and we're going to leave him to continue. You are going to rest and take it easy like the doctor said."

Dustin humphed. "Can I at least work to get things up to date in the office?"

"There's nothing to do," Emmett declared with a half smile as he left the table. "Come on, Nate. We've got a full day ahead of us." He grabbed his hat and strutted toward the door. Damn. Nate stood still, watching him as he left. Emmett was one fine-looking man, and a little confidence sure looked damn good on him.

"Shit," Dustin swore, and Giselle chastised him lightly.

"You need to do what the doctor said and rest. It isn't a sin." She sat down next to him, and Nate left to let them talk. He had to give Giselle a lot of credit if she could keep Dustin from climbing on a four-wheeler and taking a ride around to look at things. Nate had half expected to find him already out and about.

Emmett was already heading toward the barn, probably to give Sally Beth the good news. Emmett went inside the barn and then came back out. Nate pointed to the ring, where she and Holace were already at work. Emmett headed over, and Nate grabbed the four-wheeler and headed out to work for the day, hoping that Emmett and his father might finally be on the same page.

THOSE HOPES were dashed quickly enough when Nate finished for the morning and pulled back into the yard. Dustin stood at the rails, watching Holace as he worked with one of the two-year-olds. She looked good, but Dustin didn't seem happy. Nate wasn't sure if it was with the horse or with Emmett, but there was plenty of pointing and Emmett shaking his head or just standing there to take whatever his father dished out. Finally Dustin went back in the house and Emmett headed to the barn, shoulders down. What the hell had that been all about?

Nate put things away and stayed outside, not sure he even dared go in the house, opting for the barn instead. "Damn him," Emmett muttered as he worked, glaring as each horse stuck its head out. "So help me, the first one of you who decides I'm an appetizer is going to be shot and buried behind the fucking barn. Understand?"

"What's got you all wound up?" Nate asked, deciding to pretend he hadn't seen anything in the yard.

"Nothing that hasn't been the problem for most of my life. Dad was pissed about the little colt. Not that he doesn't agree that he's beautiful and that we need to get him tested. But that we don't know who the sire is, and therefore it's my fault that she somehow managed to get herself pregnant. The testing kit has been sent to the lab along with the data for the possible stallions." Emmett dropped a bale of straw on the pile.

"Your father is stir-crazy and upset, but probably not with you. He wants to get out and do things, but he can't. For the past week he's been in the hospital, where they kept him pinned down, and now he can see his life, and a return to normalcy, right in front of him."

Emmett sighed. "Yeah, I know. La-di-da. He could take his shit out on someone else for a change. But no. I'm the one he comes after all the damned time." He grabbed the wheelbarrow and shovel and started to clean one of the stalls. "I need to get this done or else my dad will say that the barn is too stinky… or that the muck pile doesn't have enough shit on it." He threw a lot more muscle into the task than it needed.

Nate shrugged and turned away, needing to answer his phone.

"I got a job working for Siras Milford," Langley told him. "He needed a general ranch hand, and I can start tomorrow. They said I can move into the bunkhouse, so I won't need the couch any longer."

Nate nodded and looked off toward the horizon. "That's great," he said. "I'm glad. We can celebrate a little this evening if you want. Did you use my name to get the job?" Something niggled at the back of his mind.

"No. They were looking, and I guess I was in the right place," Langley answered.

"Good. Say nothing about it. Keep your ears open for me. We've had a few incidents here, and talk in town started with Siras's people. Someone there knows something."

Langley hummed slightly. "You want me to let you know if I hear talk or if someone has an axe to grind?"

Nate smiled. "Exactly, but don't stick your neck out. I don't want you getting hurt." Nate leaned against the stall wall, and Virginia extended her head toward Nate and nuzzled his arm, looking for some attention. He gently patted her nose.

"I know the drill. I'll see you tonight." He ended the call, and Nate put his phone back in his pocket.

"Langley?" Emmett asked.

Nate nodded. "He's got a job with Siras, and he's going to keep his ears open for us." He patted Virginia's nose once again. "I've been wondering why it's been quiet lately."

"You thinking word got back that the sheriff's involved?" Emmett asked. "Maybe they got the revenge they wanted and are hoping they can just walk away." He stepped back from Virginia, who didn't seem to be paying Emmett any attention.

"Come over here," Nate said. "Don't worry. I'm not going to let her bite you."

"Yeah, really," Emmett said, but he took a step closer. Nate backed away and Virginia followed him, looking for more loving, paying Emmett no attention at all. Emmett patted her nose and then her neck, and she turned to him, bumping his arm but making no move with her teeth. "What the hell is going on? She always tries to go after me."

"I don't know. But something is sure different," Nate told him. "Anyway, I'll meet you for practice in the shed this evening. The rodeo is in two weeks, and we'll do what we can to make sure you give the best show possible." He clapped Emmett on the shoulder and left the barn.

Nate went inside to where Martha had put platters of sandwiches in the refrigerator. He got a couple and a glass of water and sat at the huge old table to eat so he could get back out to work.

"How's Dustin?" Nate asked as Giselle joined him with a cup of tea. He offered to get her some lunch, but she declined.

"He's sleeping. For a man who never stopped running his entire life, this has taken most of the wind out of his sails," she added.

"Have you thought of taking a vacation once he feels better? Get out, travel, see things together. Visit family, go to Paris, see the coliseum." He took another bite, and she sipped her tea with a gentle sigh.

"Dustin will never leave the ranch for long enough. This is his life." She seemed so sad. "I understand it, I really do. When I was younger, I never would have. But I do now. He's spent his entire working life building this place, and he can't seem to let it go. But I want to see the world and travel."

"Giselle," Dustin said as he joined her. He looked drawn and tired in a way Nate had never seen him. "I want to travel, but the ranch needs to be looked after. It's our living. I can't just walk away from it, and there's no one I can leave it with, not right now." He slowly sat down. "I'm sure that Nate has done a very good job, but he's only been here a short time." Nate noticed that there was no mention of Emmett. Jesus, Emmett was right, his parents didn't think of him at all. That was insulting as far as Nate was concerned. Yes, while Dustin had been in the hospital, Nate had taken on foreman's duties, but it had been Emmett who had seen to it that the ranch remained running, that everyone got paid, and that all of the paperwork and records were kept up to date. Emmett had also seen to it that supplies and feed were ordered and kept in proper supply. Nate had looked after the cattle while Emmett had looked after the ranch.

"You've been in the hospital, and the ranch hasn't fallen apart. I want to go places and see things. You promised me when we got married that when we got older, you and I would travel. I want to go to Europe and see some of the places I did with my parents. I want to go to Australia, visit the land down under. You promised that we'd do all these things someday, and I intend to hold you to those promises." She took Dustin's hand.

"And we will. But everything changed when RE died. He was supposed to take over for me. RE loved the ranch, and once he'd sown his wild rodeo oats, he'd come home and was poised to take over. But that didn't happen, and now I'm working on another plan."

Nate stuffed a good portion of a sandwich into his mouth to finish lunch and get the hell out of there before he lost his temper. Giselle and Dustin had no idea what they had in Emmett. They didn't even see him or consider him. Well, that needed to change, and maybe Nate could help with that. He wasn't sure how, but both of them needed to see Emmett for who he was and what he could do. Emmett deserved that. "Excuse me. I need to get back out to work."

"I called the sheriff this morning, demanding in accounting of what he was doing in regard to the happenings here. It seems he isn't getting anywhere." Dustin sipped his water. "I told him he needed to get on the stick and find who was behind this, or in the next election, he'd find himself out on his ass."

Nate was beginning to see how someone could dislike Dustin enough to shoot up his truck—or the truck they thought was his. The guy could be abrasive as hell, and as thoughtless as anyone he had ever met. Of course, most of Nate's interaction with him had been through RE, when things were different. Dustin lavished attention on RE. They'd talked and laughed with each other when Dustin took the two of them riding. He'd even taken them horse trekking. They'd carried only what would fit in saddlebags and spent their time outside like cowboys a hundred years earlier. Emmett, he remembered, had stayed home.

Nate excused himself and left the house before he got any angrier.

"What's with you?" Emmett asked as he approached.

Nate schooled his expression. "I had lunch with your mother and father." He rolled his eyes. "I hate to say it, but you're right. Your father only sees what he wants to see, and everything else is completely off his radar."

"I was going to get something to eat, but I just lost my appetite." Emmett turned back toward the barn. "Sally Beth and Holace are getting along really well. She just came in and shooed me out of the barn, then picked up where I left off. It wouldn't surprise me if she rearranged everything to suit where she wants it."

"And you don't mind?" Nate asked.

Emmett smirked. "Nope. It will drive my father crazy, because he always wants everything exactly where he wants it. I've never messed with his system because it made him happy. But Sally Beth can do what she likes."

"And when your father gets angry?" Nate asked. He could see Emmett's father blowing his lid completely.

"At whom? That's the beauty of it. Dustin McElroy will never raise his voice to a woman. Sally Beth will say that she did it, and my father will cave and then he'll just walk away." Emmett actually chuckled. "I was also thinking that if Sally Beth brings her son here, then we should get a dog."

Nate glanced around. "I wondered about that. Every ranch has dogs around."

"Dad doesn't like dogs. It was the one thing he told RE no about. I think he's afraid of them. If we visited other people and they had dogs, he always avoided them. So maybe we should get half a dozen."

Nate shrugged. "Again, won't your dad have a fit?" He was starting to see the game here.

"And likewise, there's the beauty—he can't. Otherwise everyone will know that the rough, cowboy, not-scared-of-anything man's man Dustin McElroy is afraid of dogs." He cocked his eyebrows. "Yeah, I know, I'm evil. But I'm also tired of being overlooked and not respected for anything I do. I love dogs, so why shouldn't I have one?" He sighed. "Well, talk is cheap, and a guy can dream."

"YOU CAN do this," Marianne told Emmett after he fell off the barrel horse for the eighth time. "The rodeo is just around the corner." She was starting to get frustrated, and Nate understood why she felt that way, but it wasn't helping Emmett.

"Don't you think I know that?" Emmett asked. "You know, all these years I thought I didn't do any of this shit because of my thing with horses. But maybe I'm just crap at it and have no balance at all. Maybe I'm complete shit at it and the best I can hope for is that I don't get stomped on or hurt too badly when I ride the damned beast."

Nate knew Emmett wasn't going to give up. After all this time and work, his own pride was on the line.

"Hopefully with Dad's health, Mom and Dad will stay away. Still, I have to make a decent showing… somehow."

"Okay. Then let's concentrate on your balance. Use your hands and hips to compensate for the movement as best you can. Part of this is just staying on, and the other is doing it with finesse."

Emmett snorted. "I think I'll stick with the staying on part and screw the finesse." He climbed on once more, and Nate and Marianne got on the ropes. The good part was that he was using his arms much better and generally staying on longer.

"Well," a voice dripping with disdain said from the doorway.

"What the fuck are you doing here?" Marianne spat at Clinton, who leaned against the doorframe.

"What do you want, Clinton?" Nate growled. "You have no business at the ranch, and especially out here." He rounded on him quickly. "Have you been the one causing trouble? Maybe I should inform the sheriff that you've been snooping around. Let him look into your whereabouts and activities to see what you've been up to."

Clinton swallowed hard, so Nate knew that wasn't a welcome thought. "I only came out here because I heard Mr. McElroy had gotten out of the hospital and wanted to wish him well."

Emmett climbed off the padding and dusted himself off. "That's a right neighborly thing to do. Too bad you aren't right about anything and you're never neighborly. So, what is it you want?"

Clinton smiled. It was probably meant to be disarming, but the Joker had a more soothing smile than Clinton Masters. In fact, when he tried, he appeared more likely to eat small children than to convey happiness. "Like I said, just being neighborly and inviting your parents to the rodeo. My father is on the organizing board, so I got them really good seats."

Emmett seemed about ready to explode. "You aren't welcome here, and you never will be."

Clinton shrugged. "I don't know about that." He came closer, looking things over. "Nice training device. I see you're trying to not make a complete fool of yourself. Like you could train the swishy gayness away." He grinned like he was being clever. "I can't wait to see you fall on your ass, and when I take the buckle, I'll—"

"Yeah. So what? I made the bet, and I'll stick to it. But it doesn't mean anything. RE was a better rider than you, and whatever I do has no bearing on that."

"We'll see. Your parents will be there, as will most of the county. And everyone is going to get the thrill of seeing little McElroy Junior fall on his ass."

Emmett turned to Nate and then back to Clinton. "What did I ever do to you? What the hell did RE do to you besides being a better rider than you?"

Clinton rushed forward and grabbed Emmett. "You little shit. I was always a better rider than him. He just got fucking lucky." Clinton shook Emmett, and Nate grabbed him by the shoulder and pulled them apart. Clinton ended up on the floor. "Don't you dare try to cast any of your depravity on me. So help me, I will grind your little pervert ass into the dust."

"Sounds to me like someone is protesting just a little too much," Marianne said, probably just to get under his skin. "What was it Sharon Lipton told me? Oh yeah, limp little gherkin." She wagged her pinkie.

"How dare you?" He postured, and Marianne rolled her eyes.

"What? You going to attack me too? I'd like that. Then the sheriff can get involved, and that will be the end of you. No one gets to ride when they're in jail."

"You keep your mouth shut about me or else," he growled at Marianne.

"And I suggest you go on home and try to figure yourself out. After all, no one else is interested."

Clinton clenched his fists and then released them and turned away, and Nate followed him to the door. "Heard your truck got shot up. Someone did one hell of a job on it." He lifted his hat, striding off over the grass back toward the main yard.

"What the hell was he doing out here, and what was he looking for?" Emmett asked. "There's no way he wanted to just say hello to my parents, and why would he come all the way out here? This isn't the most visible building on the ranch. Most of the hands don't pay it any attention, and yet Clinton is poking his nose around." Emmett stood next to Nate until Clinton disappeared from view. Nate watched until Clinton's truck headed down the road toward town.

"I wish I knew what was wrong with that man," Marianne commented.

"So do I," Nate agreed. "But I suppose we're never going to know. It isn't like Clinton Masters is going to open up to any of us about his man pain." He couldn't help smiling. "I know that at one point he and RE were friends. We all went to school here together. I didn't think much of Clinton, but RE was good to everyone, and they had a few classes together and stuff. Then, at one point during senior year, they had a falling out. It didn't seem to bother RE too much. I heard it was because RE discovered Clinton was cheating, but RE never said. The only thing I could think of that both of them cared that much about was rodeo, so I always thought that was it. RE had plenty of friends and our circle was solid, but Clinton's friendship seemed to morph into hatred at almost lightning speed, probably because his pride was involved." Nate absently held one of the ropes. "Honestly, I never really thought about it. Clinton was a pimple of a man back then, and I don't think RE missed his friendship. On the circuit, they were rivals, but Clinton was never in RE's class, and the few times they did go head-to-head, RE ended up on the top of the boards and Clinton toward the bottom."

"Then what's the big rivalry about?" Emmett asked.

Nate shrugged. "I don't know. I think it was largely Clinton's rivalry. Those events where RE fell or didn't score, which happens to everyone, and Clinton came out ahead of him, he'd crow like he was champion of the world. Then in the next event, RE would end up on top and Clinton was nowhere to be seen. It went on like that for a long time."

Marianne patted Emmett on the shoulder. "It sounds like he's transferred the rivalry to you."

Emmett shrugged. "Yeah, but I'm no rival. And I don't really care about him. He's the asshole of the county, though, and I'd like to put him in his place. I let him goad me into this, and I won't back down. I may fall flat on my face in front of the whole town, but I'll do it because I agreed to." Emmett turned to Nate. "I'd like to beat him just to shut him the hell up." He lowered his gaze. "And now my parents are going to be there. Clinton made sure of that."

"Of course he did. That way he can show you up in front of them," Marianne said. "Well, I'll be damned if I'm going to let that happen. Get your skinny butt back up there and let's do this again. We won't let you go down without a fight as long as you're willing to keep trying." Marianne was wonderful, and Emmett climbed back on and they got back to the training.

Nate wondered if Emmett was ever going to be able to ride. Some guys couldn't. It was clear after more rides that Emmett was going to be sore again, but Nate was more than willing to do what he had to in order to try to help Emmett walk out of that rodeo ring with his self-respect.

Chapter 10

EMMETT WOKE happily with Nate pressed next to him. He had always thought that sleeping with someone would be hot and sweaty, but being in bed with Nate wasn't like that at all. And now that Langley had left a couple days ago, the two of them could make as much noise as they wanted.

"What time is it? Hell, what day is it?" Nate mumbled.

"It's Friday. I thought that maybe we could go out after work if you wanted. Dad is driving everyone crazy because Mom is trying to keep him in the house. Apparently yesterday he tried to sneak out of the house to try to see what you and I were up to. Mom scolded him, and he went back inside. Martha said he was grouchy for the rest of the day, so I don't want to spend any more time in the house than I have to. When Dad gets grouchy, he always seems to find a way to make it my fault."

"Sure. But after practice. The rodeo starts in a week," Nate said, and Emmett groaned.

"I'm not getting any damned better. I think it's best if we just give up and I pray for luck when I get on the damned horse."

Nate sat up, the covers pooling around his trim waist. "Not on your life. You know how to ride and what to expect, and we covered how to fall. I think the next step is to put you on a horse again. We can't let the rodeo be only the second time you've ridden. Like I said, you just have to make eight seconds. Nothing more."

Emmett sighed and rested his head against Nate's bare shoulder. "I know. But what good is that going to do? I barely make eight seconds on the barrel horse. There's no way I can on a real one. It really looks like Emmett McElroy is going to do what he always does—end up making a fool of himself. Only this time it will be in front of the whole town, and my parents will have a front-row seat." He slid his hand over Nate's hard belly.

"I don't see you as a fool," Nate whispered. Emmett turned his head and kissed his neck. "You try your best at everything you do, and while you don't always succeed, you give it all you've got, and no one can ever ask for more." Nate used a single finger to lift Emmett's chin. "I'll let you in on a little secret. No one gets it right all the time. The only person who doesn't fall off the horse every now and then is the one who never gets on." Nate rolled toward him, pressing Emmett down on the mattress. "And I really like the way you ride. So it's worth going for."

Emmett hummed his approval, and Nate captured his lips until first Emmett's phone and then Nate's rang. He pulled back and grabbed the phone off the nightstand.

"Where are you?" Emmett's mother asked without any other greeting.

"Mom?"

"The horses are going nuts, and your father is trying to get up. I called Holace and now you. We need you here."

"I'm on my way." He hung up, and Nate was doing the same. "My mother—"

"Holace," Nate said as they jumped out of bed, pulling on their clothes and boots before hurrying out of the house. Emmett climbed into Nate's truck, and they took off toward the ranch at top speed.

"What's going on?" Nate demanded as soon as he got out of the truck.

"Bastards," Holace swore at top voice from inside the barn. It sounded as though some of the horses had calmed, but others were still agitated. Sally Beth let another horse out into the corral, and Virginia ran and threw her head from side to side before slowly calming.

What looked like snakes came out the barn door, followed by more. "Call the sheriff," Nate said, hurrying into the barn. Emmett made the call as his father came out the back door.

"What the hell is going on?" he demanded.

"It's under control. Go back inside and sit down," Emmett ordered. The last thing he needed was his father stirring things up. "Holace and Sally Beth are calming the horses." The call was answered, and he spoke to the operator and explained what he needed. Apparently the sheriff was already out on patrol and could be diverted to the ranch. Emmett hung up and went to his father. "Nate has things under control. The sheriff is on his way, and I think you need to go inside and sit down. Let us handle this, and we'll tell you what's going on as soon as we know."

"I'm not an invalid," his father snapped.

"And you can't do us any good if you get hurt." Finally the whinnying from inside the barn ended as more snakes sailed out of the barn. Emmett went up and kicked the pieces of rubber, swearing to himself before carrying one to his father. "Someone tossed these into the stalls, I'm guessing."

"Shit," his father swore.

"Go in and sit down. This is the fourth incident in the last few weeks. We need to know who might have it in for you. And the sheriff is going to want to sit down and talk to you too."

His father screwed his face into an expression of distaste. "That—"

Emmett spoke over him. "The man isn't going to want to help us if you act like that. I don't know what you have against him, but he's been helpful so far, and he is the sheriff." His father's notion that on the ranch, he was the law, was old-fashioned and not going to get them anywhere. Sometimes Emmett admired his father's strength, but at other times it took the form of stubbornness, and that could be counterproductive.

"You've gotten bossy lately, and you need to remember who you're talking to," his father began.

"All right. Go on in there and make things worse. Holace and Sally Beth know what they're doing. The horses are already calmer, and the fewer people in the barn, the less disturbance and the more evidence there will be for the sheriff to collect." He guided his father back toward the house. "Let's go get us something to drink and we can wait for Nate and the others to let us know what they find."

His father bristled and pulled away. "You think I'm going to let everyone else handle this?" He walked toward the barn.

This time Emmett just let him go. He should have known that his father would do exactly what he wanted, but he had tried. He thought about leaving him alone, but he followed his father anyway.

In the barn, everything was much quieter. The horses still in their stalls had calmed down, and Sally Beth fed them treats as she and Holace spoke softly to each one, continuing to calm them down. "How did they get in here?"

"We don't post guards at the ranch. All someone has to do is walk in either along the drive or through the field. Yes, we make sure the barn doors are closed and latched, but they aren't designed to keep people out, just the horses inside." He didn't bring up the fact that he had recommended that they get cameras around the property a year ago so they could monitor the yard and the horses, but his father hadn't seen the need for it.

"And where were you when all this was going on?"

Emmett had been wondering when his father would get around to him. "I was just getting up," he answered, purposely avoiding the question.

"I know you weren't here because I heard your mother calling you." He didn't bother to look at Emmett. "Why weren't you here? You're in charge of the horse operation. I thought you could handle that, but now I'm wondering if I was mistaken." This was his father's usual mode of operation, and Emmett was coming to the end of the line.

"Then fire me. I'll go get a job somewhere else and you can do it all here. I'm starting to like that idea more and more." He was so tired of the ridiculousness of it all. "I was at Nate's, and if you really want to know what I was doing, I can give you a play-by-play. Maybe even a blow-by-blow, as it were." He loved how his father stepped back. "Besides, I think you're obfuscating at this point. Someone came onto the ranch with the purpose to panic the horses, and I somehow doubt they were trying to get even with me. But I do think someone has a grudge against you." He held his father's gaze, noticing the wrinkles that formed around the sides of his father's eyes.

Nate joined them. "We've removed all the fake snakes and calmed the horses. Holace said he saw someone getting into a car at the road as he heard the first distress cries from the horses."

"The sheriff is on his way," Emmett told him. "It might be a few minutes."

"Sally Beth and Holace have everything under control. We gave each of the horses some extra oats, and they're munching away."

"And when all this was happening, neither of you were here," his father snapped at Nate.

"That's enough, Dad. The reason for this is whoever is behind it. You don't get to treat Nate that way. He doesn't deserve it, and neither do I." Emmett pointed toward the house. "As I said, I think someone is sending a message to you, and I'm not backing away from that."

His father parted his lips slightly, and Emmett thought that he was going to open up, but instead he turned.

"I don't know what you're talking about," he said and slowly walked back toward the house. "Tell the sheriff that if he wants me, I'm going to be inside lying down." It seemed that the stubborn cowboy in his father wasn't about to give an inch for anyone.

"I don't know how much more of this I can take," Emmett said. "I thought that standing up for myself and trying to be strong, saying what I felt, would somehow make him respect me and see that I have an opinion and that I could be more like him. But I think I've confused his stubbornness for strength." Emmett sighed. "I don't know what to do, but I don't think I can stay here much longer."

"I wish I had an answer for you," Nate said softly. "This is a great ranch, and the people who work here are pretty amazing. But I don't know about your father. Yes, he's stubborn as hell, but I think there's more to this than just him being stubborn." He looked in the direction Dustin had gone. "I think Dustin knows what's behind this—or at least he suspects—but he isn't willing to talk about it at all."

"You're saying my father has a secret?" He wondered what it could be.

"We all have secrets and things we keep to ourselves. Sometimes those secrets are hurtful enough that we will do just about anything to keep them quiet." Nate's phone chimed with a message, and he pulled it out.

"What is it?" Emmett asked.

"Langley. He's working for Siras Milford, and he says that there's a lot of whispering and that one of the men disappeared for a while, but now came back with another of the hands. He says he'll tell us more when he can talk. But the timing is more than a little suspicious."

Emmett's mind began to turn. "What could my father have to hide that includes Siras Milford? They had a falling out some time ago, and I don't know what it concerned, but according to rumor, it had something to do with my mother." He leaned closer. "I used to wonder if my mother had an affair, but then that makes no sense. One thing I can say about my dad—he may be an ass sometimes, but his world always, *always* revolved around Mom. She's been the center of his world and he hers… at least as far as I could tell." Heck, she'd stayed at the hospital every minute he was there.

"Even if something happened years ago, what would prompt this kind of action now?" Nate asked, and Emmett shrugged. "I know… it's too much to handle at one time."

"Yeah. That's just it. Something seems off to me. Like everything is piling on all at once." His mind kept spinning. "I know Dad's heart attack wasn't planned or anything, but what if someone is taking advantage of that?" Emmett asked. "What if they knew Dad was away and someone truly is after me? Dad's attitudes are pretty well-known." He sighed, because that meant that they were back at square one and didn't know anything about anything. Except that his father was definitely hiding something, which was curious enough. God, he needed to quit mulling this shit over, because it was already giving him a headache. "I just can't do all this at once."

"And maybe that's the point," Nate offered. "Maybe our first instinct was right. Maybe the incidents on the ranch are all about Clinton Masters trying to get to you. Think about it—he was actually here, ostensibly to wish your parents well. What if he really was scoping things out?" Nate's jaw set, and then he opened his arms, and Emmett went right into them. Let people look; at the moment, he didn't give a damn.

"Well, if it is that asshole, he isn't going to win without a fight." Emmett held Nate tightly. "I'm going to finish my work, and then this evening we're going back to that damned barrel horse and I'm going to stay on if I have to tie my ass to it. Then, somehow, we're going to figure out who is behind all this." With Nate holding him, Emmett felt like he could do just about anything if he really tried. "Then, to top it off, once this is over, I'm going to sit down with my father and tell him what I want. The worst he can do is fire me, or I'll leave, but things cannot continue like this. It's not what I want." Damn, saying those words out loud felt good.

"What do you want?" Nate asked, and Emmett lifted his gaze.

"You. And I'll get that tonight, loud and to the point."

SOMETIMES THE best-laid plans completely fell to shit. Emmett knew that as a certainty, and it seemed to happen to him more often than not.

"Where have you been?" his mother asked when he came inside after another one of Nate and Marianne's failed attempts to help him learn to ride that damned barrel thing. He was coming to hate the idea of it, but he wasn't going to give up. Maybe there was some of his father's stubbornness in him. Emmett just hoped he'd left the asshole part of his father behind.

"Working," he answered.

"I asked the guys, and they didn't know where you were," his mother said, fluttering around him like a hummingbird. She had herself nerved up and seemed to go from place to place with no particular purpose in mind.

"Sit down and tell me what's wrong," Emmett offered, but she seemed more content to flit around the room.

"There's nothing wrong, and yet I can feel something waiting on the horizon... and it has me worried." She paused in her wanderings. "And before you can say it, I know what you're thinking, and your mother's cheese has not fallen off her cracker... as you kids used to say."

"Then what has you flitting around here like a canary evading a cat?" She really did resemble one, in her red kimono-style robe embroidered with flowers and birds. "You can't deal with something until it happens." He glanced toward the living room, where the television was playing. Emmett suspected his father was in the chair, sleeping through whatever sport he had on. At least he was getting enough rest.

Finally his mother pulled out a chair and perched herself on it. "I don't know. This ranch is his life, but I sometimes feel like it's killing him. Dustin won't let go, and the last few nights, he's been up wandering the house or in his office, making lists of things he wants to make sure get done."

Emmett was well acquainted with those damned lists. Like he was a teenager who needed to be told to feed and water the horses. The damned things were insulting, and they pissed him off.

"Yeah, I know," Emmett said sarcastically. "They burn well."

"And that's another thing. You fighting with your father—it isn't good for him. He needs calm and for things to run as smoothly as possible."

"Then tell him to stop giving Clinton Masters a run for his title of Asshole of the County," Emmett told her. "I'm not a child, and he can't do all the work that needs to be done." Emmett stood.

"Where are you going?" she asked softly.

"To make some noise," he answered cryptically, in part to shock her and in part to get one up on her.

And danged if his mother didn't smirk. She was a lady, but it was rare to get the better of her, and apparently now wasn't Emmett's turn. "The kind of noise Martha told me about? It seems you and Nate have quite the set of lungs on you." Sometimes his mother shocked him. "I'd say well done, but the rest of the house does not need to be kept awake with your bedroom shenanigans, especially with another man." Her eyes blazed for a moment, and Emmett braced for an explosion of recrimination and disappointment. "Now if you and Marianne...." She sighed and patted his hand, fire flashing in her eyes for a moment, and then it was gone. Her gaze met Emmett's, and he tried to read her emotions, but got nothing but turmoil, maybe confusion. It was like she was trying to figure something out, one of those sink-or-swim moments when everything could change with one decision. And this was that moment for his mother, and Emmett held his breath. Then her jaw set and her eyes and mouth relaxed. "Come on, I get it. Grandchildren aren't something that's likely to happen." At least she seemed to be facing reality. That was an improvement, at least.

"Why do you think I've been over at Nate's? He and I can make as much noise as we want there and we don't disturb anybody." He could hardly believe he was having a conversation about sex noises with his mother. He put up his hands. "I think we need to change the subject."

"What?" she asked innocently. "You think you come by that on your own? My goodness, there were so many times when I had to stop your father from yelling at the top of his lungs when you were children. You know the lungs your father has on him.... Well, imagine...." She grinned.

"I'd rather not, Mom. Really." He closed his eyes and tried to will away any thought of the two of them in bed. "But it's good to know that Dad was a screamer."

"Oh no, dear, your father didn't scream. He grunted. I was the screamer." If Emmett had had a glass of water, he would have done a spit take. As it was, he coughed and couldn't get his breath. "Stop that," his mother scolded. "How do you think we got the three of you kids?"

Emmett clenched his grip on the chair in front of him. "I'm entirely happy to think that you found me under a cabbage leaf the way you told me when I was five. That's a perfectly acceptable image." Because there was no way he wanted to think of his mother and father.... Emmett shuddered. He had to change the subject. "As I was saying about Sally Beth, she'll be moving into the old foreman's house. We're cleaning it out for her, and once she does, you can spoil her son. She's going through a divorce, and her soon-to-be ex-husband is Brad Connors. I'm sure you remember him."

Oh yeah, by the way his mother narrowed her plucked and shaped eyebrows, she remembered. "You did tell her that he is not allowed on this ranch under any circumstances." She did not take kindly to anyone trying to steal one of her horses, even if they were teenagers too drunk to get the stall door open.

"She knows. But the point is that it will be nice to have kids on the ranch again, and you can spoil him rotten if you like. I think Sally Beth would like that, and I know you've been missing having children around. It will make the ranch feel younger again."

She nodded. "I wish you'd just married Marianne, settled down, and had children. I don't understand all this gay business." She patted his hand. "I know you are who you are and I'm not going to push you to anyone anymore, but as a mother, I can wish for things. Being gay is a hard row to hoe."

"Tell me about it, Mom. And it's harder when your mother pushes women at you and doesn't just accept you for who you are. You know, you're supposed to be in my corner."

"But I just want—" she began.

"I don't want to be mean, but what you want is immaterial. It's my life, and imposing your will on me isn't helping. If you're worried that being gay is going to be difficult, then please don't make it any harder." He walked toward the door.

"Emmett," she said softly. "Your father and I need you here. And things do have to change, but give your father some time. He's been through a lot, and it's hard for him to just walk away from what he's always done." She bit her lower lip. "Your father has always been a cowboy, and when he dies, I'll bury him in his hat and boots. I know that. I'm hoping that's a long ways off, but you can't expect him to change easily."

"I know, Mom. But it would be good if he changed at all." He headed to the door.

"Don't go. Stay here. With everything that's happening, I need to know you're in the house." She seemed so fragile all of a sudden. His mother had always been the steel rod in a velvet glove. To see her vulnerable was too much, so Emmett nodded.

"I'll be in the office for a while. There are things that need to get done." He left, and once he was behind a closed door, he messaged Nate to let him know what was going on.

I'm sorry. The bed is going to seem huge without you taking up three-quarters of it. The message was followed by smiley faces.

Me? You're the cover stealer, he retorted. *I wake up with nothing, and everything is on your side of the bed.* He pressed Send and waited.

You can steal my covers any time. The message was followed by a picture of Nate on the bed, bare-chested, with that come-hither look in his eyes. Emmett moaned softly without thinking, and it was almost enough for him to head on over regardless of what his mother wanted. Instead he pulled off his shirt, reclined on the old chair, and took his own selfie. He had just pressed Send when the door opened and his mother ducked inside.

She took one look at him and the phone, and her eyes widened. But instead of closing the door, she put both hands on her hips, glaring at him. "What are you doing?"

"Mother." He pulled his shirt back on. "I was texting Nate."

"Well, this isn't getting work done, and so help me, if you are sending naughty pics to your boyfriend, at least do it from your own bedroom and not from my furniture. I may have to burn that chair, and I really liked it. Your father and I once...." Her words trailed off. She turned around and pulled the door closed again as Emmett jumped to his feet, wondering what the poor chair had seen and knowing he could never sit in it again.

Chapter 11

NATE USUALLY hated Mondays, and this one was particularly grueling. A storm system had moved in from the west, drenching everything. They needed a good rain, especially this time of the year, but it meant that work was miserable. It was hot, and they had to wear rain gear, which made it even hotter. Eventually Nate called an end to outside work for the day and then got the men busy with indoor tasks. That only led to Virginia getting up to her old ways and trying to take a bite out of Emmett, which she hadn't tried to do in days. In fact, she'd been warming up to him. Either the horse was psychotic, or something else was going on.

What he didn't expect was Dustin heading into the barn as Nate was leaving late in the afternoon.

"Everything okay?" Dustin asked.

"Emmett and the guys have the horses under shelter. The herd is fine. We moved them to slightly higher ground so they didn't get mired in any mud. After this wetting, the grasses will sprout in a big way, and that should get us through the next few months. Hopefully the hay fields will yield an extra cutting too."

Dustin nodded and actually smiled. "You always did know what you were doing." He didn't seem to be looking at Nate, but out toward the horizon. "I had hoped that one of my sons would be able to take over the ranch from me. RE was supposed to be that person." He sighed. "Once I'm up to snuff again, I'll take things over like they were before and we'll move forward."

It was the first time Nate's future here had been hinted at, but he should have expected that his position wouldn't be permanent. Nate knew when he'd been hired that Dustin being in the hospital had created an opening. He'd thought that if Giselle and Dustin saw his skills and what he was capable of, they would want to keep him on. Dustin wasn't getting any younger, and his heart attack would most likely slow him down whether he wanted to or not. But to hear Dustin musing only brought home just how temporary his tenure was here. Nate tried to think of where he was would go after this. There weren't foreman jobs just anywhere, certainly not around here, so it was likely he'd end up moving on. The idea sent a chill up his spine, but he pushed it away as best he could. There was no use begging trouble. Dustin couldn't take on ranch duties at this point, and hopefully he'd see that when he did, he needed more help than before.

"Did you know that Emmett stayed up nights in your office so he could learn the systems you were using? He was determined to try to see the ranch through your illness." Nate didn't press and waited for Dustin.

"This isn't his life. He just…." And there was the limit of how far Dustin was willing to go. "Emmett doesn't have what it takes to run this place. I know that. He tries, but it isn't in him."

Nate disagreed with him, but it wasn't his place to correct him, so he tried a roundabout way. "I tried a semester in college right after I couldn't rodeo anymore. I figured I'd give it a go. Terrible decision. I wasn't cut out for a desk, school or otherwise. But in the time I was there, I took some business classes because I thought I'd come up with the next big idea and make a million dollars." He chuckled as Dustin continued looking out over the land.

"What's your point?" Dustin asked.

"That not much stuck, but in one of those classes, the professor said something that stayed with me." He grinned. "I know, miracle of miracles. But he said that a good manager knows what the people who work for him are best at and makes the most of their strengths." Nate wasn't going to push any further. The rain picked up, and Nate waited for Dustin to head back to the house, but he stood there, hair plastering to his head. Nate half expected Dustin to blow up at him, but he seemed stunned. Finally, without a word, Dustin trudged toward the house. Then Nate made his way to the practice shed to try to get Emmett ready for the rodeo, still wondering what Dustin's silence meant.

NATE WAS beginning to think this was hopeless. After a brief period when Emmett looked like he might be getting the hang of it, he was once again having great difficulty staying on. The rodeo started Friday, with Emmett scheduled to ride on Saturday. That left very little time for him to improve.

"What the heck am I doing?" Emmett asked after dusting himself off once more.

"I don't know. Maybe we should try a real horse?" Marianne offered. "We've talked about it before, and I think it's our only chance. He's going to have to ride one in the arena, so he may as well ride now."

"Okay. We'll do that tomorrow. We can try." Nate wasn't sure that was a good idea, but there was no way Emmett could step into the arena without having at least tried a few horses. He had to get the feel for them and, if nothing else, be able to get off and out of the arena as fast as possible. "Let's do a few more rides and then we'll be done for the night."

Emmett's heart didn't seem to be in it, and Nate couldn't blame him. They had been at this for weeks with some improvement, but not enough to give him any confidence that Emmett wasn't going to get hurt, never mind make the eight seconds on a live horse. They kept up their ruse and carried out boxes of junk when they left before closing up the shed for the night.

"Are you coming over?" Nate asked. Emmett hadn't stayed with him in a few days, and he was beginning to wonder if something was wrong.

Emmett sighed. "Yes. I'm going to try. Mom has been asking me to stay, but I told her I wasn't going to tonight. Let me take care of some things."

"I was wondering, have you heard anything more from the insurance company about your truck?" It had been towed away a few days earlier now that the sheriff had released it.

"They're going to total it, so I have to get a new one. They're going to give me a figure soon, and then I'll go pick one out." He seemed less than thrilled. "I'll finish things up and let Martha know that I won't be here for dinner. Maybe we can get something somewhere before going back to your place." He slid his arms around Nate's neck. "I just want some time alone with you."

"Emmett," his mother called from the doorway. In so many ways, his parents treated their son like a child, and it was hard for Nate to keep his opinion to himself.

"I'll be right back," Emmett told him, answering his mother's call. When he returned, his expression was stormy. "Let's go to dinner."

"Is something wrong?" Nate asked.

"Not really. Just Mom wanting to control my life and everything in it. I told her I'd see them in the morning." He stomped toward Nate's truck. "I'm not good enough to do anything without them looking over my shoulder, but now they want me to stay here all the time. At least she does. I suspect my father is glad to have me gone. He likes to be in charge, but the whole thing with the fake snakes has my mother freaked."

Nate opened the truck door. "Then why don't we go get something to eat and we'll come back here afterward? Let your mother know that you'll be here tonight. She'll be in bed early, and we can sneak into your room like teenagers." It was an off-the-cuff suggestion that had Emmett smirking. Nate got in and closed the door before starting the engine.

"Did you ever sneak anyone into your room growing up?" Emmett pulled open the truck door and slid into the passenger-side bucket seat.

"God, no. Did you?" Nate asked.

Emmett snorted. "Are you kidding? Who was I going to sneak in? Though if we're talking about sneaking, I remember you and RE bringing in that bottle of cheap rum. Dad was in town and you and RE were supposed to have gone camping, but you both got drunk. Mom and Dad never said anything, but I knew what you did."

"You did?" Nate hummed softly. "I thought he and I got away with that. He got sick that night, and I didn't feel well. We stayed out late because we wanted a chance to sober up before we had to come back and face our parents."

Emmett grinned as he drew closer. "I followed you out when you went camping. I was fifteen, and I so wanted to be part of your fun. But I was too young, and you didn't want me along. I saw you start drinking and then went back home. Then I saw the two of you come in the next morning all haggard with circles under your eyes. Mom thought it was because you had been up all night."

"And you never said anything," Nate said, kind of surprised as he pulled out of the drive and made the turn to town.

"I told RE about it a while later."

Nate nodded as understanding washed over him. "Is that why RE insisted that you come camping with us that next summer? He never told me why he asked you along, but...."

Emmett nodded. "Yeah. I had kept his secret, and he rewarded me. After that, our relationship was different, better. He looked out for me and included me in things. RE was always a good brother, but he became the big brother that I miss even today. I'd give just about anything to have him back."

Nate would too. He missed his best friend every single day.

Nate didn't want to go to the tavern, so he parked in front of Eric's. It was a nicer restaurant, and at least there were tablecloths and cloth napkins rather than paper.

"Why here?" Emmett asked.

"I wanted to take you someplace nice," Nate answered, and they got out of the truck and went inside.

For a Monday night, the place was rather full. The hostess found them a table, and they took off their hats and placed them on the empty chairs as they sat down. "I haven't been here in years," Emmett admitted. "This is sort of Mom and Dad's place. They come here when they want dinner in town, which isn't often since they have Martha. In fact, other than an occasional night at the tavern, I rarely came into town to eat before I met you. I think Martha is starting to wonder if I've gone off her cooking." He smiled and looked through the menu as their server filled their water glasses.

"Do you have any questions about the menu?" a familiar and somewhat surly voice asked.

"Reid, what are you doing here?" Emmett asked, and Nate looked up from his menu. "I thought you were working from home while you took care of your mom."

He rolled his eyes. "I am, but Eric was shorthanded, and Lord knows I needed a little time away." He leaned over the table. "Mom has decided that she's going vegetarian, and man, she went big. Now for breakfast she makes these wheatgrass shakes that a cow would throw up. I had to get some real food, and Eric called in desperation. So I came in, and he says he'll feed me." He straightened up again. "I used to wait tables in college, but God, I must be getting soft, because my feet are killing me."

Nate chuckled. "You better take care of them or you'll get cankles, and no man wants that."

"Smartass," Reid retorted. "For that I'll bring you yesterday's bread and last week's roast beef." He leaned against Emmett's chair. "What's going on with your truck? Are you getting a new one?"

"Eventually," Emmett said. "They said the check is on the way, so I'll get one when it arrives." He didn't sound excited. "I keep wondering if I should wait in case someone decides to go after the new one as well. Whoever is doing this shit at the ranch is really pissing me off, especially since I have no idea who it is."

"The rumor mill has been surprisingly quiet, at least as far as I've heard. I'll ask Mom—she usually has an ear to whatever is going on." He leaned even closer to Emmett, and Nate tensed before he could stop himself. "What about the riding?"

Emmett rolled his eyes. "I swear the only way I'm going to be able to do it is if I get a horse that's nearly dead or if I can figure a way to tie myself on."

"You'll do great. I have faith in you, and I'll be there to cheer you on. I promise." He patted Emmett's shoulder. "Do you know what you want to eat, or should I come back?"

"I want the filet, please. Medium with all the fixings," Nate said, and Emmett ordered the same thing.

"Oh, thank God," Reid said as he jotted down the order. "I was starting to worry the entire world had been reduced to eating rabbit food." He took the menus and hurried away before returning with their salads, slathered in lots of house-made ranch dressing. Reid set down the plates and hurried back to the kitchen. Apparently chatting time was over.

"I've been trying to think of how we can find out who's behind the stuff at the ranch, and I have no idea. On television, the amateur sleuth always figures it out."

"Yeah, and they are always snoops. They go into everyone's house to try to find stuff. Could you imagine sneaking around other ranches?" Emmett shivered. "Imagine the things we'd see. Siras and his wife in bed," he whispered, and Nate shivered. "Or worse, Clinton Masters. I always wondered what kind of kinky shit he was into."

Reid set down their bread. "Now, boys. That isn't very nice." He leaned down. "One of the other servers, I won't say who, was talking, and apparently she went out with Clinton a couple days ago. Let's just say there were things that he wanted her to do that left her... a little weirded out and on her way home, quickly."

"Great. Sex rumors we can get, but nothing about what happened at the ranch," Nate groused and took a bite of his salad.

"Can't help you there, big guy." Reid patted him on the shoulder. "I only work in kinky. You're going to have to check another branch of the town gossip line if you want anything more." He flounced away, and Nate rolled his eyes. But Reid had him thinking, and he messaged Langley.

We need to talk, Langley answered. *I can be at your house in an hour or so.* Nate relayed the message to Emmett, hoping that Langley might have some answers for them. In the meantime, he was determined to enjoy his meal with Emmett.

"I still think things revolve around my father," Emmett said as he finished his salad. "If cattle get lost or hurt, it's my father who suffers most. The same thing if they burn down some of the buildings. And my truck is close to the same color as his." He bit his lower lip, and Nate knew Emmett wanted this to be about his dad. It was easier than knowing that someone hated you enough to want to cause you real harm.

"One way or the other, we'll find out." Nate was determined. "But for now, let's just enjoy our dinner. Eric always knew how to make an amazing steak." He took a bite, and the luscious, rich beef melted in his mouth.

"He really does. And the company is nice too." Emmett flashed one of those shy smiles he got whenever he opened up a little to talk about his feelings. In some ways Emmett was so much like his father it was frightening. Even if he didn't realize it, he was a cowboy through and through, and that was sexy. It wasn't the horses or the clothes that made someone a cowboy—it was the attitude and the way they held themselves. Like the way Emmett didn't give up on the barrel horse no matter how many times he fell on his ass. "It's a shame that we didn't figure things out a long time ago."

Nate had told himself the same thing more than once. "I think if we had, we'd have messed it up somehow. RE was the best friend I ever had. I somehow doubt he would have been happy that I was dating his younger brother. You were a kid, I was older… it wouldn't have worked. I think things had to be more equal for us to have a chance."

He watched Emmett nod slowly. "I suppose you're right. But it would have been nice to know that I wasn't the only one. Reid and I spent a lot of time alone in school. He was out then, and he was my best friend, and I stood by him. Mom and Dad couldn't figure it out, and I just told them that I stuck by my friends. I was too scared, especially after I saw how Reid was treated, to come out myself."

"It wasn't any easier for me. I suppose if we'd grown up in the city then things would have been different. There are so many more people, and they encounter different folks all the time. Here, everyone is the same. They grew up here and were raised here, so everyone pretty much thinks alike. It isn't as though they encounter a lot of gay people."

"Did you have to fight sometimes?" Emmett asked. "How did you get on in the rodeo?"

"I pretty much kept to myself. The Professional Bull Riders has nondiscrimination policies and doesn't stand for any bad behavior. But that doesn't mean that some of the judges wouldn't sway things a little because of how they felt. I wanted to ride and didn't need the distractions, so I never said anything. RE knew, though. I told him right after high school, and he always supported me. I don't know if you ever told him, but he would have been in your corner there too, just like Suzanne in the end." He met Emmett's gaze. "You do know that the guys on the ranch may pick on you, but they think a great deal of you too. They know you watch out for them, and they do the same."

Emmett shrugged.

"Did you know that Holace asked what was going on in the shed? He said that we had been spending more time in there than that shed deserved cleaning. Then he leaned close and told me that if we was helping you with the rodeoing, then that was a good thing and that he wouldn't say nothin' if that was what you wanted." Nate nodded for emphasis. "I bet you thought you were just a joke to them."

"Yeah. They laugh at my ridiculous antics." Emmett lowered his gaze to his plate and began eating faster. "I figure I'm the laughable bright spot in their day."

"They may be amused at some of the things that happen because… okay, sometimes they're funny. But if you were to get hurt, they'd be the first ones there to pick you up again. You make sure that the work is doled out evenly and that those who work hard get rewarded. And don't tell me different, because I hear them talking. And I dare say that all of them who can will be at that rodeo cheering you on."

Emmett shook his head. "And that's what I don't want. They'll all see me fall flat on either my face or my ass. Actually, I think I'd be safest if I fell on my head. All us McElroys have thick skulls and fat heads. It's the hardest thing on us." He ate the last of his steak and the potato. "I just want this entire episode behind me. What the hell was I thinking?" He barely paused before answering his own question. "I wasn't. I was drunk and got it in my head that I could somehow defend RE's honor. He didn't need me to take up his honor. RE was always the best of any of us, and I feel bad that I forgot that."

Nate took Emmett's hand. "You stood up for your brother because you loved him and you knew that Clinton Masters could never hold a candle to RE no matter how much he boasted differently." He leaned over the table. "You should have seen your face that night. The way you stood up to Clinton was impressive. He boasted, and you let him run on and then took up his challenge with all the bravado of any cowboy." He pulled his hand away from Emmett's and finished his dinner.

Reid returned to ask them if they wanted dessert and left the check. "Thank goodness this is just one night."

"Sometimes you whine worse than a teenager," Emmett teased, and Reid smacked his shoulder.

"You can run with the cows all day, but I'll put a dinner service against anything you do anytime." He turned and strode back toward the kitchen, but Nate could tell his feet hurt.

"Come on. Let's get back to my place and see what Langley has to tell us." He was hopeful that maybe Langley could help shed some light on the happenings.

"I SEE YOU started the party already," Nate said when he found Langley on his sofa, beer in one hand and a sandwich in the other. "Don't you guys eat out at Siras's place?" Langley screwed up his face for a few seconds before taking a big bite. "I take it the food isn't very good."

"It's okay. But I needed to get out of there, and since you and the noisemaker here were gone, I thought I'd make use of your television and a little quiet." He tipped his beer, and Emmett took off his hat and seemed to get comfortable as well. Nate wondered what the hell was happening until Langley set down his beer.

"What's going on, Langley?" Emmett asked. "I know for a fact that Siras has a wonderful cook. Greta has been with him for years. When the town used to have big picnics in the park, she used to make this blueberry buckle that was to die for."

"That may have been the past, but not now. Greta isn't there anymore. I was curious and asked why. Everyone was closed-lipped, and I didn't want to press and arouse suspicion." He took another bite and swallowed.

"Do you even bother to chew, or do you just inhale your food?" Emmett teased. "Maybe we should just arrange it in lines and you can snort it." He got up again and returned with a couple bottles of beer, handing Nate one.

Nate thanked him and leaned forward. "Okay. Get to what was so important." He scowled and tried to be patient as Langley finished his sandwich.

"Okay. So a new guy started, name's Wes. He's a real bully, and he had his eyes on me until I knocked him down a peg. I'm not taking that kind of shit from no one."

"Wes Marcourt?" Emmett asked, and Langley nodded. Why was it that in a small town, every dickhead you went to high school with returned once they grew up into a complete asshole?

"Yeah. He's the worst kind of dumb, because he thinks he knows shit and draws other people in. Anyway, he was yammering on about the goings-on at your place. Honestly, it sounded like he was repeating what he heard rather than having been there. Another guy came in and shut him up right away. Name was Brad, and he was pretty urgent. I got the feeling that Wes was telling Brad's story. Anyway, I didn't make a big deal out of it and pretended like it wasn't important."

"I didn't know those two worked for Siras," Emmett commented. "I thought they worked with Clinton out at his father's place."

"Clinton Masters?" Langley asked. "I heard talk about them too. It seems the Masters' place is having trouble, and the other two were let go and needed to find work." Emmett caught Nate's gaze, and Nate nodded. They must have been thinking the same thing. "Let me in on whatever ESP you two got going on," Langley said. "And I don't care if getting buttfucked gives you ESP, I still ain't interested."

Emmett gaped at Langley for about two seconds and then whapped him across the back of the head.

"Hey," Langley protested, rubbing the back of his skull.

Nate chuckled. "The only reason he did it is because I'm over here." He glared at Langley for a second and then shifted to smile at Emmett, pleased he was getting when Langley was being an ass. "Anyway, that explains why some of the rumors seemed to start from Siras's place. Maybe Clinton and his friends are behind what's been happening."

"We figured that," Emmett said. "But what do we do about it?"

Langley sipped his beer. "What I don't get is why now? You guys all have a history. Right? Clinton and RE were always huge rivals. I remember some of those weekends. RE left Clinton in the dust most of the time. But that was some time ago. Why the animosity now? Why cut fences, set fires, shoot up Emmett's truck...."

"And panic the horses with rubber snakes," Nate supplied, picking up on Langley's train of thought. "Why now, and could Clinton be behind it... or Siras? The more we learn, the less we know about who's behind this shit." These incidents seemed to be escalating, and it was a matter of time before Emmett or someone else on the ranch was hurt. It was really getting frustrating.

Emmett sighed. "I wish I knew. But I keep wondering if those answers don't lie with my father. I tried to ask him what was going on and who he had pissed off, and Dad got really tight-lipped. I think he knows something he doesn't want to talk about."

"Oh, great," Nate mumbled. "That means we need to get him to open up. I'd much rather be Geraldo Rivera standing at Al Capone's empty vault on hyped national television. Your father won't open up about anything until he's ready, and that could take decades, if it ever happens."

"Tell me about it. I swear if my father had a staring contest with a fish in a bowl, the fish would lose. He is the most stubborn man on earth." Emmett blew out his breath. "But maybe I can appeal to him through the one thing he loves almost as much as my mother—the ranch." Still, poor Emmett. He looked like he was going to be led out to the firing squad.

Nate finished his beer and sat back. Emmett did the same, but Langley seemed to be settling in for the long haul. Nate shared a look with Emmett, wondering how to tell him that he and Emmett had things they needed to do and that they couldn't have a repeat of the other night when Langley drank all Nate's beer and then basically passed out on the sofa.

Langley got up, and Nate heard him rummaging in the refrigerator, bottles clinking. "Dude, you need to drive back to Siras's," Nate called. "Emmett and I are heading back to the ranch." The refrigerator door closed, and Langley appeared in the doorway, empty-handed. "It's a workday tomorrow for all of us."

"Yeah, I know," he said. "I need to get back anyway." He returned to the kitchen and the refrigerator door opened and closed. Then Langley returned with a bag, no doubt filled with Nate's beer. He then said goodbye and practically skipped out the door in delight.

"I bet he took the last of it," Emmett said.

"It's okay. I have some more. I keep it under the sink. It's the one place I know he won't look for it." Nate grinned.

"You do realize the bag he took was too big for a bottle or two. He looked way too pleased with himself." Nate stood and hurried to the kitchen, then pulled open the cabinet door to find the place where he kept his extra six-pack empty. The little thief. He closed the cabinet and hurried to the door just in time to see Langley's red taillights disappear from view.

"Bastard," he swore, closing the door more forcefully than he needed to.

"Come on. I need to get home. Mom and Dad should be in bed. You and I have something much more enjoyable planned for the rest of the night. As long as you promise you'll be quiet."

"Look who's talking. After our last time, there are cemeteries in the county that have been emptied because of your cries of ecstasy." He puffed out his chest a little. After all, those noises had been because of him. "Hell, I think if we can't keep quiet, the entire area will see its version of the zombie apocalypse."

Emmett snorted softly and put his hand over his face. "More like my entire family will be the zombies if we keep them up all night. The last time we were there, it took poor Martha a day and a nap before she looked all right again." He giggled almost like a schoolkid as he got his hat, and they left the house. "I feel like some errant teenager sneaking home in order to make out while Mom and Dad are gone."

"RE did that, you know," Nate confided. "He had this thing for Debra Mell, and he used to sneak her into his room sometimes. You might remember her father. Huge scary man, and yet he liked your brother. That is until Debra thought she might be pregnant. After that it seemed RE was no longer welcome."

"I see."

Nate shook his head. "RE never did that with her. They used to sneak into his room, and the two of them would talk all night. He had a girl all alone in his room and did nothing. Yet you're the gay one." He rolled his eyes. "Debra, on the other hand, was in love with Chip Larson, and he treated her like shit. I like to think it was RE that helped her get away from that asshole. Last I heard she was married and living up in Boseman. RE stood by her, and thankfully the whole thing was a false alarm." They got into the truck and drove slowly back toward the ranch. Folks often thought that country roads were open places to go as fast as possible, but hitting a cow with a car was a surefire way to end up with an entire cow through the windshield and in your lap. It was not pretty. Besides, there were plenty of other animals out at night, including deer.

"I'm curious. I thought I heard howling the other night," Nate said.

"Me too. Dad will come unglued and start pulling out his gun, so don't mention it. There's a wolf pack to the south. They broke off of the ones from Yellowstone, and occasionally they make it up this far, especially when times get tough for them. But I suspect that they're still far enough away that we don't need to worry. If my father heard me say this, he'd kill me, bring me back to life, and kill me again, but I love hearing that sound. To me it means that nature can repair itself, especially if we're willing to give it a little help and then get the heck out of the way. I know the ranchers hate the idea, but wolves have been in this area since long before the first herd of cattle ever set foot on this land."

Nate huffed because he knew as Emmett did that they were a fact of life. "They are a nuisance and a threat to our business that we're all better off without." He made the turn into the yard, and Emmett got out. The house was mostly dark as Emmett took his hand and led him inside and, surprisingly, into the office, where he closed the door. Nate hoped they weren't in for a repeat of their earlier embarrassment. "Are we watching porn?" Nate asked as Emmett woke up the computer.

"No. I'm looking for something." He pulled up YouTube. "Here it is. *How Wolves Change Rivers*. I found this some time ago. It's pretty amazing, and it proves how wrong you are." Emmett got up from the chair and stood back as Nate sat to watch the five-minute video. About halfway through, a tingle went up his back. It made sense and proved everything Emmett had said.

"That's pretty cool," Nate said when the video ended.

"I know, and that's what I want to do here. Well, not the wolf part, but I want the ranch to better fit into the environment. I want to figure out how to keep our water cleaner and reduce the chemicals and pesticides we use, because they hurt the good insects as well as the bad ones. We can make a difference that will help save the ranch and ensure its resources for the next generation and the one after that." He avoided the chair his mother had indicated and leaned against the doorframe. "Not that any of those plans matter."

Nate knew that Dustin wasn't going to just give Emmett free rein to do what he wanted. "What other ideas do you have?"

"I was thinking that there are those areas down by the creek that wash out when it rains. Over the years, we've brought in fill to try to stabilize the area, but I think we should plant trees there and let them go. The roots will stabilize the ground and keep it in place. Like I said, instead of fighting it, work with nature and let it help us too." Emmett crossed his arms. "I put together a whole plan, and I keep thinking I should show it to my father, but he won't even leave a breeding plan we went over together alone." He pushed away from the doorframe and shut down the computer.

Nate sighed. "You know that your parents hired me temporarily," he said, and Emmett nodded. "I had hoped that they might realize what I can do and keep me on, though you know your father is anxious to get back in the saddle." The last thing he wanted was to leave Emmett behind. A job… well, jobs might be hard to find, but there were more of them. But there was only one Emmett.

"I'm aware of that. But I also know that like it or not, my father isn't going to be able to go back to the way things were." Still, some of the energy drained from Emmett's eyes, and Nate knew there was little that logic was going to play in this decision. Dustin would do what he wanted, and no one could stop him. It was his ranch, after all. "I'll fight for you." Emmett took his hand and turned out the lights before opening the office door.

The house was indeed quiet, with only a single light in the kitchen to show the way. Everyone else was in bed as Emmett guided Nate down the hall to his room. Nate went inside, and Emmett closed the door behind them.

Now that the two of them were alone and in the quiet, Nate was afraid to move. Whether he was acting like a naughty child or not, he wanted to be with Emmett. They worked hard and long hours, so being together in the quiet darkness, just them, was precious. Nate reached for Emmett, tugging him close, just holding him. He'd done this many times, but surrounded by darkness, they seemed nearer and the need more immediate, like the world had grown smaller until it ended just beyond where they could see and feel. Nate tugged off Emmett's shirt while kicking off his own shoes.

It didn't take long or much effort to divest each other of their clothes. Unlike their earlier amorous endeavors, they were silent, letting their hands and bodies do the talking. There was something exciting and dangerous about the need to make no sound, so even their breathing became a tell.

The bed squeaked softly as Emmett climbed into it. Nate felt his way around and joined him, the covers sliding up and then Emmett slipping into his arms. Nate used his breathing as a guidepost to find his lips, then took them in a gentle kiss that deepened quickly as heat built between them. Not being able to see left the feel, scent, and soft sounds of Emmett even more exciting.

"Nate," Emmett whispered, pressing him back on the mattress, Emmett's weight settling on top of him. Nate stroked down Emmett's back, cupping his butt, kneading the firm globes.

"I know. It's strange not to see you, and yet I know what you look like." He squeezed, running his hands back up his sides, just to create the entire picture in his mind. "I like seeing you with my hands. It's like getting to know you all over again." He smiled as slightly rough skin passed under his palms. "Do they give you anything for your skin?"

Emmett hummed softly, pausing in his own explorations. "Yes. It was really bad when I was a kid. The doctor gave me special soap and shampoo to use. It's supposed to help keep my skin from drying out." Nate paused and drew his hands away, lightly cupping the cheeks of Emmett's face.

"Do you still use it?" Nate asked.

"Yes. Every time I shower. Well, at least when I do it here. I didn't use it after staying at your house. Why? It's just special soap. It isn't going to hurt you if you use it."

Nate held Emmett tighter. "Do you remember the other day when Virginia came up to you and bumped your chest for attention? You'd stayed at my house and showered there. Then, later, after you'd stayed home, she was back to her biting ways?"

Emmett paused, and Nate could almost see him staring at him in the darkness. There was no moon and no light coming in through the window. "What are you saying?"

"That tomorrow we do an experiment. I want you to shower, and don't use your special soap. That could be the issue. Maybe it's the soap that has some scent that either Virginia hates or that makes her think you're tasty." He held Emmett, rubbing his back.

"But…." Emmett paused. "You think it's been the soap all along?"

"Don't know. But Virginia doesn't always try to bite you. A lot of the time she ignores you. Same with the other horses. Maybe they only react when the scent is strongest. But it would explain this strange fixation they seem to have with you. And it could also be the reason you haven't been able to ride ponies or horses. I want to do a test in the morning." Nate guided Emmett's mouth to his and tasted his sweetness, and they kept kissing through the lovemaking, each swallowing the gasps and groans of the other until they were both spent and fell asleep together as fatigue overtook them.

HE AND Emmett were up early and out before breakfast. There was plenty to get done, and Nate wanted to conduct his little experiment first thing. "Did you bring the soap?" Nate asked as he met Emmett at the barn door. It was quiet, so he tugged him into a kiss, taking his lips hard. He loved the time he spent with Emmett.

"You made me get up early so we could do this and then you ravage me in the barn? We could have stayed in bed where it was a heck of a lot more comfortable." Emmett chuckled, and Nate warmed at the sound. If he had his way, Emmett would laugh all the time and be as happy as possible.

"Good point. But come on." They went inside, and Nate hung on to the bar of soap that Emmett had slipped into a plastic bag. "I want you to slowly approach Virginia and see how she reacts to you. You haven't used this soap in a while, so hopefully the scent will be gone."

Emmett cautiously approached Virginia, who remained calm, and when Emmett stroked her neck and nose, she bumped his chest lightly, looking for more.

"This seems like she was the other day," Emmett said, rubbing her nose gently.

"What's going on?" Dustin demanded. Virginia threw her head back, and Emmett calmed her.

"Dad, you should know better than to snap around one of the horses," Emmett said calmly, but with a definite bite. "We're trying something." He stroked her neck once again, looking like an old pro. Then he stepped away and Nate pulled out the soap. Almost instantly, Virginia became a different horse, extending her head and snapping her teeth as she tried to reach it. Nate backed away, put the soap back in the bag, and set all of it outside.

"What the hell was that?" Dustin asked.

"My eczema soap," Emmett answered. "All these years I thought horses hated me, and here it was that damned soap. The doctors said I needed to use it to keep my skin from drying out and flaking. I have all this time and...." He rubbed his backside. "I can't tell you the number of times I've been bitten or kicked." He turned to his dad. "I never rode because the horses turned on me all the time."

"That's a bunch of hogwash." Dustin went outside and returned, rubbing the soap on his arm. Then he strode up to Virginia, and she snapped at him more like a rabid dog than a horse. Dustin jumped back, and Nate caught him before he fell to the ground. "Well, I'll be damned. And here I just thought you were afraid of them."

"You would be too if that came at you all the time." Emmett might have been trying to keep the amusement out of his voice, but he wasn't successful. "We should have figured this out years ago. God, I could have ridden as a kid and...." He shrugged. "At least we know now."

"Yeah. And it seems that Virginia doesn't hate you after all." She nudged Emmett's chest when he got close enough. "Maybe she feels bad for all the times she's gone after you."

Dustin huffed. "I'm glad that's cleared up." He looked both of them over. "I heard the two of you come out of Emmett's room. That means that either Emmett didn't stay home as he promised his mother or the two of you snuck into the house last evening. You know how your mother and I feel about that kind of behavior under our roof." He turned on Nate in an instant. "And—"

"What?" Emmett snapped. "We weren't working, and I live there too. Or am I not part of this family any longer? Mom knows that Nate and I have been seeing each other, so don't put your own squeamishness on her. She and I have talked, really talked, but you and I are never on the same page. You don't listen and you never have." Emmett left the barn, and Nate turned to find himself something to do. The tension between those two hung over the ranch most of the time. It probably had for a very long time, but Emmett seemed much more willing to push now. Nate wondered how long it would be before Dustin either shoved back or just exploded in a fit of rashness. Either way, it wasn't going to be pretty. In many ways, Nate liked that Emmett had become more willing to challenge his father when he thought he was out of line, but it also wasn't helping Emmett's cause very much.

In Nate's opinion, the two of them needed to sit down and talk things out, but neither of them seemed willing to do that. Nate didn't like that he could be caught in the middle, but he wasn't going to withdraw his support for Emmett.

"Sometimes I wonder if I will ever understand that boy," Dustin groused.

Nate bit his tongue to keep from responding. It definitely wasn't his place, and he wanted to keep his job. Nate had always thought that Dustin didn't see what Emmett was doing around the ranch. That he didn't understand all that Emmett contributed. But now he was starting to see that wasn't the issue at all. Dustin didn't respect Emmett as a man or as a son. He was just a replacement for RE, and since Emmett wasn't the perfect son that Dustin always wanted, it was too easy for him to look past him. Nate wanted to help, but he didn't see how he could. Besides, after the last time he and Dustin had talked, Nate's position here wasn't on solid ground. It was definitely best if he stayed out of Dustin's way.

Chapter 12

EMMETT SPENT the rest of the week steering clear of his father and trying to figure out how not to make a fool of himself at the rodeo. At least after ditching the soap he had used for years, life with the horses had become much easier.

"Are you ready?" Holace asked as Emmett checked everything in the barn before getting ready to go to the rodeo grounds in the new deep red truck he'd picked up two days ago. It had everything, including Bluetooth to his phone and all the safety features. The heated and cooled leather seats were amazing and more comfortable than most of the chairs in the house.

"As I'll ever be." He had managed a couple of rides on Ringo. They hadn't gone particularly well, but he had lasted longer than the first time he'd tried to ride him. "Nate made sure I know how to fall and get the hell out. I suppose that's all I can hope for. At least I'm keeping my word."

"You don't need to do this," Holace told him. "No one here is going to think the worse of it if you don't." Not that most of the hands knew anyway. They had kept his training a secret as much as possible. But they couldn't keep everyone completely in the dark, especially when he'd ridden Ringo.

Emmett shook his head. "I have to. I opened my big mouth, and now I have to pay the price. I won't back down. I may fall on my ass or my head, but I'll keep my word, and then once I get thrown, I'll pick myself up and know I did what I set out do to."

"And what if you get hurt?" Holace asked.

"Yeah," Sally Beth chimed in. "No one wants that. And you do know that your parents are going to be watching. Your mother is going to pitch a fit when she sees you out there. I'm assuming they don't know you're riding, since she hasn't screamed the house down." She definitely had a way of phrasing things.

"I'll do my best." His mind was made up. At some point this had become not only about his pride, but a point of honor. Succeed or fail, he was going to give it his very best.

"Is Nate going with you?" Sally Beth asked.

"He has some things to do here and will be there before I have to ride." Emmett forced a smile to try to hide his nervousness and got into the truck. His gear was already inside. After taking a look around the ranch as though the place wouldn't be the same, he climbed in and headed for the rodeo grounds, where he was given a number and told where to change.

"If it isn't little McElroy Junior," Clinton sneered as soon as he entered the area reserved for the riders.

"What is it with you?" Emmett asked. "Did RE do better than you so many times and do you have so little self-worth that you think beating a member of his family will make you feel like a man?"

A laugh went through the six or so men in the room. "He's got your number, Masters," one of the men said, earning a sneer from Clinton.

"Leave him alone. Whatever business you have, take it out in the arena," another told him, pushing over. Clinton turned and went back to his area, leaving Emmett to finish getting ready. Once he was dressed, he took his things back to the truck. He wasn't going to leave them where Clinton could get anywhere near them.

When he returned to the arena area, Nate met him. "Are you ready?" Grandstand bleachers had been set up around the field used each year for the county rodeo, and Reid had already gone up to take his place to watch and cheer him on. There was a carnival, along with a midway for games and rides. Food vendors and local clubs had booths set up for food. It was always a festive atmosphere. But for Emmett, it was nothing but nerves. "You don't have to do this."

"Why does everyone keep telling me that? I thought that maybe you would understand why I have to do this. I can't back down. I know no one thinks I can do this—hell, I doubt I can do it either, but I'm going to try, and I'll do my best. At least then I'll be able to look at myself in the mirror each morning instead of wondering what would have happened if I'd had the guts to go through with it." He hardened his jaw. Emmett had hoped Nate would stand behind him.

"I understand. But it isn't going to change the way I think of you." Nate drew closer.

"Maybe not, but it affects the way I think of myself. It's also what RE would do, and for once I'm going to live up to what my brother would have done." Emmett began walking back to the competitors' entrance.

"Stop," Nate said sharply from behind him. "I do believe in you. I have for a long time." He strode closer. "I don't want you to get hurt, that's all. Riding a bronc can be dangerous. I thought I could teach you how to ride well enough so you could be safe."

"But you did. And like it or not, I have to ride today, and I will." Emmett's stomach fluttered with anxiety. All he wanted was for this to be over.

"Then come on. We'll go in together, and I'll be there at the gate when it opens." Nate motioned ahead, and Emmett led the way out to the rails to watch the other riders. "Some of the guys will stay in the changing area until it's their turn. I never liked to watch the riders before me. RE always did. He said there was something to be learned in every ride and he wanted to know all that he could." Nate stood next to him, watching as the first rider exploded out of the chute, almost instantly flying off and hitting the dirt. The audience seemed to hold their breath until he got up, waving his hat, heading for the fence.

Emmett tensed and wished he'd stayed in the dressing room. Watching was only making him more nervous. The next rider made the eight, but the one after flew off in spectacular fashion. "I think I'm next."

Nate nodded. "Then let's go. Let the men help settle you on the bronc. The gate will open, and then it's just you and the horse. Hold on like we told you and use your arms. If you fall, tuck and roll just like we practiced... and for God's sake, don't get hurt." Nate hugged him, and then they went to the chute. Emmett climbed up and lowered himself onto Tsunami, a dark-brown coiled bundle of energy ready to explode between his legs, and so not in a good way. Emmett was about to tell them to just let him get the hell out as Tsunami fidgeted and quivered in the chute, but then his courage rose. He took a deep breath and settled in the saddle, knowing it was now or never, and nodded.

The gate opened, and all hell broke loose. At least it seemed like it. The damned horse seemed to move in all directions at once. All Emmett could think of was that he needed to make the eight, and that meant moving with the fucking animal. Tsunami jumped up and then to the side, twisting slightly, then jumping again. Emmett did his best to keep his legs down and around the damned horse. It was hard, but he flopped less than he thought he would. Of course, that could have been because he was completely out of his mind to have done this in the first place.

The horse jumped again, this time sending Emmett's rear end upward. He crashed back down and gripped as hard as he dared, hoping to keep from bouncing back. It helped somewhat. At least his legs stayed down and he remained upright.

Tsunami turned and jumped again, higher and harder. Emmett sailed upward and back down once again, barely hanging on. His arm felt like it was on fire, and he waved the other one to try to counter some of the movement, but it was too much. The next jump sent him up and off the horse. He flew through the air. When his feet hit the ground, he did what Nate said, rolling down and to a stop. Emmett quickly took stock, realizing that he might be okay.

"Get up!" someone yelled, and he climbed to his feet and raced for the rails, glad to all that was holy that the ride was over.

"Emmett!" Nate cried as he tugged him down and over the fence, right into his arms. "You fucking did it."

"What?"

Nate swung him around. "You made the eight. I have no idea how, and all the gods in the universe must have been looking out for you, because that was the worst ride I have ever seen, but you did it."

"Really? What's my score?" Emmett asked. "If I did the damned event, then I want my score." He pulled away and looked up at the board. It was a sixty-three, and for now, he sat at the top of the leader board. "Take a damned picture. It isn't going to last long." Nate snapped one of the board with his phone. The next rider and horse were being prepped, so Emmett made his way out of the area to the grandstands.

"What do you think you were doing?" his mother asked, hands on her hips, blocking his way forward. "You scared half my life out of me."

"Giselle," his father said much more sedately, "calm down. He's fine."

"But... he...." She turned on his father.

He shook his white-cowboy-hatted head. "Giselle, that's enough. Don't embarrass him—he's a cowboy just like the rest of us." With that, his father turned and led his mother back up into the stands. Emmett had no doubt that his mother was giving his dad an earful, and then she'd move to the third degree about whether he knew about all this. He watched them go, unable to move.

"Emmett?" Nate said from behind him. "We're holding up traffic."

He took a step to the side and slowly turned back to Nate. "That's the first time in my entire life that he's ever said that to me. Even when I was a kid, he never called me that." He searched his memory, but he was certain of it. "My father said that I was a cowboy."

"Emmett, you always were," Nate told him, and Emmett found his feet and moved toward their seats. There was a place empty next to them, and Emmett took off his chaps and laid them over the bench before sitting down.

"Are you a real cowboy? Like those men out there?" a boy from behind asked after tapping Emmett on the shoulder.

"He sure is. He rode just a few minutes ago," Nate said. "This is Emmett, and he's one of the finest cowboys I know. He takes care of horses and everything." Nate smiled, and the little boy's eyes widened under his cowboy hat.

"I'm Emmett."

"This is Jimmy," the man Emmett presumed was his father said, extending his hand. "I'm Howard. This is my weekend to have him, and he's wanted to come to the rodeo for weeks." Apparently this wasn't Howard's thing, but Jimmy was sure enthused.

"I brought some snacks," another man said, sliding in next to Jimmy.

"My husband Raymond." Emmett shook hands with him once Howard took the cardboard box of food.

"And this is my boyfriend Nate," Emmett said.

"See? I told you there would be gay cowboys," Raymond said. "It's good to meet you both."

"Did you win?" Jimmy asked, and Emmett glanced at Nate before smiling broadly. He opened his mouth, but Nate beat him to the punch.

"Yes, he did," Nate said, and Jimmy predictably looked up at the leader board. Emmett knew his name wasn't there. "Jimmy, winning doesn't always mean coming in first. Sometimes it's doing something you've never done before and succeeding." Nate took Emmett's hand and squeezed it hard.

"Like riding a horse even though you're scared?" Jimmy asked.

"Yes. Are you scared of horses?" Emmett asked.

Jimmy nodded. "Sometimes. They're so big. But I rode a pony, and Papa and Daddy say that maybe I can get one, and when I grow up I won't be scared anymore and I can ride a horse."

Emmett bumped Nate, and he pulled out his wallet and handed Howard a card. "The Rolling D is Emmett's family's ranch here in the area. Give us a call, and Jimmy can meet lots of cowboys who will be happy to show him that horses aren't scary." A cheer went up through the crowd, and they all turned as a rider waved his hat and took his place on the leader board. "Clinton is next," Nate told him quietly, "and it looks like he got the money ride."

"Oh?" Emmett snarled, shaking his head.

"Do you know this Clinton?" Raymond asked. "Are you fans?"

Emmett snickered. "Yes, we know him, but we certainly aren't fans. He also lives here in the area, and he's a real…." The words stuck in his throat as a pair of bright blue eyes stared up at him from a cherubic face.

Raymond patted his arm. "We get the point. Let me guess—winning is doing better than him."

Emmett nodded. "And he drew the money ride. The easiest horse there is. That gives him a chance to get a really good score." He tried not to let it bother him. Emmett had set out to do what he wanted. His goal had been met.

"There he goes," Jimmy cried.

Emmett turned back to the arena, his gaze going to Clinton as the horse bucked, jumped, and launched Clinton Masters into the air like a rocket.

"And there he went," Jimmy added with a giggle. Emmett wanted to share a high-five with the little guy, but that would be bad form, so he smiled at him instead. Jimmy put his hands over his mouth as he laughed. "Is he okay?"

Clinton got to his feet, but he was wobbly. Two men hurried over and escorted him to the side, where Clinton waved his hat and then disappeared behind the rails and probably right into Medical for a review.

Emmett patted Nate on the hand before sliding out of their row and then down to the ground level. He made his way around to the competitors' area and was let through.

"Is Clinton all right?" he asked one of the men outside the medical tent.

"Yeah. He'll be fine. The asshole just broke his arm and got shook up," one of the men answered after rolling his eyes. "You'd think he got hit by a semi, the way he was bellyaching like a little girl." Clearly they didn't think very much of him. "You his friend or something?"

Emmett coughed and tried not to choke. "Are you kidding? I just wanted to make sure I beat him fair and square."

The man grinned. "I heard he had some sort of bet on this ride. It's all over town. Your ride was pretty awful, if you don't mind my saying, but you stayed on, and that's saying something."

"Well, let's just say that after that ride, I've decided my bronc-riding days are over. I'm going out with an eight-second ride and knowing I beat Clinton Masters," he said loudly enough that he knew his voice traveled far enough for Clinton to hear him. "That should settle any questions of my family's honor or that fact that my brother was head and shoulders better than that asshole in every way."

Clinton stumbled out of the tent, his eyes filled with rage. "You little…!"

"What's with you, anyway? I know RE was better than you, but what does my family have to do with all this animosity? What did any of us do to you?"

"Besides thinking you're better than everyone else? That your family is the cream of the crop and the rest of us are just second-best?" Clinton spat. "I should have been good enough, but I never was. It was always someone from your fucking family standing in my way."

"You need to go back inside and calm down," one of the medics said, trying to guide Clinton back. He shrugged the guy off, one arm cradled to his chest.

"And you need to let me finish with this little piece of shit," Clinton spat. "Your father lorded it over mine, and your brother always thought he was so much better than me."

Emmett cleared his throat. "And now you lost to the black sheep of the McElroys. A guy who never rode in a rodeo before today. Hell, someone who hasn't been on the back of a horse since he was eight years old. And I beat you. I made the eight and am standing here. And look at you. You not only didn't make the grade, but you fell off the money ride in front of everyone here." Clinton looked about ready to explode, and Emmett had had enough. "You stay away from my family and my ranch, you hear me? If anything happens again, I will come after you, and so help me, I'll kick your ass into next week." He turned to the medic. "Take him back inside and check him for alcohol while you're at it.

He's been drinking. I can smell it on his breath. No wonder he fell off." Emmett turned and almost ran straight into his father. "Dad...."

"Emmett," he said softly, their eyes meeting, his father's shining with pride and maybe respect.

"How long were you standing there?" Emmett asked, waiting while his father stared at him. Then Dustin McElroy, the epitome of what Emmett thought of as the stoic cowboy, who never, ever backed down, lowered his gaze.

"Long enough," his dad said. "Long enough." He shook his head. "Damn, boy, I've been stupid blind for a long time." He stood quietly for a few seconds. "Come on. It's time to go." He turned, and Emmett followed his dad back up toward the stands. They separated, and Emmett went back to sit next to Nate, who was talking to their neighbors, explaining all about the judging and how things worked. Emmett took his place, and Nate's hand, squeezing it. He didn't know what the interaction with his father meant, and he was cautious about reading too much into it, but his gut told him that things had changed, and Emmett knew that was in large part due to Nate.

"I STILL CAN'T believe you did that and didn't bother to tell us," Emmett's mother said as she and Martha finished setting the table that evening.

"Leave the boy alone, Giselle," his father said. "He did good, and he knew you'd fret over him." He gently patted her hand before kissing the back of it. "How long before dinner?"

"Half an hour or so," his mother answered.

His father nodded. "Nate, Emmett, I think the three of us need to talk." He turned and went to the office.

Emmett met Nate's gaze, tension rising. He took Nate's hand and followed, unwilling to let go. Nate closed the door behind them.

"Sit down. There are things that need to be said, and I think it's best to get them out in the open now, rather than later." He took his place at his desk chair, and Nate and Emmett sat on the sofa. "You both know that I'm feeling better every day—"

Emmett shook his head. "You are not letting Nate go," he interrupted. "That isn't going to happen."

"And who are you to call the shots here?" his father drawled. "This is my ranch."

Emmett stood. "And I'm your son and the future of this place. You know that. I may not be the son you want right now, but I'm the only one you got left alive. Nate is doing an amazing job. Actually, the two of us together are, and you know it."

"Is that so?" his father countered. "You're saying you can run this place and you don't need me?"

"Dustin, I don't think Emmett—" Nate began, but Emmett turned to him with a glare.

"We don't need you the way things were. No, sir," Emmett said, meeting his father's steely gaze. "Things need to change. Holace and Sally Beth are more than capable of managing the horse operation with proper oversight. My plan is that Nate will stay on as foreman and run the cattle and horse operation. You are the ranch owner, and it's time you act like it. You don't need to be busting cattle or riding out every morning to check on fences. That will be Nate's job."

His father crossed his arms over his chest defiantly. "So what will I be doing on my own spread?"

"You're the head of the place. Let Nate run the day-to-day things. He's damned good at it. Better than me, and almost as good as you were. I won't have him run off or let go, because then I'll go with him." There—he'd laid his cards on the table. "We need to figure out how we can expand and use our resources better. Make the land pay as much as it can without hurting it." He sighed. "You would be the one to plan for the future, to drive our business forward. And that doesn't mean that you can't help out, just that you let Nate do his job." Emmett smiled. "And maybe you can take Mama on one of those trips she's always wanted to take."

His father didn't loosen up an inch. "It sounds to me like you got Nate's life planned out, as well as mine and your mother's."

"Come on, Dad. You know you want to make her happy. You've lived your entire life here, and you worked yourself into the hospital. Don't you deserve to see some of the rest of the world?"

Some of the rigidity slipped out of his father. "And what about you?" his father asked. "You have this big plan for everyone else."

"I'm going to be the ranch manager," Emmett pronounced and reached for the ranch books. He handed one to his father. "I found a lot of money in the accounts when I reconciled them with the bank statements. You just transferred the same amount of money each month—most of the time more than you needed—and it sat there because it was easier."

He didn't say that doing things the right way took effort and energy that his dad didn't have any longer. "Dad, there's been a ton of money just sitting. I want to go over all of it with you, and I'd be the one to manage the books and the herd records, along with Nate. You and I would then develop strategies for moving the ranch forward. Let's set the stage for the future... for all of us."

"Damn, boy, that almost sounded like a speech." His father snickered and then stood up. "If it was, it was a good one."

"Just think about it, Dad," Emmett said.

His father sighed. "What do you think I have been doing for the last five years? Here I thought RE dying would be the end of the ranch. That you didn't have the heart for it. Fuck, and you were just sitting here waiting that entire time for me to see what I really had." Before Emmett knew what was happening, his father extended his hand. Most fathers might have hugged at this moment, but Emmett took the handshake. His father recognizing that he was his own man and capable of taking on the family ranch was more than enough. "You really want to do this? I thought that after today you might want to be the foreman."

Emmett shook his head. "Nate is best for that. He does it without thinking. It just comes naturally to him." He took Nate's hand. "And we're a team. A damned good one, just like you and Mom are a team. I think I'm more of a strategy person." He came closer. "Dad, I have so many ideas I want to run by you. I want to change some of the things we do to make sure the land is in better shape for the next generation, like planting trees by the creek in those erosion-prone areas. There are so many ideas, and I want to do it together." He felt like he had a single chance to get his point across.

"Okay," his dad said.

Emmett took a step back. "Huh?"

"I said okay. To all of it."

Emmett narrowed his gaze. "Why?" That clearly caught his father off guard. "Is it because I rode that stupid crazy horse today? That was the stupidest thing I have ever done, and I will never do it again. Nate worked with me for weeks so I didn't get hurt, and the only reason I stayed on was pure luck. So if that's the reason, then maybe you need to reexamine your thought process." Jesus, he'd won. Why did he have to press further? But Emmett couldn't seem to stop it. He must have taken Ex-Lax for the mouth or something.

"But you...." His father seemed lost. "You actually did it."

"So what? I did it. That doesn't change the person I am—the person I always was. It just made you see me differently. Just like the fact that someone shot up my truck and you seem to have an idea who it could be and won't talk about it. Was it someone trying to send you a message?"

His father huffed, and Emmett knew a blowup was on the way. He braced for it, but then Dustin McElroy seemed to deflate.

"About seven years ago, we had a hand here on the ranch. Your mother and I were going through a rough patch with you kids growing up. She and I didn't see eye to eye for a while, and this particular hand got it in his head that your mother needed rescuing and that he was Prince Charming. Now, I can understand a man standing up for a lady, especially your mother. But he took things too far." The fear that flashed in his father's eyes, as well as the color that rose in his face, told Emmett that what had happened had been terrifying for his father.

"Dad...."

"I will not go into it further, other than to say that the incident had the opposite effect, and it snapped Giselle and me out of our complacency. We rediscovered what made each other special."

"Why didn't I know all this? I knew you fired Foster, but not why." Emmett had heard rumors and knew he was gone, but he'd been unaware of the sheer level of animosity.

"It was while you were away for a time," his dad said gently. "I thought Foster had left town, but he returned a few months ago, and Siras hired him on. Siras didn't realize what he'd done, but Foster holds a deep grudge toward me. I know that." He nodded and then stood. "We should get ready for dinner." That was his father's way of cutting off the conversation. Emmett was certain that they had gotten all that his father was ever going to tell him.

"And you think he could be behind all this?" Emmett asked.

"It's possible. I called the sheriff and told him everything. He said he'd look into it." Dustin cleared his throat. "It seems I'm realizing I need to bury the hatchet with lots of people. The way I'm thinking, it's better than sinking the danged thing into someone's head."

"We'll be right out," Emmett said, and once his father had left the office, Emmett closed the door. "Damn.... Who the hell would have figured that?"

"It's all about respect. Your father saw something today that he never realized before. He saw the man that you are."

"But why the hell today? After all this time and frustration." That made Emmett's head spin.

Nate shrugged. "Emmett, you never met him on his own playing field before. Dustin understands being a cowboy, and today he saw you as one for the first time. It's like you suddenly started speaking his language." He hugged him hard, and Emmett held him back. "And thank you for sticking up for me."

Emmett didn't let go. "I was standing up for *us*... because I want there to be an us." He lifted his head off Nate's shoulder. "I've had a thing for you for years, but I never, ever thought that you'd come back into my life, turn it upside-down, and somehow actually make things better."

"So you really want to do this? Us?" Nate asked quietly, and Emmett nodded. "Because I want that too." Nate kissed him gently and then backed away. "I knew you when you were like a tagalong little brother, and now I love you in a way I never thought possible. Who in the hell meets the other half of them when they're sixteen years old?" Nate kissed him again.

"Are you two going to stay in here all night making out, or are you coming to eat before my dinner gets cold?" Martha asked from the doorway, loudly enough to ensure everyone in the house knew what was going on.

Emmett glided his gaze toward the door. "If I have a choice...."

"Get out here, smartass, before I swat your behind the way I used to when you were eight." She closed the office door, and Emmett rested his head on Nate's shoulder once again, trying to stifle his laughter, but Nate's broke the last of his control.

"Before someone else comes back in here, I love you too," Emmett told Nate. "Now we better go eat, and then we can go to your place for dessert." That got a nod and a flare of fire in Nate's eyes. They left the office, and Emmett held Nate's hand until they reached the table. He was making a statement and making sure both his parents saw it. His father joined the table, putting his phone away.

"That was Sheriff Bridger," his dad announced, scowling. "Siras Milford just reported that Brad Connors and Foster Hadden both quit, took their pay, and left with no notice or reason. He's mad as hell, I understand, because he didn't get the chance to fire their lazy asses. He called to tell us to be on the lookout in case they cause trouble." He pulled out his chair and sat down.

"You think that confirms it, then?" Emmett asked as Sally Beth came in with her son, who she introduced as Adam. He looked just like her, with his big smile, huge eyes, and long blond hair that he apparently refused to let her cut.

"Just sit right here," Emmett's mother said, putting Adam next to her. It seemed she instantly shifted into full grandma mode. Apparently his mother had been over to Sally Beth's to help her settle in. "Sally Beth, honey, you sit on down." Mama fussed and helped get the food on the table before getting Martha settled too.

"I think it's a possibility that the two of them were in this together. Masters is another one. I suspect between the three of them, they have enough bad blood to fill a swimming pool." He spoke softly, and Emmett straightened up as the chicken, potatoes, carrots, and beans were passed around the table.

"Mama," Adam whined when beans were added to his plate.

His mother leaned close. "You gotta try some of everything because you don't want Martha to feel bad. Afterward for dessert, she has chocolate cake, and you can add your own sprinkles."

"Can I have sprinkles on my cake too?" Emmett asked.

Martha pointed a fork at him. "No. You're way too noisy for sprinkles." Nate coughed, and Emmett patted him on the back. "You too, mister." Now she was smiling. "I think Adam gets your share." She winked at the little boy, who was eating steadily, probably dreaming of the pile of multicolored jimmies he was going to get on his cake.

"Is it good?" Giselle asked Adam, who nodded and continued eating.

"I can never get him to eat his vegetables," Sally Beth said. "And here he is shoveling them in."

"Emmett was the same way. My cooking he'd never touch, and then we found Martha and he cleaned his plate every time," his mother said.

"It's Martha. She's magic in the kitchen."

Martha lowered her gaze. "Oh stop, Emmett," she demurred, but it was plain that she was very pleased.

A bang from outside pricked at Emmett's hearing. He stood and went to the back door, listening as he opened it.

"How dare you!" Holace bellowed as a figure took off around the side of the house. Emmett raced out after it, knowing the lay of the land well in the waning light. The man—from the way he moved—was dressed in dark clothes, and if he'd stayed still, he would have been much harder to spot, but his movement gave him away. Emmett continued the chase across the yard toward the barn. Holace hurried over, and Emmett dodged back toward the house.

"That's enough, Bradley Connors," Sally Beth said from the back door. "I'd know your snakelike movement anywhere. Now stop these games." She stomped out and grabbed him by the arm as he tried to pass her, pulling him to the ground. "What the hell do you think you're doing?"

"I won't let you steal my family," he growled, facing Emmett. "You buttfuckers think you can take whatever you want. But you can't have my son. I won't allow it." He slowly got to his feet as Nate and Emmett's father joined them, ensuring that Brad wasn't going anywhere.

"You don't get to choose anything for us anymore." She reared back and smacked him hard enough to send him reeling.

"She hit me. You saw it."

Emmett shrugged. "None of us saw anything of the kind." He narrowed his gaze. "Have you been out here before? Was it you putting snakes in the stalls?" He drew closer and grabbed Brad by the collar, shaking him with fury. "So help me God, if one of those horses had been injured, I'd take you out back and put you down for the good of humanity and all horses alike."

"I was just trying to see my boy," Brad said, the fight going out of him. "I just wanted to see Adam. Sally Beth said I wasn't allowed out here and that I had to arrange a place to see him." He covered his face. "I just wanted to see my boy."

"Then maybe you should have stayed out of the beds of half the women in town, and maybe you should have provided for us instead of drinking away all your pay. I'm through with you, and after this little episode with the horses—" Damn, Emmett never wanted to get on Sally Beth's bad side. She was fierce, and Brad backed away from her.

"So you put the snakes in the stalls so everyone would race out and you could try to sneak in to see Adam?" Nate asked. "Or did you intend to take him?"

"I just wanted to see him, but he wasn't there. I heard later they hadn't moved in yet," Brad said plaintively. The fight gone out of the fool.

"Did you also cut our fence and set the fire to the field?" Emmett asked.

Brad shook his head, and Emmett pulled him up onto his toes. "Did you?"

"Foster said…," Brad began. "He said he wanted to make old man McElroy pay. I didn't want to do it, but they were determined to make you all pay."

"So the three of you rode out here that day," Emmett said as calmly as he could. "And who cut the fence? Was it Foster?" Brad nodded. "Then Clinton set the fire?"

"Yes. I was with him in the truck, but he didn't get out. He set the grass on fire with a cup of gasoline from the can he had in back. He said he wanted to do the barn as well, but the cry went up fast, and he hurried away."

Emmett swallowed as bile rose in his throat. "And you're telling me you innocently sat by and watched as he did this? You know the sheriff isn't going to see it that way. You may as well have started the fire yourself."

"What about the truck?" Nate demanded. Brad shook his head hard and fast but didn't say anything. "That was you, wasn't it?"

"No. After the fire and the fence didn't work, Foster was all about making old man McElroy pay for what he did to him. Or what he thought he did to him." Brad shook his head.

"Were you there?" Nate asked, and Brad drew up silent, his mouth closing. "You can talk to the sheriff, then, and tell him everything you know."

"Giselle already called him, and he's on his way. All of us have heard what you confessed, and he will be told all of it. Sally Beth, go inside with Giselle and Adam. Holace, thank you for your vigilance. The three of us will stay with him until the sheriff arrives, and then he can cart him away."

Brad seemed to curl into himself. Thankfully, the sheriff's car pulled into the yard shortly after, and once questions were finished, he put Brad in the car and put out a call for Foster and Clinton.

"Remain vigilant until we have them in custody. I don't know what they might do if they come out here." He shook all their hands. "Call if you need anything. I'm going to assign a deputy to this area of the county for the next few days as a precaution. But I suspect they're already out of the county and possibly the state, considering that they left the Milford ranch this afternoon. But we will find them one way or another. They aren't going to get away, not if I can help it."

Emmett watched as his father nodded. "Thank you. And if they show up here, I hope you have something to cart them away with. Preferably a hearse." Emmett shrugged to himself. At least some things stayed the same.

"Now, Dustin…," the sheriff began.

"No. Understand. He has attacked my ranch and my son. I will not stand for it. If he comes on this land, my land"—he turned to Emmett—"*our* land, we will shoot, as is our right, and you know it. So if either returns, bring a hearse." His father went back into the house without another word, and Emmett couldn't blame him.

"Make sure you catch them before my father does," Emmett told him. "Don't make him prove that he means what he says." Then Emmett followed his father inside, with Nate behind him.

"Is everything okay?" his mother asked.

Emmett kissed her cheek. "It is now." He didn't want to talk about what happened in front of Adam, who sat at the table eating a huge slice of cake with enough multicolored sprinkles to float a battleship. At least Martha and his mother had prevented Adam from seeing his father taken away in handcuffs. That was one small blessing.

"Thanks," Sally Beth told him quietly as he sat down, and Emmett squeezed her hand.

"We protect our own," Emmett told her, catching Nate's grin. Suddenly, to Emmett, it felt like he was in tune with things for the first time in his life. He understood his role and his place in the world. Up until now, the ranch had been his father's, and all the people on it hired by him and loyal to him. Now that was beginning to change. Nate was here and would run things, he'd brought in Sally Beth… and Emmett would bring on other people as time went on. And like his father, Emmett would protect them to the best of his ability, because that was what a good cowboy did.

"As long as you protect the rest of us from your loudness," Martha mumbled under her breath.

Okay, so not everything had changed. Sometimes it was hard growing up in the eyes of people who used to wipe his nose and doctor his skinned knees.

Emmett ate the last of his dinner, and Martha reluctantly brought him a piece of cake, but apparently no sprinkles. After the meal, he and Nate helped Martha clear the dishes before joining his father in the office, where Emmett showed his father what he'd found in the accounts and why all that money was there doing nothing. He also went over some of his plans for the future and how he hoped to grow the ranch, until his father's energy began to wane. Then they brought their review to a close, and his mother took his father off to bed. Emmett turned out the lights and took Nate's hand, leading him through the quiet house and to his bedroom.

"I feel like I've run a marathon," he admitted as soon as he closed the door.

"You did. You conquered a bronc, your father, and quite possibly Clinton and his cohorts all in one day." Nate pulled off his shirt and went into the bathroom. Emmett did the same and stood behind Nate as he brushed his teeth. He slipped his arms around his waist, resting against him. For the first time in years, Emmett was content. Hell, he was almost giddy.

"Come on. Clean up and come to bed," Nate said softly.

Emmett took his turn in the bathroom and joined a very naked Nate in bed, sliding in just the right spot next to him.

"God, I'm tired," Emmett whispered, turning out the lights, darkness surrounding them.

"Too tired?" Nate asked, already rolling over, his warmth enshrouding Emmett as Nate settled on top of him.

"Are you kidding?" Emmett cradled Nate's cheeks in his hands, drawing him down into a kiss as Nate flexed his hips. Emmett groaned softly as their lengths slid past each other. Damn, Nate knew just how to touch him. "Do that again." He held Nate tightly as passion built between them, with Emmett wrapping his legs around Nate's waist in invitation. "Damn, I love you."

"Love you too," Nate growled softly in his ear as their passion built.

Bam! Something in the bed frame slid into place, the sound echoing in the room.

"Emmett!"

"Crap!" Emmett swore under his breath. "We definitely need a house of our own, preferably as far away from this one as possible."

Nate chuckled and buried his face in Emmett's neck. Oh hell, who cared if everyone was awake all night long? If Nate kept doing that, the teasing would definitely be worth it.

Epilogue

"DAMN YOU," Emmett snapped, turning back to Virginia. "I thought we had come to an understanding. I don't use that soap, and you stop biting my ass." He rubbed his cheek, and Emmett swore the horse laughed at him.

"And such a sweet ass it is," Nate commented as he strode up the barn to where Emmett was still glaring at the cantankerous horse. "You want me to rub it and make it better?"

"You can kiss it," Emmett snapped as Nate wrapped his arms around his waist.

"Later," he whispered, sending a surge of heat through him that burned hot enough to ward off the wintry north wind that blew outside. "It's just starting to snow again."

"And that's supposed to make me feel better? It's almost February, and I'm ready for spring already."

"That's just because your parents are on a two-week Caribbean cruise. Think about it, we have the house to ourselves," Nate nuzzled the base of his neck.

"Bullshit. We have bat-ears Martha to contend with." Emmett was more than ready for their house to be finished, and it wouldn't be long now. The foundation and exterior were done, and it was all interior work now, which would go on for the next month. In order to save cash, Nate had given up his place and they had moved into the ranch house for the time being, taking the extra bedroom next to theirs as a small media room for themselves.

"Don't worry. I bought her the mondo package of earplugs," Nate said, and Emmett snickered.

"Get a room," Sally Beth said as she came in holding Adam's hand.

"Did you want to see the horses?" Nate asked Adam as his heat slipped away. Of course he did. Adam loved the horses. Emmett hadn't told him or his mother that the ranch was taking delivery of a pony in the next few weeks. Adam, as well as Howard and Raymond's son, Jimmy, had both wanted to learn to ride, so Emmett figured the ranch could get a pony, and Sally Beth and Nate could teach the two fast friends to ride. When Emmett had explained his plans to his father, he'd expected pushback, but instead his father had smiled.

"Boy, you gotta teach the next generation of cowboys." He'd actually seemed pleased. Emmett and his father didn't see eye to eye all the time, but over the past few months, they had worked out a way to work together and built up enough respect that they could disagree without killing each other.

Sally Beth led Adam to Milly's stall and lifted him up so he could pet the horse. "Did your father really give you permission to reforest some of the ranch?"

Emmett hummed. "I know it sounds crazy, but there are areas that wash out every couple of years and those that just aren't conducive to grazing cattle or horses. He fought me on it tooth and nail, but in the spring, I have three scout troops and a 4H group that are each going to take a section and do the planting. It'll stabilize the land nearby."

"How did you ever get him to agree?" she asked.

Emmett snickered. "I tried a new tack. When he told me no, I simply took all my notes and plans and put them in a folder I'd marked DEAD. He asked what that was for, and I told him it was all the things I intended to do after he dies."

"You're kidding," Sally Beth said, shocked.

"Nope. He looked at me about the same way you are, grumbled, and said, 'Aw heck, go ahead,' or a version of that with more expletives. Then he and Mom left on their cruise."

"Is Grampy Dustin going to die?" Adam asked.

Emmett took Adam and lifted him high in the air to happy giggles. "Nope. Grampy and Grammy are going to live a long time. And when they get back next week, you can come over and spend time with them. I promise."

The past few months had been hard for Sally Beth and Adam. The custody fight had been pretty much over with Brad's arrest, but he had testified against Foster and Clinton, so he got a lighter sentence. All three were currently serving their prison time. Sally Beth no longer had to worry about Brad contesting her custody of Adam, but the entire situation had made things difficult for her.

"Is Valentine's next week?" Adam asked.

"Yup. They'll be back in plenty of time, and I'm sure Grammy will have special valentines for you." Emmett put an arm around Nate. As much as he was ready to move out of the house and have a life of his own, the big ranch house and its huge family dinner table would always be the center of their extended family.

"And is that when you plan to break the news to them?" Nate whispered from right behind him once, he'd put Adam down and he'd gone on to say hi to the horses.

"Possibly." He liked him and Nate having a secret.

"You haven't told your parents about your plans yet?" Sally Beth asked. "You know things are going to start to show in the next month or so." She rubbed her belly absently.

"I know. I was planning to tell my parents at Christmas, but it was way too soon." Sally Beth had agreed to be the surrogate for his and Nate's child. The chance to have a family of their own was something they both wanted, but neither thought they'd have the chance to have. They had expected the process to take a while, but everything came together the first time. "I figure it can be their Valentine's surprise." Along with their engagement and wedding plans. He was thinking May. Reid had already agreed to be his best man.

"I bet your father goes straight out to get a baby cowboy hat and boots," Sally Beth said, and Emmett turned to look at Nate. There was no way he was going to take that bet. "Come on, Adam, it's getting late and we need to get home for dinner." She held out her hand, and Adam raced up to take it.

"Bye, horsies, see you tomorrow," Adam said as the two of them left the barn.

"Let's get everything closed up here for the night," Emmett said, and they checked the stalls for water and hay before turning out the lights and pulling the doors closed behind them.

The wind bit as they headed across the yard toward the house, snow falling heavily now. "You know, I was thinking that maybe we should start getting you ready for next year's rodeo," Nate told him as he turned toward the old shed they'd used for practice.

"No way in hell," Emmett retorted. "Once was more than enough, and you know it." Emmett pulled Nate close, his big body blocking the wind.

"I'm serious," Nate said, humor dancing in his eyes.

"So am I. If I want to ride, I know exactly where to go to get one that's a hell of a lot more fun." He smiled and drew closer. "You can buck me any time."

Keep reading for an excerpt from
A Courageous Ride
by Andrew Grey.

Chapter One

MARSHALL HARRINGTON took a deep breath. He felt as though within seconds he might split into a million pieces. Travel upon travel, a different hotel room almost every week. Not that he really had a home. He wouldn't until he'd managed to land a job, but the search, the auditions, being a finalist for every position he applied for and coming in second each time to someone else—it all had his nerves about shot, and he couldn't take much more. Maybe his parents were right and he should have gone to business school. All his father talked about was having Marshall come work with him on Wall Street. But music was in his blood, and no matter how many talks he'd had with his folks about his future, it wouldn't leave or be pushed back. He'd worked hard, studied with some of the best conductors in the world, and now he was out on his own trying to get his first real job. He hadn't expected a position with one of the top orchestras, but Marshall was talented and he had the gift. He had hoped one of the many smaller orchestras in the country, like the Glenn Arbor Symphony, would give him a chance. Up till now, though, none of them had, and he was so exhausted he could hardly move.

He heard the orchestra warming up and tuning, the familiar sound infusing him with a modicum of energy. "Thank God," Marshall whispered under his breath. He heard applause, and the door in front of him opened. Marshall strode out onto the stage to take his bow. The auditorium was only half full, and Marshall groaned softly but pushed it away. He'd been working with the musicians on the stage every evening for the past week, and they were ready and deserved his best. Marshall turned to the musicians, lifted his baton, and began the first piece of music. He loved the energy in music, but the pieces that had been chosen for the program were lethargic and deep. Not the music Marshall had expected the attendees of a small symphony outside Houston would go for, and he'd been right, judging by the attendance. Marshall and the orchestra had worked to add some punch to the rather obscure, almost funereal pieces. He figured if he had any chance to get this job, he would have to shake things up a bit.

Halfway through the Mahler piece, his energy kicked in, the music working its way inside him. He picked up the pace just a little, and the orchestra followed right along with him. Suddenly, they were having a good time. He saw feet tapping and that extra little bit of—zing—excitement crept into the music. Marshall felt it now, reverberating off the walls of the concert hall, filling the air with anticipation. By the time the first half of the program was done, Marshall was back. After taking his bow and motioning to the musicians for their accolades, he strode off the stage with a spring in his step. He had no idea what the board members would think of the performance, but right now he didn't care. He'd spent a year trying to be whatever he thought they wanted him to be. Tonight, he would be himself, and that meant taking a risk and doing things his way.

After taking a drink of water and clearing his mind, he returned for the second half of the program. Whoever had put this together must have been on crack, because the second half of the program was completely different from the first. Thankfully, he'd seen that and had been able to add vitality to the first half, because the Mozart in the second was lively, fun, and just wonderful.

The musicians let him take them where he wanted to go, and they seemed to have a great time. Between movements they smiled, and anticipation for what was to come filled the stage and drifted out into the audience. Marshall knew that kind of positive vibe always got carried along with the notes, and it lasted until the final piece ended and the music faded away.

The audience applauded, and Marshall took his bow and then stepped aside, motioning to the concertmaster and then the musicians. He left the stage and then returned for one final bow before leaving once again. As soon as the stage door closed behind him, the last of his energy left him. Fatigue, lack of sleep, strange beds—all of it caught up with him and his knees buckled. He managed to catch himself, but not before one of the stagehands saw him and rushed over to offer assistance. He helped Marshall to a chair and got him some water.

"I'm okay," Marshall said as musicians and other people began gathering around. "Please, I'm fine. I just misstepped." He drank from the bottle and slowly stood up. He met the gaze of each person around him and straightened his tuxedo jacket, forcing a smile he hoped appeared genuine. People drifted away as he thanked them for their concern. Honestly, Marshall wasn't sure how much longer he was going to last, and he still had to put in an appearance at the after-performance reception. Taking a deep breath, he called on the last of his reserves of energy, put on a smile, and walked through the backstage areas and out through the auditorium to the reception in the lobby of the building.

A few people applauded politely when he entered, and then he joined the fray and spent the next hour talking to people and shaking hands. He got many compliments and thanked each person.

"Did you enjoy the performance?" he asked for what seemed like the millionth time.

"It was lovely and had such energy," the late-middle-aged woman answered with a smile just like the dozens of others he'd seen that evening. Not that he expected anyone to tell him otherwise. If they hadn't liked it, they'd still smile and then talk to their friends or other patrons when he wasn't around to hear. "It's about time we had some of that here. My husband and I have had season tickets for years, but after this year we might give them up. We want to support the arts and enjoy coming, but lately Reggie sometimes falls asleep." She colored. "He didn't tonight, though," she added hastily before turning to look around. "Reggie," she snapped more loudly than was necessary. Her husband disengaged from the couple he'd been talking to and walked over. "This is Maestro Harrington, the conductor. I was just saying how much we enjoyed the evening."

"Best we've had in a while," Reggie said as he shook hands with Marshall.

"I'm glad to hear it," Marshall said.

Reggie moved closer. "Do you know who picks the stuff they play?"

"Usually the conductor also acts as music director and chooses the program. It's generally given final approval by the board, but the programs I'm seeing were probably developed by committee." Marshall felt they had little cohesiveness, and the ones he'd seen appeared to have been developed with a little something for everyone, but nothing that worked together. So either the person developing the programs was a schizophrenic drunk, or it was the result of an inept committee. Neither choice was particularly comforting.

"You didn't pick this program, did you?" Reggie asked.

"No. I was given the pieces to conduct and tried to make the best of them." Marshall smiled and stopped short of saying anything derogatory. He didn't know who might be listening or what would get passed on to whom. "They're good pieces...." He let the rest of the thought trail off. That would only lead to a discussion of the disjointed program, and he didn't need to go there. Not with members of the board heading across the room with their eyes on him.

His heart beat a little faster. They seemed pleased and complimented him on the performance. Marshall could have sworn he'd had other jobs sewn up, but he'd been disappointed up to this point.

"Great program tonight," Eleanor Beard, the head of the board, said, and Marshall knew it had been she who'd most likely put the program together, or had at least exerted her influence to get what she wanted.

"It was interesting. The audience members seemed to enjoy themselves." He kept his true opinion to himself and his words bland and neutral. His legs ached and he was so tired he could hardly think, but he had to keep up appearances. This business was as much about how things looked as how they sounded, at least when you were trying to get yourself a job offer. "The musicians did, as well."

They gradually made their way toward a table with glasses of sparkling wine. Each of the board members took one, so Marshall did as well. He sipped it but drank very little. Alcohol of any type was not going to help him. He needed quiet, sleep, and to get laid—most definitely in that order. Normally he'd put sex first, but he was too tired to do anything, even if the grandest über-stud in all of Texas were to walk through the door.

"So, where do you see this organization headed musically?" Marvin Thompson asked. He seemed to be the only board member willing to step out from Eleanor's shadow.

"Anywhere they want to go," Marshall said. "You have a very talented and dedicated group of musicians. Most symphonies your size would give anything to have that kind of talent available to them." It was an honest answer. The musicians were indeed very gifted, but nothing was being done to foster the talent and bring them together as a cohesive group. Marshall liked to think he'd done some of that over the past week, but it wouldn't last if it wasn't constantly nurtured.

"You know that funding of any type is tight and getting tougher every day for this kind of organization," Eleanor began, and Marshall suddenly wondered if her day job was as an accountant. They were good at watching the money, but tended to lack any sort of vision or imagination when it came to developing this type of organization, where the best and most important results were hard to quantify.

"Of course, and I'm aware the orchestra, while healthy now, is on a trajectory where that could change in the future. Part of the conductor's job is to help make sure that doesn't happen." He also knew the cause of the financial troubles. But he couldn't tell them that the organization needed vision and programs that got people to come to the performances. Butts in the seats were what every orchestra needed—people who enjoyed the music enough to dig deeper and be willing to write checks or act as performance sponsors. That was not going to happen with a half-empty performance hall. The orchestra also needed to record and sell those recordings for extra revenue. He wanted to say something, but knew that would not get him anywhere, at least not today. He had to get the job before he would be able to make the changes that needed to be made.

"Thank you for your interest in our organization," Eleanor said, and Marshall nodded. He'd known he wasn't going to get an answer tonight, but he hadn't expected an obvious brush-off either.

"I appreciate you having me," Marshall said and set his glass on one of the trays before turning and heading back to his dressing room. He changed clothes, left the building, and walked out to his car.

Somehow he made it to his hotel and got to his room before collapsing on the bed. He woke a few hours later still in his clothes. He undressed and dug around in his bag for something to eat. He found a granola bar and wolfed it down, along with some water. Then he got undressed and climbed in bed, falling back to sleep.

When he woke next, Marshall was slightly disoriented and it took him a minute to remember where he was. He'd been in so many places—Dallas, Seattle, Cincinnati, Minneapolis—over the past few months, it took him a while to get his bearings. He tried to remember where he was supposed to be next and then sighed softly. He had no place to be. Last night had been his final audition, at least until more calls were put out for conductors, and that might not be for months. He figured he might as well go home for now. At least he could regroup and figure out his next move. Although that course of action would come with a healthy dose of "I told you so," along with plenty of advice and guilt over his choices and what he wanted to do with the rest of his life.

He was still thinking about his next move when his phone rang. It was muffled and he barely heard it. He got up and searched for it, finally locating it in the bag he'd taken to the concert hall the night before. He pulled it out and answered it just before it went to voicemail. "Hello," he croaked and picked up one of the bottles of water from the nearby counter.

"Hey, Marshy, how's it hanging?"

"God, Terry, it's too early in the morning." He shook his head. "But since you asked, the hanging parts are fine, but haven't seen much action lately, except...."

"Whoa," Terry, his best friend since they'd been kids, said in his deepest voice. "It was just an expression. I'm not interested in hearing anything about your little dude, okay? I'm a doctor, so I've seen plenty of little dudes in my time, but I don't need to hear about yours."

Marshall laughed; it was a long running joke between them. "Fine, but for the record, you did ask." He took a drink and his throat felt less like it had been scraped with sandpaper.

"Duly noted, but still TMI. So, did you get the job?"

"I don't know, but I doubt it. The head of the board was pretty cool after the performance. But I won't know for certain for a few weeks. I was the last person they had up for consideration, so hopefully they'll make their decision soon. In the meantime I was going to head home, spend time with the folks, and listen to my twice-yearly quota of recrimination about my career choice. You know, the usual." Marshall yawned and tried to stifle it. "I'm so tired. Last night after the performance my knees buckled. I caught myself and sat it out. Somehow I managed to make it through the evening, but I don't know if I have the energy for the parental units."

"Listen, take my doctorly advice: find a place to rest for a while. Do something different. You've been immersed in your music and trying to get a job for so long, and with such focus, you need to give your system a break."

"Yeah, but what?" Marshall heard papers shuffling and figured Terry was on a break at work. Dr. Terry Millard was a brilliantly gifted surgeon at Columbia Medical Center. He was making a real name for himself with a number of successes and techniques that had proved lifesaving for heart patients who previously would have had no hope.

"I don't know, but I'll give it some thought. Where are you right now?"

"Houston. I have the hotel for another day, and I figured I'd try to relax today and then see if I can catch a flight home tomorrow." Marshall yawned again and moved through the room to gather the clothes he'd strewn across the furniture when he undressed the night before.

"Get some rest and a good lunch, preferably nothing fried, maybe some light exercise, and try to relax and recharge. I'll call you later and see how you're doing."

"That's some house call—all the way to Houston," Marshall said.

Terry chuckled. "It's just sound advice. Besides, I know you almost as well as you know yourself. You've been so focused on your goal throughout this audition period that you've probably been living on granola bars, caffeine, and pure guts. Last night it caught up with you, and it'll get worse and make you sick if you don't give yourself the chance to recharge." Terry paused. "And don't make me come there. I will, and then you'll be sorry."

"I know. You'll come to Texas and drag me to every rodeo event known to man." One of the little-known things about the East Coast born-and-bred Dr. Millard was that he adored rodeo. He watched it on television and attended events when he could, which unfortunately wasn't often, with his busy schedule. "I promise to be good and get some rest. I'll talk to you soon."

"Okay. And get some decent food," Terry said with a smile in his voice. They disconnected, and Marshall headed for the bathroom. He cleaned up and then dressed before leaving the room and heading down to the lobby, where he asked the clerk for a good place for lunch. The clerk checked his watch.

"It's too late for barbeque," he said softly. Marshall nodded slowly. He knew the drill. The good places only made so much, and you had to get in line and wait. Once it was gone, it was gone, and eleven in the morning was too late to get in line on a Saturday.

"I want something light and healthy," Marshall said. The clerk nodded and looked at him rather blankly. "It's okay, I'll find something." Marshall thanked the clerk and left the hotel. He walked down the street near his hotel and found a small restaurant. He sat at a table and ordered a salad and soup. When his food came, he ate it all and realized just how hungry he was. He thought back and realized he'd skipped lunch most days, and his dinners had been sporadic. No wonder he'd felt light-headed and had little energy. He'd done this before—become so focused on the one thing he wanted that he forgot to eat. Marshall ordered another bowl of soup and finished that. Finally full, he sat back at the table and thought about what he was going to do next. Going home was about his only option at this point, unless he simply wanted to travel a while. A vacation sounded good, but wouldn't get him closer to his goal. Yet the more he thought about it, some time away to relax sounded better and better.

After paying his bill, Marshall left the restaurant and went for a short walk. His phone beeped, letting him know he had a message. He pulled it out and saw a message from Terry, asking him to call. Marshall messaged him back and was about to call when his phone rang.

"I have to get ready for surgery in ten minutes, but I might have a solution for you. How about a vacation?"

"I was just thinking about that," Marshall said with a smile.

"Excellent. Phillip, one of my rodeo buddies, has a friend who's just opened a ranch for tourists."

"A dude ranch? You have to be kidding."

"Why not? It's about an hour outside Houston, and Phillip says there's some rodeo folks in the area. The owner's name is Indigo Santana. He was a bull rider a few years ago. I saw him ride once. According to Phillip, he inherited the family ranch and is opening it to guests. It should be a lot of fun, with no pressure. You don't have to do anything you don't want, but it'll be quiet and it will give you a chance to think about what you want to do. You also won't have to go home to face your folks, at least until you hear if you got the job or not." That did sound appealing.

"My idea of a vacation is an all-inclusive resort with pool boys, fruity drinks with umbrellas, and all the sun I can soak in," Marshall said. "A ranch is hardly my idea of fun." He didn't share Terry's fascination for all things rodeo.

Terry sighed, and Marshall thought he heard a door close in the background. "I can't believe I'm going to say this, but according to Phillip, there are few things better-looking than tight cowboy butts in tight jeans and chaps." He could almost see Terry shuddering. "Now, you are forbidden from telling anyone I ever said that, and if you do, I'll say you were drunk and don't know what you're talking about."

"Okay, I get the point." The image that flashed through his mind was most definitely intriguing.

"Good. I'll email you the details, and you can call the ranch. They're just starting out, so they have plenty of room and should be able to accommodate you for as long as you want to stay. Phillip said they usually book by the week, but they'll be flexible." Terry paused. "Go have some fun with the cowboys."

"Straight cowboys," Marshall grumbled.

"I wouldn't be so sure of that. Phillip said Dante Rivers lives in the area. He was a champion bull rider and is gay. It doesn't mean anyone there will be gay, but you're there to de-stress and have a good time, not hook up with everything that moves."

"Look who's talking—the playboy heart surgeon," Marshall countered. "Fine, I'll call and see what they have to say, but I'm not making any promises."

"I gotta go, but I'll text the number in a second." Terry hung up, and true to his word, a text came through with a phone number and a message less than a minute later: *This will do you good. Think of the view. LOL.* Marshall rolled his eyes and shoved his phone back into his pocket. He walked back to the hotel, trying to decide if he wanted to do this or not, and he was definitely leaning toward not. His phone rang again and he pulled it out and answered the call.

"Terry," he said with a smile.

"Excuse me," He sighed when he heard the voice on the other end. He should have looked at the display.

"Hi, Mom," Marshall said.

"How did the performance go last night?"

"Very well. The two halves of the program were really different, but I managed to tie them together and make them work. I just don't know if that's what the board wanted. They'll let me know in a few weeks if I've got the job."

"Well, if you don't, you can always come work with your father. You know he'll always bring you into the firm." That was their answer for everything.

"That isn't what I want, Mom," Marshall said. "I hate the thought of that kind of work. It's dull and uninteresting. I know Dad loves it, but

I can't stand the thought of it. If I come back to New York, it will be to take up a position there with one of the musical groups, not Wall Street."

"But you are coming back, aren't you? And when you're here, just go in to work with your father one day and give it a try. You'll eventually inherit the firm, you know." The thought was enough to give Marshall a migraine. "Someone will have to lead it."

Suddenly the thought of spending a few weeks on a dude ranch sounded like an appealing proposition. "I've decided to take a few weeks' vacation. I've been very tired and I need some time to myself."

"You can rest while you're here." *Yeah, rest combined with pressure to do what they want, and guilt piled on every time I say no.*

"No, Mom. I don't think so. Going to New York is not what I think I need right now."

"But...."

He knew she was disappointed. His parents were good people, and they wanted the best for him. Unfortunately, what they thought was best was different from his own vision, and Marshall wanted to make his own way, at least partially. Marshall had enough money of his own that he didn't have to work. His grandfather had founded the brokerage firm his father now ran and owned. He'd also set up Marshall, as well as his cousins, with generous trust funds, so Marshall didn't need to work for a living. He wanted this job because it was what he truly wanted to do, what got deep down into his soul and moved him. The money was secondary, although it would be nice to earn money for himself rather than requesting funds from his trustee whenever he wanted cash, especially since his trustee was his father. But not for long. Next year he came of age at twenty-seven, as far as the trust was concerned.

"Mom, I'm not staying away forever. It's just a few weeks of rest and relaxation. I'll call you when I can, and you have nothing to worry about. I promise." They talked for a few minutes more and then hung up. Marshall walked the rest of the way back to the hotel. It was a beautiful day, warm and sunny, and he found he was now in a great mood. When he got back to his room, he pulled out his phone and made a call to the ranch.

"Yeah," the man said who answered the phone.

"Uh, yes. I was given this number as that of a dude ranch. I'm interested in spending some time and was curious about your availability. I got the number through a friend of a friend. Phillip." He hoped he had the right number.

"This is the Circle R, and, yeah, you got the right place. Hang on a minute." The phone was set down and Marshall waited. He wasn't sure what kind of place this was, given the initial reception. But he waited for a few minutes.

"Hello. You wish to stay with us?" said a man with a deep, rich voice.

"Yes. I was wondering if you have any vacancies. I'd like to spend, say, a week at your ranch." Who knew? Marshall figured he could always stay longer if he liked it, and if he didn't, he could leave and go back to New York.

A deep laugh followed. "Of course. I'm Indigo. We've just begun accepting guests. But we should be able to accommodate you. When did you want to arrive?" A smooth Texas accent, combined with a smooth, almost musically rich voice, had Marshall's heart pumping for a second. Then he shook his head to return his attention where it belonged.

"Tomorrow, if that's okay." Marshall's answer was met with a pause.

"That will be fine. I'll put you in the book. I'm assuming you need directions?"

"Just the address. I can use GPS to get there." Indigo laughed. "I take it there's a problem." Now Marshall was worried.

"GPS doesn't seem to work very well where we are. We're off the beaten path, and the GPS programs haven't done a good job figuring out where we are. Have you got a piece of paper? I'll give you directions you can use that won't get you lost." Marshall reached for his folder and found a sheet of paper. He wrote down the directions as well as the other information he needed to know. He gave Indigo his information as well. Then Indigo said, "We'll see you late tomorrow morning. If you get here in time, you're welcome to join us for lunch."

"Thank you, I'll see you then." They ended the call, and Marshall smiled. He found he was looking forward to getting away. Maybe this wasn't such a bad idea after all.

ANDREW GREY is the author of more than two hundred works of Contemporary Gay Romantic fiction. After twenty-seven years in corporate America, he has now settled down in Central Pennsylvania with his husband of more than twenty-five years, Dominic, and his laptop. An interesting ménage. Andrew grew up in western Michigan with a father who loved to tell stories and a mother who loved to read them. Since then he has lived throughout the country and traveled throughout the world. He is a recipient of the RWA Centennial Award, has a master's degree from the University of Wisconsin–Milwaukee, and now writes full-time. Andrew's hobbies include collecting antiques, gardening, and leaving his dirty dishes anywhere but in the sink (particularly when writing). He considers himself blessed with an accepting family, fantastic friends, and the world's most supportive and loving partner. Andrew currently lives in beautiful, historic Carlisle, Pennsylvania.

Email: andrewgrey@comcast.net

Website:www.andrewgreybooks.com

Follow me on BookBub

Rafe Carrera hasn't seen his Uncle Mack since he was a kid, so when he inherits his ranch, it throws him like a bucking horse. He's been on his own for a long time. Now suddenly everyone wants to be his friend... or at least get friendly enough to have a chance in buying the ranch.

Russell Banion's family may own a mega-ranch in Telluride, but Russell made his own way developing software. He misses his friend Mack, and purchasing the ranch will help him preserve Mack's legacy—and protect his own interests. It's a win-win. Besides, spending time with Rafe, trying to soften him up, isn't exactly a hardship. Soon Russell realizes he'll be more upset if Rafe does decide to leave.

But Rafe isn't sure he wants to sell. To others in the valley, his land is worth more than just dollars and cents, and they'll do anything to get it. With Russell's support, Rafe will have to decide if some things—like real friendship, neighborliness, and even love—mean more than money.

www.dreamspinnerpress.com

ANDREW GREY

Two cowboys.
Twenty years together.
One chance to save their love.

SECOND
GO-ROUND

Former world champion bronco rider Dustin and rancher Marshall have been life partners for more than twenty years, and time has taken its toll. Their sex life is as dusty as the rodeo ring. Somehow their marriage hasn't turned out how they planned.

But when a new family moves in up the road with two young boys, one very sick, Dustin and Marshall realize how deep their ruts are and that there might be hope to break them. After all, where they're from, the most important part of being a man is helping those who need it.

A new common purpose helps break down the deep routines they've fallen into and makes them realize the life they've been living has left them both cold and hollow. Spending time with the kids—teaching them how to be cowboys—reignites something they thought lost long ago. But twenty years is a lot of time to make up for. Can they find their way back to each other, or are the ruts they've created worn too deep?

www.dreamspinnerpress.com

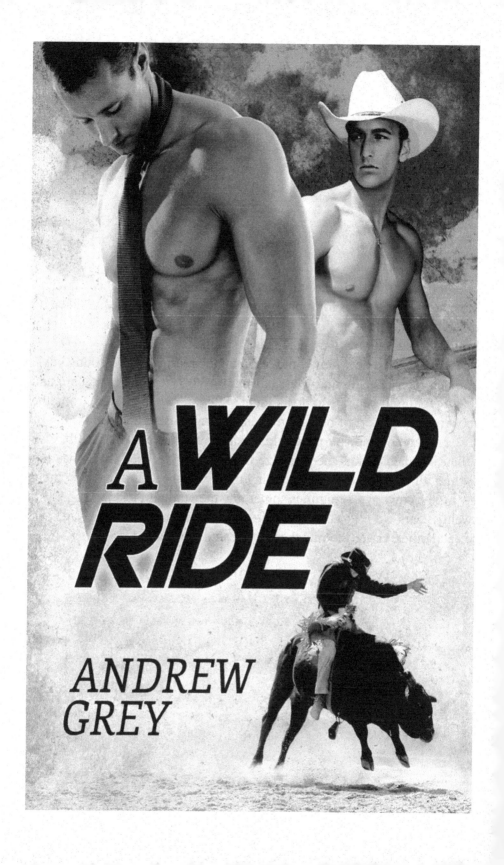

A WILD RIDE

ANDREW GREY

The Bullriders: Book One

Dante Rivers just lost the rodeo by two one hundredths of a point:
he's frustrated as hell, needs to get laid, and he knows just where to go.
That night he meets Ryan Abbott and catches his eye—Ryan watched
the rodeo and is still riding high on the rush. The chemistry between
them ignites, but Dante, unable to deal with complications, leaves while
Ryan's asleep.

Ryan figures he'll never see Dante again, but they're fatefully
reunited when Dante's grandfather, Hy, hires Ryan to help straighten
out some old investments. The attraction between Ryan and Dante still
sizzles. Sex slowly turns to more, but obstacles abound: Hy's failing
health, Dante's homophobic sponsor, an attack on Ryan, and Dante's own
struggle with his identity. Any one thing would be enough to separate
them permanently… unless they both decide to hang on for the wild ride.

www.dreamspinnerpress.com

ANDREW GREY

A DARING RIDE

The Bullriders: Book Two

Simon "Frizz" Frizzell sneaks away to the rodeo on weekends, and it's not until after he wins a buckle that he tells his parents about his bull-riding. He knows they won't approve of his choice of sport, but his parents own a Christian bookstore, and he couldn't possibly tell them the whole truth: he's gay. And so are some of his rodeo friends, like Dante and Ryan, and Jacky—a young man he wishes could have been more than a one-night stand. When Simon sets his sights on his dreams, he finds work with Dante and Ryan, and bumps into Jacky on the job.

Jacky Douglas is a rodeo fanatic, plain and simple. He loves the ride, and he loves the cowboys. He fell hard for Frizz when they met, and theirs was a one-night stand made in heaven. When they meet again, Jacky thinks it's a stroke of luck. Frizz takes some convincing, but once he's on board, they begin a relationship. The fledgling romance faces a challenge when news of it travels all the way to the one place Frizz doesn't want it to go: his parents' bookstore.

www.dreamspinnerpress.com

A COURAGEOUS RIDE

ANDREW GREY

The Bullriders: Book Three

Aspiring orchestra conductor Marshall is exhausted after months of auditions without a single job offer. Marshall's friend, Terry, recommends a change of scenery and points Marshall in the direction of a dude ranch run by former bull rider Indigo Santana. Marshall is understandably skeptical, but his friend is convincing, and Marshall needs a break, so he agrees to go.

Indigo captures Marshall's attention but leaves him confused. Indigo's confidence is shot after an injury ended his rodeo career, and he walks with a slight limp. He hasn't been anywhere near a bull since he was hurt, and he's not the most accommodating host. After all, the only reason he keeps guests is because his family ranch is all but bankrupt.

Marshall's attraction doesn't go unanswered, which leaves him with a huge dilemma. He's torn between the possibility of love, something he's searched for all his life, and the career he's worked toward for as long as he can remember, which is miles away. From his side of the fence, Indigo doesn't see how the ranch could ever be enough.

www.dreamspinnerpress.com